February 2004 he was voted Britain's most admired
contemporar   by the British Journalism Review.

Keith Waterhouse

Bimbo

SCEPTRE

First published in Great Britain in 1990 by Hodder & Stoughton

This edition published in 2014 by Sceptre
An imprint of Hodder & Stoughton
An Hachette UK company

1

A CIP catalogue record for this title is
available from the British Library

ISBN 978 1 444 75387 5

Typeset in Sabon MT by Palimpsest Book Production Limited,
Falkirk, Stirlingshire
Printed and bound by Clays Ltd, St Ives plc

Hodder & Stoughton policy is to use papers that are natural,
renewable and recyclable products and made from wood grown
in sustainable forests. The logging and manufacturing processes are
expected to conform to the environmental regulations of
the country of origin.

Hodder & Stoughton Ltd
338 Euston Road
London NW1 3BH

www.sceptrebooks.com

I

My Early Livelihood

Now it can be told. The biggest majority of the Debra Chase By Herself series in the *Sunday Shocker* which I am sposed to of written was a load of rubbish, a virago of lies from start to finish.

Frinstance it is just not true that I had one-night stands with half the Seathorpe Wanderers team before I was seventeen. If it is of any concedable interest I did not even meet most of the lads until I had been selected Miss South-east Coast and that was when I was eighteen at least as I can prove.

Not true that after sex romps with playboy MP Sir Monty Pratt – The Sir as I always called him – I threaten-ised I would swallow a whole bottle of aspirin to stop him bringing our sizzling romance to an end. I do not even like aspirin, it just so happens it always gives me a headache. All right, so at the death The Sir was pressured into choosing between I and his wife Pussy as all the world now knows – but Debra Chase is still alive and kicking, thank you very much.

And it is defnitely not true that me and rival model Suzie Dawn, reel name Norma Borridge, fought like alley cats over super soap stud Den Dobbs, two-timing mini-cab driver Terry of the chart-topping series *The Brummies*, whose reel-life scorching romance with barmaid Sally – raven-haired sexpot Donna Matthews – was the cause of a love-tug punch-up with burly boy friend Bruce Bridges, ex-welterweight boxer who is now a top DJ. For the record saucy Suzie, now owner of the swish Pampers nails boutique off London's exclusive Knightsbridge, just so happens to be my best friend. So sposing she didn't say No to randy Den's advances when she knew I fancied him, so what, she might just of saved me from getting trapped in a sordid three-in-a-bed situation like she nearly was herself. I shall be spilling the full can of beans on that one, and anyway it's highly difficult to say No when you can't finish a sentience. She's ever so funnee the way she talks is Suzie. Where you or me would say, 'Shall we go out for a meal or stay in with a takeaway?' Suzie will just say, 'Shall we have a meal out or?' and leave you to guess the rest. Sometimes you have to have three or four guesses before you know what she's trying to say, it's like a game, she makes me laugh.

Oh, and talking of who, another thing which isn't true, it is not true what the *Sunday Shocker* made the accusal of, namely that I gave sex favours to most of the judges when I went in for the Miss Seathorpe contest before becoming Miss South-east Coast. If I did, how come I only came in second to Suzie in that particlar contest? No one can answer that question.

Yes, it is true I was brought up by my Dad and his second wife Babs, I will never call her stepmum, Babs has always been more like a big sister to me even when I was small, in fact when I was fifteen we had quite a little fling with two sailors we met on Seathorpe front whilst Dad was up in Town once – 'two ships that passed away the night' as Babs called them – so you can see we were more best mates than me her step-daughter. But I can say here and now it is not true my reel Mum walked out on us when I was three, if the sad truth be known she mysteriously disappeared with the insurance collector.

These are just some of the lies and halved truths which have been told about me, I may of said some of these things, I can't remember, but if I did it was only because Barry Butcher of the *Sunday Shocker* kept on twisting my arm by saying that if I did not come up with the goods as he put it I could whistle for my money. This was another lie, cos later I met Barry's editor at Bonks, plush Mayfair layby for the fast lane hellraisers, and he was reely sweet, he said I would of got the money even if I had only come up with the Ode to a Nightingale whatever that is. But it was too late by then, Debra Chase By Herself had already hit the fan. I reely needed that £25,000 to sink into the business intrests I had gone into with Dad and Babs as partners, to wit the Debra Chase Diet Nibble Muffin plus the Debra, Babs and Eric Chase Academy of Dance, plus there was something I wanted the world to know, so I let Barry put words in my head.

But now I want to set the record straight. I have a dinky little tape recorder in the shape of a pair of Marilyn Monroe lips which I kindly had bought for me in a Covent Garden gift boutique, and am dictatorising this all by myself, strictly no lecherising reporters present, alone on my ownsome in my Mayfair luxury pad – not lovenest as the *Sunday Shocker* made me call it. Now the world will see the reel Debra Chase, not the sex-mad gold-digging bimbo I was made out to be. Not that I have anything against s-e-x in its place (which is not always the bedroom!!!) but I am just not made like that. Neverthemore this does not mean to say I am just a smalltime girl who struck lucky, even though I am sticking to the truth this time round there will be some starting relevations with the aid

3

of my hithertofore unpublished Sex Romps Diary, so pin back your ears for the reel Debra Chase Story as told by herself, exclusive.

To begin at the beginning as they say, my incredulous life started when I became born plain Marjory Linda Chase on May the eighteenth 19 – no I am not going to give my age away but it was the year the Beatles made *Sergeant Pepper's Lonely Hearts Club Band*, it makes me feel reely old.

Of course I cannot remember very much about those far-off days but for my eighteenth birthday my boy friend or one of them, hunky half-million-pound ace goal poacher Brian Boffe of the Seathorpe Wanderers, gave me a copy of a newspaper called *The Times* for the very day I was born. It was ever so clever of him, he saw it advertised where you can get *The Times* for any day in history except Sundays, not a factsimple, it is the reel thing so he sent off for it. It was one of my favrite prezzies and I still have it.

It is like stepping back into a different age. Frinstance there were only three TV channels, ITV, BBC1 and BBC2, whilst radio did not even exist except for three boring-sounding channels called Home, Light and Third. No Radio One, no Capital, Babs says it was like living in the Dark Ages. The TV progs sound boring too, nothing but plays and classic music, though in fairness you could watch *Coronation Street*, whilst for teenagers there was a programme going by the strange title of *A Whole Scene Going*, it sounds reely Victorian.

The adverts are fascinating, would you believe only £2,357 for a new Jag 3.8 in Warwick grey with red interior, fitted power steering? Also you could have an all-in dirty weekend (no they didn't call it that!) at a luxury hotel in Bournemouth for just £13, that must of been before inflation. There was no fashion page in *The Times* but the clothes the women wore in the photographs were awful, all right so they were minis but they were like potato sacks.

There was no news, not what I would call news. No pop charts, also no soccer it being May, so where Seathorpe Wanderers stood in the League tables we shall never know. But the most intresting thing about my birthday copy of *The Times* was that it was price six dee, so it brought home to me with a bang that Debra Chase is pre-metric!

I was an only child. Mum and Dad did try for a boy to keep me company, what with them being out so much, but it was not to be, maybe that was what started to drive them apart. We lived at No 23 (Garden Flat) Dunkley Road in the better part of Sydenham, quite near where my Auntie Doris still lives although her flat is a council one. We could of had a council flat too as both Mum and Dad worked for them, but Dad has always said he does not agree with council estates, he would sooner live in a cardboard box under Hungerford Bridge. Auntie Doris says he might as well of done, the size of our Garden Flat and the state it was in, she says it was like a tip. I wouldn't know but I must say I am sprised, as Dad had quite a good job as the youngest ever superintendent of Conduit Street Swimming Baths, on top of which he has always been ever so finnicky, scrupefully keeping his nails clean and if you should leave a wet towel on the bathroom floor he goes barmy. My belief is that my Mum was overworked so could not keep the Garden Flat looking as nice as she would of wanted.

By day Mum worked in the Rates Office but three nights a week she was also a hostess at the Regal Bingo

Hall. I think this was to pay for her little luxuries as they were still thought to be in those days, such as the telly (black and white would you believe!), spin-drier, holidays in the luxury chalet Dad used to rent on Canvey Island, and of course she had to have new clothes as she was expected to dress nicely at the Bingo Hall. It was there she became friendly with Mr Gibson apparentlee, Mr Gibson was the insurance collector I made referral to earlier but I should of made mention that he did not collect insurance from us, Dad did not believe in it.

In case of anyone running away with the idea that Dad did not pull his weight moneywise in our little menagerie, I would like to put it on the record that he too had a night job, this enabled him to run his first car, a powder-blue Morris Minor which I can just remember (I used to get car sick something rotten when I was little!), nick-named Dinah the Minor. It so happened that Conduit Street Baths besides being used for swimming was also the vendue for all sorts of evening events like boxing matches, wrestling and ballroom dancing comps. Of course they would cover the pool up on these evenings. Dad earned extra by staying on to see that the Baths were proply prepared for these events, switching all the lights off when they were over, locking up, everything like that. It was doing this overtime that sparked off his livelong intrest in ballroom dancing, you should see the rows and rows of cups and medals Babs and him have won since they teamed up together. I forgot to mention that that is where he first met Babs, at the Conduit Street Baths quarter finals for the South-east London Ballroom Dancing Championships.

For the first three years of my Life, what with both Mum and Dad working all the hours God sent, I spent more time with my Auntie Doris than at home, but it is not true that I was dumped on her as the *Sunday Shocker* made me say. I am sure they must of come to some amiable agreement though I have never discussed how much. Each day Mum would wheel me round to Auntie Doris's place on her way to work then Dad would pick me up in Dinah the Minor on his way home. It does not show on my glamour pix because I am always careful to touch it up with a blemish wand, but I have a tiny scar just below my hairline where I was thrown sideways off of the back seat and cracked my head on the door handle when Dad went into a skid after braking sharply to avoid a dog in the road, some people would of just run over it but that is typified of Dad, he would not hurt a fly and has never lifted a finger to his favrite daughter. Although he has a foul temper his bark is worse than his bile.

Now what happened between Mum and Dad is shrouded in history, he will never talk about it, not that I have ever asked him. When I was about twelve I did once ask Babs but she just laughed and said it was all water under the Thames. So all I reely know is what I have got out of Auntie Doris, and without knocking her I guess she is a bit prejusticed when it comes to my Mum (she is my Dad's sister not my Mum's) but it is the only version I know not counting the one that appeared in the *Sunday Shocker*, so here goes.

The way Auntie Doris tells it, it all began with Dad starting to get hooked on the ballroom dancing comps at Conduit Street Baths, that was before he'd met Babs though the *Sunday Shocker* makes out different, the way they twisted it round he didn't get hooked on dancing until he'd already got hooked on Babs, but if that's so why would he of tried to get Mum to take dancing lessons with him? Anyone who doesn't believe that can ask Auntie Doris, cos she was there. One night when there was a programme on telly called *Come Dancing*, Mum, Dad and Auntie Doris were watching all these couples doing the Moonlight Saunter round the Winter Gardens, Blackpool, when all of a sudden Dad says, 'Do you know, Norah' (that is my reel Mum's name, Norah), 'do you know, Norah, I bet with a bit of practice you and me could give a good half of these semi-finalists a run for their money, what do you think, what do you think?' He's ever so funnee when he gets excited, Dad is, he always chews his cabbages twice.

Apparently Mum just laughed. 'You've got to be joking,' she says. 'The last time we took the floor on Canvey Island, Doris, he nearly had *me* on the floor, and that was just him trying to turn in a foxtrot I think it was, none of this fancy stuff.' I just can't believe that, not that my Mum would ever lie, because the one thing Dad can do is ballroom dance, I just can't picture him ever making a spectrum of himself on the dance floor except when he tries to bop which I wish he wouldn't, he knows all the right moves but it is just not his scene. Anyway, no way could he intrest Mum in taking lessons to get up to comp standard, she just couldn't care less but so what, that was her privilege, even though Auntie Doris has always dropped mystic hints that she had other fish to fry. So at the death, just to stop Dad banging on and on about dancing lessons so she could watch some variety programme she wanted to see in peace, Mum said if he felt all that keen why didn't he take a course by himself, so he did no more, that's exactly what he did.

What these other fish were that Mum was sposed to be frying I never found out. All Auntie Doris would ever say vacantly was that she liked a good time but then who doesn't, so do I if it comes to that, must be in the blood, and anyway it cannot of been much fun bringing up little me, apparently I was a right little cry-baby never giving them a night's peace, on top of that Mum had two jobs to hold down so who is to begrudge her a bit of pleasure? Besides which you have got to bear in mind that all concerned – Mum, Dad and Babs – were then nearly as young as what I am now, but without my worldy experience. All except Mr Gibson, who was an older man.

So off Dad trots to learn ballroom dancing, which I can reveal he did at night school over at Forest Hill. Yes, I know the *Sunday Shocker* made the allegoration that he learned all he ever knew about the Natural Promenade Turn from Babs and I freely admit having said sunnink on those lines to Barry Butcher, but only because I thought the world would not be all that intrested in Dad's dancing lessons and I wanted to get on to where I start to grow boobs and the story begins to hot up and thusly get it over with. In actual fact both versions are true, what happened was that Dad and Babs got chatting over coffee and Jaffa cakes one night at the Baths when she was sitting out the Doriz Waltz cos her partner Ronnie was late or so it was demised, it turns out he had come off his motor bike. Toyboy Ronnie and gay divorcee Babs, not that she was all that much older, both worked for a travel agency up West, I think they were having a fling at the time, in fact I know they were because to Dad's relief it was Ronnie who was named in her divorce from this washing machine salesman she had met at aged eighteen,

9

not Dad. (When I called her a gay divorcee, I meant she became one later.)

I have got all this from Babs, seems that with being seprated from her hubby she was giving dancing lessons at the Forest Hill Evening Institution to make ends meet (same as Mum reely, except that with her it was checking bingo cards), so course, once Dad let drop over the Jaffa cakes he was thinking of taking it up, dancing that is, it was a case of, 'Ooh, well you must come over to Forest Hill every Tuesday and Friday because although I say it myself you won't find a better teacher, not unless you pay someone private.' So the whole thing took off from there. Babs has always said she never meant anything to happen as she knew Dad was married with a kiddy, but she was living on her own, Ronnie was flat on his back in hospital with a ruptured spleen so what else could she do, she was only human.

Whether it would of fizzled out or not if Mum hadn't gone away with this Alan Gibson we shall never know. Seems Mum had been seeing Mr Gibson for some time, in fact the story goes that often when she was sposed to be at the Bingo Hall she was reely round at his place, according to Auntie Doris Dad went to fetch her one night when I had ear ache and was crying for my Mummy but of course she wasn't there, the Bingo Hall that is, well that was her privilege, no one is forced to do two jobs and if she wanted a night off occasionaly whom can blame her? Both Mum and Mr Gibson had a big intrest in going to the cinema so maybe that is what drew them together style of thing. The same as Mum did not want to take up ballroom dancing Dad did not want to go to the pictures, he has always called it a waste of money when you can watch Fred Astaire (his hero) on the box for nothing. So I spose it was fate reely.

Insofar as I personaly are concerned, all I can remember is playing with my Looby Loo dolly on the hearth rug at Auntie Doris's when Mum came in wearing her red coat and crying for some unknown reason. She gave me a ginormous box, whole quarter pound it must of been, of Smarties, my favrites specially the dark brown ones (they still are), then went into the bedroom with Auntie Doris. When they came out Auntie Doris was crying too. Mum picked me up and gave me a big hug and told me to be a good girl, her last words being as I remember, 'Oh God, now she's dribbled chocolate juice all down my lapel, have you got such a thing as a J-cloth, Doris?'

My next memry is being wheeled round by Auntie Doris to Conduit Street Baths. I had never been there before so far as I know, I can remember staring up at these big iron girders and hearing a lot of splashing and shrieking, I think they must of had a class of schoolkids in but I couldn't see the actual pool with my head being tilted right back cos of being strapped in my pushchair, all I can remember seeing is those girders. I think Dad and Auntie Doris must of gone into the office because I can remember lolling my head to one side and seeing them come out of a green door. Auntie Doris was crying again. This time it was Dad's turn to tell me to be a good girl. I don't know what I thought was going on but I knew there was something, cos Auntie Doris bought me a bag of crisps on the way back and that was most unusual, she couldn't be doing with eating between meals except mint imperials which she lived off.

According to Auntie Doris, Mum going off with Mr Gibson was quite a local talking point. From what I can gather, though no one can prove it and he was never had up in court, he had been dipping into his satchel, not only the insurance money he was collecting but also £70 he was supposed to be paying out for somebody's furniture destructed in a fire, the woman is supposed to have asked him to cash the cheque for her and she never saw him again. I don't know whether this is true or not, because when Auntie Doris tells the story it is £70 and a sideboard but when Babs tells it, it is £60 and a cocktail cabinet, and what would an old woman who doesn't even have a bank account be doing with a cocktail cabinet I should like to know. Anyway, for whatever reason Mr Gibson decided to do a disappearing trick to the Isle of Man, he was born there and had come into his mother's house some say so it could have been as simple as that, and he gave Mum the optic of going with him or staying behind, so after much thought and heart searching she said Yes.

There was one more historical meeting between Dad and Mum by all accounts and that was when he went out to Fleetwood wherever that is to thrash things out. Mum came over by ferry from the Isle of Man and they lunched off prawn cocktails and scampi washed down with hock at a place called the Captain's Table so Babs tells me, whilst they decided what to do about little me. Just what transposed between my parents I have never had deluged to me in any detail, but it seems that as livelong confirmed bachelor Mr Gibson could not stand the sight of kids there was no way I could live with Mum. Auntie Doris's chronic asthma was playing her up so I couldn't live with her although she didn't mind looking after me for a bit till things got sorted out, so that left me living with Dad, or Dad and Babs as it would turn out. After much agonisal Dad thought it best for my happiness to make a clean break with Mum rather than have her shuttling like a yo-yo between the Isle of Man and Sydenham to see me, it would of been unsettling for me besides there was the cost to think of. In exchange for the divorcal proceedings naming Babs instead of Mr Gibson, who apparently had a mordant fear of publicitee – nothing to do with the insurance Co finding out his whereabouts I spose! – my Mum tearfully agreed.

So it was that Mum passed out of my life, or nearly so. Every Christmas and birthday without fail she would send me a card and a prezzie. Trouble was, what with not seeing me Mum did not seem to reelise her little girl was growing up! I got a Barbie doll for my twelfth birthday when Babs had already showed me how to put on lipstick and eye make-up, whilst for Xmas when I was fourteen and into stuff like *True Romance* and *Boy Friend* I got a Pony Annual!! So if you're reading this Mum, no more dollies' teasets, all right? (Only joking, now I'm grown up she doesn't send prezzies any more.)

After Mum went I guess I stayed with Auntie Doris for a while but I have no clear remembrance of this, I often used to stay with her for a few days even when Mum was at home, so it is all jumbled up.

I do not have another memory of those times until the day came when I was taken by Dad to meet Babs under the public library clock. I thought she was beautiful and still do. I had on a little tartan dress with a tartan bow in my hair which was already quite long, white socks and black patient leather shoes, it must of been summer because I was not wearing a coat. I can't remember what Babs was wearing but she says it was her powder blue suit which she then had with a high-necked blouse, this was aiming at a simple affect as she did not wish to give me the impression she was in any way pushy even though I was not yet four and did not know about such things. What I do remember is her striking blonde hair done up in a beehive which then as now was her crowning asset. I was fascinated by her bright orange lips all shiny like an iced bun, and by her big fluttering eyelashes which I did not reelise were false till in later life when I was about seven when she let me watch her putting them on and showed me how to do it.

We went to a Wimpy House where I had my first ever Knickerbocker Glory, but my most vivacious memory of that day is of Auntie Babs as Dad wanted me to call her though I wouldn't and never have, dabbing her lips with a paper serviette and making a perfect lip-print like Marilyn's. I wanted her to give it to me and she would of done but Dad screwed it up and put it in an ashtray and I cried and cried until Babs calmed me down by fishing a Cadbury's Milk Flake out of her bag and sticking it in my Knickerbocker Glory which was then even more delicious.

Going home we left Babs waiting at the end of the street whilst Dad took me back to Auntie Doris's. She wanted to kiss me but Dad said, 'I don't want to take her back all smothered in lipstick' so I kissed her instead and she said I was a little love and that we were going to be big friends, which we are to this day. On the way across the waste ground in front of the flats Dad told me not to say anything to Auntie Doris about 'Auntie Babs' but course being young and being me I blabbed out the whole thing the minute we got indoors, telling her all about this lovely lady with the orange mouth and white hair as I called it who'd stuck a Cadbury's Milk Flake into my ice cream and jelly (I couldn't say Knickerbocker Glory!).

Whether it was on that particlar occasion or some other, because after that it was a reglar recurrence to meet Babs and go on to the Wimpy Bar, there was an almighty row with Auntie Doris storming, 'God almighty, Eric, why don't you show some sense for once in your life, if you want to stuff her full of ice cream and chocolate of a lunchtime get a Wimpy and chips down her first, she can't live on all sweet stuff.' I think he must of taken this advice cos I have a distinct remembrance of Babs scraping the onions out of my Wimpy, I have always had a thing about onions even from birth.

The years rolled by. Then, when I must of been getting on for five, came the day when Dad took me off to play in the park, this time Babs was not there, but as we watched the toy boats sailing on the pond he suddenly asked, 'By the way, we're not talking about tomorrow poppet or even next week so don't get over-excited, but how would you like to go to the seaside, eh, how would you like to go to the seaside, I mean to live?'

It was all right Dad saying don't get over-excited, I was that excited I finished up being sick. I had never been to the seaside, Mum and Dad used to leave me behind with Auntie Doris when they went to Canvey Island, but I must of seen it on the telly cos I know I babbled on for days about catching fishes and building sand castles. I can remember Auntie Doris packing all my clothes into a big suitcase and my toys into one of those black plastic rubbish sacks, this was so full with things Dad and Babs had bought for me on our outings such as my bendy giraffe I was very fond of and my blue brushed nylon teddy bear, that she could not make a neck on the sack to get the string round, so when Dad came to collect me she said, 'Does she really want all this stuff?' Dad turned to me and said, 'Why don't you leave some of your toys with Auntie Doris for when you come to see her, just take your favourites, eh, you'll be getting plenty of new toys at the seaside' but I made such a fuss that at the death we took the lot, I remember Dad staggering down the steps with the sack in his arms and Auntie Doris humping the suitcase with one hand and holding me with the other, and my dolly's manicure set that Babs had bought me falling out of the toy sack and the nail varnish bottle breaking and dripping down the steps. I burst into tears and Dad said, 'Now there's not need to turn on the waterworks, no need to turn on the waterworks, we'll get you another as soon as we get to the seaside,' but Auntie Doris said disapprovefully, 'She should never have been given it in the first place, I wish people wouldn't give her things she isn't old enough for,' this being a veiled referral to Babs. Then it was Auntie Doris's turn for the 'water-works' as we bid a tearful farewell, that is Auntie Doris was tearful, but having got over the upset with the dolly's manicure set I was too excited about going to the seaside.

Babs did not come with us in Dinah the Minor, it transposed she had gone on ahead to get things ready at the Seathorpe end. I was car sick as usual after eating all the Jelly Fruits Dad gave me to keep me quiet. 'I didn't tell you to eat the whole box, I didn't tell you to eat the whole box!' I can remember him saying as we pulled up for me to bring up the Jelly Fruits. There was a pile of builders' sand by the roadside which with my then tiny mind I thought meant we were already at the seaside! This made me so excited that all thoughts of being sick left my head until we were back in the car, when I brought up the Jelly Fruits just as Dad hit the motorway.

*

To begin with we lived in digs in Albert Street, just two rooms with shared loo and bath on the half-landing. They were on the second floor and if I clamoured up on the window sill I could just see the sea over the rooftops. All through my childlihood I longed for a place on the front with a balcony like the Regalcy houses diverted into flats they had along the prom, but it was not to be. Dad and Babs were set on a bungalow, and by the time I myself could afford a sea view, Seathorpe and me had long since parted company.

I don't think we could of been all that well off at first. Dad had taken quite a step down careerwise by excepting a post as assistant manager of the King George VI Open-air Swimming Pool, a right dump it was with all the plaster flaking and tiles coming off and half the cubicle doors missing, whilst Babs could only work half-days, she just took the first job going, behind the counter in a chemist's, because although I had just started at the infants' school it was only in the mornings so I had to be picked up and looked after. These must of been hard times for Dad and Babs but I guess they wanted a clean break from Sydenham and a fresh start, I reely admire them for sticking it out, it can't of been easy.

As for me, they were happy days mostly. Whilst I called Seathorpe all the names under the sun when I got to be a teenager – Sleepythorpe it used to be known as to the Wet Set as me and my friends liked to call ourselves on account of spending most of our time hanging around Dad's Pool (though I should say this was not till both myself and the Pool had developed out of all recognisance, the Pool to have a complete facelift and get upgraded to the Seathorpe Open Air Swim Pool and

Fitness Centre, and me to grow boobs) – it was a nice little place from a toddler's point of view. There were the sands and amusement arcades and the dodgems and swingboats on the Pier, as well as the Dairymaid ice cream kiosk where I always got an ice lolly moon rocket and a bag of crisps on the way to the beach and very often a Mister Softee cone on the way back if I promised to eat up all my tea! Babs took me down to the beach nearly every afternoon, where I played with whatever kiddies might be there whilst Babs sunbathed in her bikini. Before that first summer was over she was as brown as if she had just come back from Badedas and she has been that way ever since.

But the ridiclous thing about these blissful days of paddling and being held up to play the fruit machines is that young as I was I thought we were on holiday, specially as we were in digs with none of our own furniture which turned out to be in store. Therefore I thought that sooner or later we would be going back to Sydenham. Therefore when it started to rain for days on end I thought our holiday was over and I wanted to go home and see my Mum, who in the confusal of my five-year-old mind I had forgotten was no longer there, in fact Babs found me putting all my dolls in the suitcase I had dragged from under her and Dad's bed.

I must of gone on and on about Mum, being dead boring in fact, because one night when putting me to bed which was a cot in the corner of their bedroom (I never understood why some nights I was carried back into the living room and tucked up on the settee!) Babs told me a story which instead of reading it out of a Rupert Bear book she made up. I still know it off by heart, it went like this:

'Once upon a time there was a little girl whose Mummy loved her very much, but then she, the Mummy that is, had to go away. It is anybody's guess why she did what she did but she must've had her reasons and it turned out for the best, because after that the little girl went to live at the seaside where she was very happy and had lots of lovely sweeties and ice creams and Polo mints and so she lived happily ever after with her Daddy who loved her just as much as her Mummy and his lovely lady who loved her too, now try to get off pet and tomorrow if it's still raining we'll go to the Aquarium and look at all the fishes.'

Babs told me that story many many times and it must of sunk into my sub-conscience, because one day at the infants' school when everyone in the class had to tell a story, I stood up and told Babs' story word for word as she had told it to me, the upshot of this being that the teacher took me to this other teacher, then both of them took me to the headteacher who sat me up on her desk, giving me a Quality Street out of a big tin then accusing my Mum of being dead. At first I believed her and this became a very convoluted time in my life, until at the death Dad had to take time off and go down to the school and sort it all out, but not before I don't mind saying I had wet the bed a few times.

Here I am revealing facts that the *Sunday Shocker* knew not the first thing about because I never told them, but it was after this that Babs reely began to take me in hand, becoming a second Mum to me as well as my big sister, telling me about Mum running off with Mr Gibson in a guardful sort of way and saying I must not worry about it any more, which for most of the time I didn't, she said they had a muted intrest in the cinema which seemed quite reasonable to me.

There were acceptances to my not thinking about Mum any more such as one Monday afternoon when the Open-air Pool always closed, all three of us went to a reprisal of *Mary Poppins* at the Essoldo, in spite of Dad grumbling that he didn't agree with the cinema. I didn't go much on the film tell the truth, I had a pash on the James Bond films which Babs used to take me to see even though I was under the recommendal age cos she had got to know the manager, so I suppose my mind began to wander and I started to think if only Mum and Mr Gibson being the movie buffs they apparently were had taken me to the pix just once, and I cried and cried and had to be taken out to the foyer by Babs and given a Twix bar. So began the growing up of Marjory Linda Chase as I was still called in those far-off days of the forgotten Seventies.

2

I Grow Boobs

The next event in my interesting livelihood is that I was a bridesmaid at Seathorpe's glamour wedding of the year, that of Dad and Babs at the Registry Office in East Street. So presumptiously divorcal proceedings must of come through for both of them, but this was never mentioned. I wore a dinky little pink taffeta dress with matching sash, cute little halo of plastic rosebuds, white net gloves, white lacy tights and pink ballet pumps. Babs wore yellow. Dad wore his blazer and flannels. Norma Borridge, the future Suzie Dawn, tried to put it about the school playground that I wasn't a bridesmaid at all, I was just there, seems her Mum had told her you do not have bridesmaids at Registry Office weddings, you only have witnesses. I'm afraid she was just jealous, anyway I wasn't a witness because two friends of Dad and Babs were those.

After the ceremonial we were all driven to the Royal Talbot Hotel on the seafront for a champagne lunch. But what made the day so memorous for me was not only that it was the first time I ever tasted champagne (you are not sposed to like it your first time but I took to it like the provisional duck to water, in fact I got quite tiddly and nearly spoiled the reception by being too noisy, Dad had to keep telling me to put a sock in it), it was also the first time I ever had my picture in the Press. There I was on p3 of the *Seathorpe Clarion*, standing in front of Dad and Babs on the Registry Office steps with my little bouquet. Yes, a Page Three girl already! What a pity I was squinting.

By this time we had moved out of our digs into a proper flatlet being the first floor of a little terrace house in Castle Street near the ice rink, where as some people may know the South of England Ice Queen finals are always held (I never went in for it as you have to be able to skate). We now had our own furniture back plus Babs's bits and pieces, so we were one of the first families ever to own two TV sets, one in the living room and one in the airing cupboard, besides a record player and a cocktail cabinet belonging to Babs. I was fascinated by it, it lit up and played a little tune when you opened it, I used to play with it for hours till Dad would say, 'Will you stop that, you'll run the batteries down, you'll run the batteries down.' Dad and Babs having spent nearly their last penny on the deposit on the flat and doing the place up, they did not have a proper honeymoon, they just took advantage of one of the Royal Talbot's Bargain Off-peak Weekends whilst I was looked after at the flat by Auntie Doris who came down for the wedding.

After that, nothing much happened till I was twelve. Dad became Manager of the Pool whilst once I had started proper school Babs was able to take a full-time job which she did at the Seathorpe Snappy 24-hour Foto Developing Service, where she too rose to be Supervisor. With extra money coming in we were able to move to the bungalow of their dreams, Oceanview, Sowerby Crescent, West Seathorpe, which although they were to live in London again on account of our business interests, they kept on as a weekend place – and I am pleased to say guess who paid off the mortgage once she had hit the big time?!

Till I was old enough to go home by myself, Babs used

to pick me up from school and if it was one of her busy times she would sometimes take me back to the shop where I was allowed to help by putting people's snaps in their envelopes. Being as we lived in a seaside resort, quite a few of the snaps were guys and gals in swimsuits, some of them very skimpy, the swimsuits that is, not their wearers! I think this was what first made me intrested in people's bodies, especially the guys, they were reel hunks some of them, and from there on in it was but a short step to wanting to be a model.

All this time they were reburnishing the Pool and putting in the ride-of-a-lifetime wild water flumes, solarium, martial arts hall and fitness centre, then came the day when it was officiously opened by Seathorpe Sound DJ stunna Bob Bradfield. By this time I had my own latchkey but instead of going home to an empty bungalow to make myself a crisp sandwich and watch the cartoons, now that we had a proper Leisure Pool instead of just a tatty old open-air swimming baths, I used to like to go there after school when Dad would let me lie on a sun lounger and do my homework whilst watching the swimmers. Course, I could swim myself by now and I am afraid I spent more time splashing about in the Pool or sliding down the wild water flumes than filling in the blanks in my Look & Tell book – specially after meeting Pete!

I guess Pete was my first boy friend. We were both about ten and I reely had a crush on him. He had blond hair and freckles and a gap in his teeth, he looked so cute he could of been a child actor in a sweeties commercial, I'm sure he could of. I met him by pushing him in the Pool, I had seen him looking at me and this was the quickest way I could think of to make his acquaintal and how right I was, he responced by dragging me in by my ankles and then splashing water over me till Dad came round the side of the Pool and stopped the fun. There was a bit of a row cos although I had on my swimsuit I was still wearing my dress on top of it, I wanted to see Pete rolling his ice-blue eyes when I slowly took it off, I was a right little minx I can tell you! After that we used to meet up at the Pool every day. I would save the Crunchy bar or Smarties Babs gave me to eat in break and share them with Pete. In return he gave me a piece of bubble gum, it was the first prezzie I ever had from a boy (but not the last!) and we had a lot of fun blowing bubbles at one another. But came the day when Pete had to go home to Croydon, he was only on holiday in Seathorpe and though we promised to write I guess it was too much hassle for both of us and anyway writing has never been my strong point so we never saw one another again. I was to meet other boys round the poolside, a whole raft of them in fact, some of them quite good lookers, but I never forgot Pete and his cheeky grin.

As for school I hated it, complete waste of time from my point of view. Whilst I still did not know exactly what I was going to do for a career, modelling and actressing were utmost in my mind and I knew I did not have to know anything about the Battle of the Roses in order to get on, except maybe for historic parts if I became an actress which as a matter of fact is still very much on the cards although I cannot see myself doing Shakespeare, there is too much to learn. New Maths was a closed book to me, but fortuitously before getting reely bogged down with it we got a new teacher who did not believe in it either, so from there on in we did all our sums with pocket calculators, not that I'm much good with those either, having long nails your finger sometimes slips and you can make a lot of big mistakes, luckily I do not have to worry about figures as it is all done for me these days by Dad and Babs and top accountant Mr Cuthbertson.

Also to be fair we did have another reely good teacher, Ms Banks her name was but she let us call her Roz. She taught English reely well even though she did not seem much older than we, at any rate she was a lot younger than Babs, she must of been straight out of training college. We thought Roz was smashing, she wore jeans and that reinsured us that she was one of us, that she was on our side style of thing. I was reely nervous about moving up into her class out of junior school because English had just been a big headache with me, I could never get the hang of it, but Roz just said as soon as she saw I was worried which she did when she gave us our first project and I could not do it (Write a letter to the Council about something you would like something done about, it could be more amnesities for the old folk, it could be dog dirt, it could be anything), 'Look, love, language is just what we all speak, you have been doing it all your life, you didn't have to take lessons in how to talk now did you, any more than you had to in how to walk so don't let it bug you, just express yourself what you want to say and as for grammar, frankly don't quote me on this but I think it's crap.'

Roz reely was fantastic. You didn't have to read books in her class, she said they were elitist, she used to say, 'I'm a big believer in reaching kids where they're at' so instead of having to imaginate we were somebody in a Roald Dahl story and write out what was sposed to of happened to us after the story had ended, which was what we had to do in the juniors, she let us bring the *Beano* or the *Sun* or the *Daily Stunner* to school and write stories as if we were Dennis the Menace or a *Sun* reporter.

Sprisingly enough I had never seen the *Sun* before cos Dad doesn't believe in newspapers, and I reely took to it, specially the Page Three girls (not that they are in the same legion as the *Daily Stunner*'s Page Three Popsies, but Debra Chase would say that, wouldn't she?!). This was the only part of the paper Roz didn't agree with, she said there was nothing wrong with seeing the human body but this was just titivating and degradeful to women, I thought her theorem a load of codswallop quite frankly but I didn't say anything. But where I did agree with Roz was when she went on to say if men could ogle scantly-clad girls on Page Three, why shouldn't women ogle scantly-clad men? (Actually these days you can, though it is usually Page Seven.) So for one English lesson we had to make up a caption for an imaginative Page Three Fella.

I can still remember what I wrote for that project, I had a crush on a bloke called Matt at the time, he worked with Babs, in fact a little bird told me Babs quite fancied him too, he was sweet seventeen and a reel hunk. This is what I wrote: 'Matt by name and Matt by nature – with that hairy chest this he-man heart-throb could double as a Welcome mat, he would be Welcome on my front door-step any day! Matt works at Seathorpe's Snappy 24-hour Foto Developing Service but snaps are not the only thing he develops, just look at those muscles gals!' Roz fell about, she thought it was brill, she made me read it out to the class and they all wet themselves too. I wanted to keep it and let Matt see it accidently on purpose but Roz said better not in case Dad got hold of it, she didn't like parents seeing our schools work on account of a lot of them would not understand. But she said if I could write like that I ought to go in for journalism when I left school. I did toy with the idea of becoming a *Sun* reporter but I guess I did not have the qualifications, and anyway I now knew what I reely wanted to do with my life. I wanted to become a Page Three girl.

Just after my twelfth birthday I woke up one morning to find I was suddenly growing up in the most alarming way, I was both puzzled and frightened. Babs had told me the facts of life but this was one particlar fact she had been quite vague about, firstly as to why it happens (I still do not understand human biography to this day, tell the truth) and secondly what to do about it when it does, she said the easiest thing would be for me to come to her when it did happen, when she would show me what to do, she said it was no great hassle. But as luck would have it the Snappy 24-hour Foto Developing Service had to pick that day of all days for Babs to go up to their Head Office for an interview so of course she had taken the early train long before I was up. Turns out they were promotionalising her to Supervisor so when we finally did meet up Babs made a joke of it, saying we had both grown up on the same day, but it was no joke to little Marjory Linda Chase as I still was believe you me. I couldn't bring myself to tell Dad and I didn't know who else to turn to, I would of talked to Roz but it was the school holidays so I did something incredulously stupid, I ran away to find my Mum.

After waiting for Dad to leave for work I packed a spare pair of jeans, T-shirt, make-up, can of Coke, crisps, the Twix bar Babs had left for me and that week's *Jackie* into my school duffel bag and set off, but not before writing a note to Dad and Babs saying, 'Do not worry, have got a problem so have gone to find Mum and will be back as soon as everything has been sorted out, I love you both but I need Mum at this moment in time, lots of love Linda xxxxxxxx.' (At this period, no pun intentional, I had a big thing about not wanting to call myself Marjory, I had never liked it for a name, I didn't go much on Linda either but it was better than Marjory. Little did I know I would return to Oceanview with a brand new name for myself!)

I had about £3.50 left out of my pocket money and this I thought should get me to the Isle of Man. I knew the Isle of Man was an island, I'm not stupid, and that it was off the coast of Fleetwood, but for some reason I had it firmly fixed in my mind that Fleetwood must be somewhere near Southampton. I now know I must of been thinking of the Isle of Dogs and that the Isle of Man is between England and Ireland but I do not blame myself for this, all I ever learned in Geography was how to make a model of some mountains out of wet paper.

There is a bus service between Seathorpe and Southampton but only about every hour and as all it said where the bus stop timetable should of been was SOUTH COAST SAVERS – FAMILY FARES YOU CAN AFFORD there was no way of knowing when the next one would be. I waited and waited and then did something Dad had told me I never should, I hitched a lift in a TV rentals van. I did try to get a lift by car but none of them would stop, they probly thought I had a boy friend lurking round the corner who would appear out of the blue as soon as they had said Southampton, yes, hop in darling.

The driver was called Terry. He was about twenty-something, straight brown hair, little moustache, not good looking, not bad looking, but nice with it. Terry asked why I was going to Southampton and I said to stay with my Mum, I didn't mention the Isle of Man or he might of sussed I was running away, he said Oh, didn't I live with my Mum then, I said No, she and Dad led separate lives, she went her way and he went his style of thing, it was what both wanted. Terry said and hadn't anybody ever warned me against excepting lifts from strange men and I said yes but he had laughing eyes and I trusted him. After that we talked about the pop scene and whether I had ever been to a Seathorpe disco called Sparkies. At that time I had not but I did not want to admit it so I said I had and he said I didn't look old enough. So I told another little white lie and said I was older than I looked, I was sixteen if I was a day if the truth be known. Then Terry asked if I liked a band there used to be in those bygone days called Street Cred and when I said I did he reached out to put a tape of them on, no prizes for guessing that in so doing his hand accidently on purpose brushed against my knee. I didn't mind cos I was wearing jeans so he didn't get to touch bare flesh, but very soon after that, when we had left all the houses behind and were driving through some big woods, the New Forest I think, he pulled into a layby on the excuse of lighting a ciggy. I knew he was going to suggest getting out of the van and stretching our legs and my heart was pumping as I wondered how to tell him No, my Mum would be waiting for me and besides I was not that kind of girl. But then having given me a cigarette, when I coughed after taking the first drag (it was only the third cigarette I had ever had, it has never become a habit with me although I do like the occasional cig in the middle of a reely good dinner), he put his hand under my chin and turning my head to face him said, 'Well you don't look sixteen to me, sweetheart, you look more like jailbait' and with that we drove off again, so I think I probly had a narrow escape.

But Terry was still quite chatty and started telling me stories about all the women he was sposed to of pulled whilst installing their new videos, how one of them went to get him a cup of tea and came back wearing just stockings and suspenders, and another answered the door wearing only a housecoat which flapped open just as he was carrying in the new TV set which according to him he dropped on his foot in his sprise. I didn't believe a word of it, if this kind of thing was always happening as he claimed it was, why would he of been sprised? If you ask me he got these adventures from some book like *Confessions of a Windowcleaner* which I had heard of at school but not read, I have never been a big reader. But I had a pretty good idea that telling them to me was making him quite horny and sure enough we stopped at another layby on the far end of the forest where he made a suggestion. I was amazed. I had heard of people doing that sort of thing but not in reel life, I thought in my innocents it was something only call girls did. Thinking quickly I said I was sorry, I was not a call girl and anyway I had a sore lip, which was perfectly true as I had torn off a bit of skin where my ciggy had stuck to it. I must say Terry once again was the perfect gentleman, just gave me a crooked grin and said, 'Ah well, you can't win them all Terry, you can win most of them but there will always be the one that got away, it's like in fishing,' and with that he drove off again.

As we got to where the houses started he asked me where I wanted dropping off. I had never been to

Southampton in my life before so I said, 'Anywhere near the bus station' knowing there must be one. Terry asked for my phone number saying he might take me to Sparkies some time, so I gave him the number of Norma Borridge, now Suzie Dawn, but he never called her or if he did she never let on.

At the bus station I wandered about looking for a Fleetwood bus but with no luck, so I asked one or two people but they'd never heard of the place, they just said, 'Fleetwood, Fleetwood, that's a new one on me, no, I should ask at the Inquiry Office' so I did. This wrinkly old inspector with white hair coming out of his nostrils gave me a funny look saying, 'Why do you want to go to Fleetwood, love?' so I said, 'I've got to go over to the Isle of Man to see my Mum,' so he said, 'Oh, I see, well I'm afraid you're a long way from the Isle of Man, a very long way indeed, but if you'll just sit down for a minute I'll see if I can find a lady who can help you, now don't go away will you?' But I did, as soon as he went into the little office behind the counter and shut the door I was off like a greased bat, cos I knew he was calling the police.

I ran to the far end of the bus station and mingled myself in a bus queue till their bus came and they started to get on it, then taking care I was not being followed I found a big destinator board with the names of all the places the buses went to, both short distant and long distant. I couldn't find Fleetwood under the letter F and couldn't think of any other letter it might come under except maybe P if it was spelt like phone or photo. I was just looking hopelessly under the Ps when I felt a hand on my arm and I looked round to find this dumpy young policewoman saying, 'Excuse me, are you the young lady who's trying to get to Fleetwood?'

I was reely scared, I thought in my ignorsense it was probly a crime to run away when you were under age and I had visions of being put in care like a girl at school called Julie Cutteridge who was whisked off by the social workers and never seen again, all because she kept running off to the bright lights of the West End with its tawdry values (that's if you don't know which bits of the West End a nice girl should keep out of, or don't care more like in Julie Cutteridge's case). So although she looked friendly enough I said, 'No, not me' and tried to tug myself free, but she kept a firm grip on my sleeve saying, 'Well I think you are and I'd like you to come with me for a little chat at the station, now don't worry you're not going to be locked up.' I must of gone pale because she added, 'Now you look to me like a girl after my own heart, someone who likes Cornish pasty and chips, I bet you haven't eaten today, have you?'

Truth to tell I hadn't even thought about eating, but apart from my Twix bar and Coke which I had consummated in Terry's van I'd had nothing since breakfast, and that was only a bag of crisps and a Fanta orange, having told Dad I would have my Sugar Puffs and banana later. So yes, being as how it must of been getting on for lunchtime I suddenly reelised I was ravishing, so whilst I won't say I went wilfully with Janice as she said she was called, she never told me her second name, I certainly went a lot more wilfully than if she'd just said, 'All right, sunshine, come on, I want a word with you,' specially as everyone was staring at us.

She had a panda car waiting just outside the bus station, driven by a male policeman. By now Janice had asked me my name and not wishing to tell her it I said in a flash of aspiration, 'Debra', after sultry songstress Debra

Dawson whose hit single 'I Don't Wanna Cry For You, I Don't Wanna Sigh For You' happened to be No 1 for the seventeenth record-breaking week. So the world can believe it or not and by the way this exclusive revolution never appeared in the *Sunday Shocker* so you are reading it here for the first time, but that is how Debra Chase came to get her name – being led to a police car on the way for interrorisation at the station!!

As we got into the car Janice said by way of introducing the policeman driver who was quite a good looker in his way but not my type, too old for one thing, 'Now this is Mick, Debra, and he's going to drive us in the general direction of that Cornish pasty and chips.' Mick was the strong silent type, he just said, 'Any excuse for a nosh-up Debra, that's our Janice.' I hoped he would switch on his siren as we drove off but it was not to be.

Janice was reely kind to me when we got to the police station, true to her word she sent down to the canteen for Cornish pasty and chips twice, tea for her and Diet Coke for me, saying to Mick who took the order, 'And tell them we've got two growing girls up here so they needn't go easy on the chips.' Then she took me into a little cubicle off the main charge room or whatever it's called where we just chatted. It wasn't a case of, 'Right Debra, now I want to get to the bottom of this, what's it all about, eh?' which would of made me clam up, she was just saying things like, 'So what do you think of Southampton, Debra, is this your first visit, has anyone been showing you round at all, we've got some very nice wine bars,' and 'Just say the word if you want to spend a penny,' drawing me out style of thing. Course, they are trained for it. The upshot was that as she did not ask what I was doing in Southampton or how I came to be there I was aching to tell her, though not of course why, that was something I wanted to be between I and Mum.

The next thing is that Mick brings in the Cornish pasties and chips on a tin tray with the Queen's Coronation on it. Saying, 'You don't mind if I pinch a couple of chips, do you, Debbie?' he showed signs of malingering on, but Janice said sternly, although I think she was only joking, 'Thank you Constable Patterson, this is girls' talk in here,' so I thought as he went out shutting the door behind him, Right, this is where we get down to the nitty-gritty. But no, Janice just started tucking in with the words, 'Why is it that all the nicest food has the most calories?' then with a glance at my waistline adding, 'I bet you're the same as me, Debra, you find it easy to put on but hard to take off.' I don't think I've yet mentioned that in those days I was a right little pudding what with all the chocolate and crisps and chips I used to stuff myself with before Babs took me in hand, but that is to come later.

She was reely crafty was Janice, they should of made her a plain clothes detective, cos before I could stop myself I heard myself saying, 'I know, Babs is always going on about if I want to be a model I'll have to go on a proper slimming diet as soon as I've stopped growing.' Quick as a flash she said, 'Oh, so we're still growing are we, lucky you, I could do with growing a couple more inches myself, so how old are you really Debra, just between you and me and these four walls, you're not quite sixteen yet, are you?' In the car I had told her I was, this being the age of consent as regards running away, but now I told her my true age, twelve.

So then Janice ever so casual says, 'And who's Babs then, your sister?' to which I responded, 'No, not reely, although I'd like her to be, but she is married to my Dad.'

This led Janice to say warmly, 'So your Mummy's not with you any more, I expect you miss her, I know I would in your place, Debra,' and upon that I just broke down and sobbed. Trouble was I had a big piece of Cornish pasty in my mouth and I nearly choked on it so Janice had to hit me on the back, so there I was spluttering bits of mince and carrot and pastry all over the Queen's Coronation tray, I even coughed some of it on to Janice's plate, I was never so humilified. But Janice just put the tray on top of a green filing cabinet saying soothfully, 'Well, I don't think it'll do our sylph-like figures much harm to leave a few chips, so why don't you just drink up your Diet Coke and relax and tell me all about it?' which in response to Janice's gentle questionising I started to do, though to the question, 'And why did you decide at this particular moment of time to seek out your Mum, are you in some sort of trouble at home, I know I always was at your age?' I only said, 'I was bored and just felt like seeing her.'

'And she lives in the Isle of Man, you say,' went on Janice. 'And who told you the Isle of Man was anywhere near Southampton?'

'I just thought it was,' I said. Just then there was a tap on the door and in came another lady policewoman who gave me a big smile and handed Janice a slip of paper, whilst Janice said, 'Hello Meg, this is Meg and this is Debra,' but then as Meg went out again she said, 'But it isn't Debra, is it? Because I'm afraid we've had to go through your duffel bag that we've been looking after for you while we had our chat, and according to your bus pass in your purse your name's Marjory Linda, now isn't it?' So now the world knows why Debra Chase cannot stand being called by her given name, in fact I do not agree that it even is my given name any more because I have given it back, Marjory Linda Chase does not exist, if I hated my name before I now reely loathed it.

I just shrugged. The thought crossed my mind to ask, 'If it comes to that, where is your search warren?' but Janice had been so nice to me I couldn't. I also knew that if they had gone through my duffel bag they must of found my diary, not that it had any sizzling secrets in it at that age but it did have my address and phone number and Dad's number at the Pool, so the game was up as regards any hope I might of had of getting back to Seathorpe without him hearing of my escalade.

So I just waited for the next question which was, 'Now you didn't come to Southampton on your bus pass did you, Marjory, because the Seathorpe buses don't come as far as this, do they?' I knew that if I said I had come on the long-distant bus she would of started banging on about what time it set off and how long it took and what the fare was, she was so sharp, so antipathising what she was duty bound to ask next I said, 'No, I got a lift.'

'I see, you got a lift, did you?' said Janice. 'And would that be in a car or a van or a truck or a lorry or what?'

I did not want to get Terry into trouble because so all right, he might of had some funny ideas whilst we were driving through that forest but he was not exactly the Yorkshire Ripper, so instead of saying a van I said a BMW, my favrite car at that time, and instead of saying Terry when Janice asked, 'And how would you describe the driver, did he tell you his name at all?' I said he was called Klaus and that he spoke in a foreign accent with staring eyes.

Upon this, Janice got up, saying, 'Would you just hang on a jiff, Marjory, only I want to get Meg in on this, don't be alarmed, it's just that she's a trainee and it's useful for her to sit in on questioning procedures sometimes,' and with that she went out into the charge room where I saw her talking conspirationally with the desk sergeant, then with Meg who by the way was very nice with big blue eyes and Welsh I think with a reely good figure, then they both came back into the cubicle and sat down, both very smilingly. Meg got out a notebook and Janice said, 'You won't mind if Meg writes one or two things down, she has a terrible memory,' and Meg said, 'Like a sieve', then Janice started to cross-examinate me about this lift into Southampton that I'd got, whether Terry or I should say Klaus had stopped off anywhere, whether he'd made a pass at me, did I know what she meant by pass, could I remember this fictionile BMW's number (I said it began with C nine something, I hope they didn't have a nation-wide search for it if the computer found there reely was a BMW starting C9), and on and on and on.

'I'm just going to ask you one more question,' Janice said at the death, 'and then I want you to come with me upstairs to see a nice lady doctor who just wants to satisfy herself that you've come to no harm. Now the question I want you to answer is this Marjory, and think very carefully. You said he didn't make a pass at you, now no one's going to think any the worse of you but did you make a pass at him?'

I could feel myself blushing all over when I said No, so she probly didn't know whether to believe me or not but it reely was true, I wouldn't of dared, I had read too many true stories in *True Story* about girls who took a hitch-hike to horror, starting out with them encouraging the driver cos he seems reely dishy but finishing up with a dangerous ordeal of nightmare and terror.

Saying goodbye to Meg, Janice and me then trooped up some stone steps to another small room where there was this woman in a white coat with thick glasses and bobbed black hair who looked like a wardress, praps she was one as they must of had cells there, but she was also a doctor called Dr Ross. Although she was very unsmiling she turned out to be quite nice reely, in fact awfly nice before I left. Dr Ross said, 'Now I'm just going to give you a little examination like I'm sure you must have had with your own doctor, so if you'll just go behind that screen and undress I'll be with you in a minute.' This I did in fear and tremblidation, you see I don't know how to explain this but owing to my discovery that morning that I was suddenly growing up, this of course being the whole reason for being in Southampton, I was by now quite frankly I can only say in a bit of a messy state under my jeans. But it was all right, Dr Ross must of seen it all a thousand times because all she said when she came behind the screen was, 'Oh, tt tt tt tt tt tt tt, I hope you've got a change of clothes with you, would you be very kind and pass me that bag of cotton wool balls next to you, Janice?' This brought Janice behind the screen and as soon as she saw me lying there in the nude she took one horrible look at the state I was in and cried, 'Oh, my God, you poor child, what's the beast done to you!' But Dr Ross calmed her down saying, 'Don't leap to the wrong conclusions yet, Janice, she's just started that's all, and let's hope it *is* all that's happened to her today.'

Which of course it was, as her examinating proved. It was time then for Dr Ross to get me fixed up with what I needed for growing up and how to do it, as well as telling me the facts of life that Babs had missed out. She did this in such a matter of fact way that she made it sound like the most ordinary thing in the world which of course it is if you're a girl, though it can be a nuisance if you're modelling swimwear. When Dr Ross had finished I felt very relieved and in a strange sort of way no longer needed to see Mum, though of course it would of been nice if she had walked in.

So the only thing left to worry about was what Dad was going to say, Babs I wasn't bothered about, I knew she would stand up for me. They had rung him of course, as became plain as apple pie when I had finished with Dr Ross and Janice took me up to the canteen for a farewell orange squash and cream slice for me and tea for her. We sat in a corner away from all these policemen who were eating baked beans and laughing, and Janice started, 'Now you've been a very silly girl today Marjory, you do know that, don't you, anything could have happened to you when you took that lift and I do mean anything, I don't want to give you nightmares but you could have been murdered and cut up into pieces, you know these things do happen, you must have seen them on television.' I hadn't actually, because Dad didn't believe in the News, he said it was too gory.

Janice went on, 'And apart from your own safety, you must have realised your Dad was going to worry himself sick until you were found, you've caused him a lot of anguish today Marjory, a lot of anguish.' Actually it was news to me that Dad even knew I was missing till he heard I was found if you can follow that, as he was at work and would not of seen my note yet. Turns out that one of our nosy neighbours from next door at Balmoral had seen me standing at the long distants bus stop on her way for a jacuzzi at the Pool, so she had told him, thank goodness she had not seen me getting into Terry's van,

39

he would of gone beresk. I was truly sorry to of caused Dad this needles heartbreak but I hope I made it up to him in later life when the cheques started rolling in.

Dad came to collect me in Boris the Morris as he called our Metro, Dinah the Minor of course having been confined to the scrapyard by now, and after a privatised word with Dr Ross and Janice he drove me back home, stopping only at a Happy Eater for a quick beefburger each. I kept waiting and waiting for the storm to break but apart from saying, 'Right, let's be having you, young lady' as he came back into Janice's cubicle where I was waiting for him, and some bitter remarks about the Southampton one-way system as we drove round the same set of streets three times, he did not say anything at all, bar, 'Oh, Babs called from Town just as I was coming out, you'll be glad to hear she's been made up to Supervisor, meaning touch wood we should be able to afford that holiday in Spain you both keep dropping hints about, I haven't mentioned this unfortunate business up to press but she'll have to know sooner or later, she'll have to know sooner or later.'

In a funny sort of way instead of scolding me he seemed anxious to please me, probly it was the thought of his little girl growing up, presumptiously Dr Ross had told him all about that. I hoped it would stay that way and began to think pleasant thoughts about that dream holiday in Spain Babs and me had been nagging him about, but as we turned into the Happy Eater car park Dad started breathing heavily and clearing his throat as he always does when he is getting himself worked up. Waiting till he had to reverse into a parking space so he could look into his wing mirror instead of at me he said, 'Before we go in Marjory, there's just one thing I want to say to you young lady, and then we'll drop it, all right? If anything of this sort happens again, for whatsoever reason, for whatsoever reason at all, you'll feel the back of my hand, big as you are, now I suppose you're starving as usual so out you get, I'll treat you to a burger.' Who says I haven't got the most wonderful Dad in all the whole wide world?

Babs was super too. Instead of being in any way reproachsome for having given Dad white hairs she just said, 'Well, flower, you've reached a milestone in your young life and so have I, so this calls for a double celebration.' With which she made Dad book a table at the Three Seasons (the reason it wasn't the Four Seasons was that it always closed in winter), a gourmet candlelit restaurant in a reel manor house just outside Seathorpe. This was absolutely typified of Babs. It was my first grown-up restaurant meal outside their wedding breakfast, and even though there was nobody else taking dinner except for a couple of old wrinklies who didn't speak to one another the whole evening, I had a ball apart from being car sick on the way home. I had quails' eggs Muscovite, some kind of chicken dish with a creamy sauce and all the trimmings, and my first ever potiferoles, all washed down with I think it was claret, then coffee and after dinner mints.

During the sweet course, by which time we were all a bit squiffy, Babs announced that to round off our double celebration, her being made Supervisor of the Seathorpe Snappy 24-hour Foto Developing Service and me beginning to grow up, she was going to buy me a little present, anything I liked within reason, and what did I want? I replied that apart from having my ears pierced and a pair of dangling blue bobble ear-rings I had seen in Mancowitz's the High Street jewellers' window, there was nothing in the world I wanted more than to be called Debra from that day hencetofor.

Dad said, 'Debra, Debra, there's millions of Debras, what's wrong with the names you were born with, if you don't like Marjory you can call yourself Linda and if you don't like Linda you can call yourself Marjory, that's why you were given two names.' But as I pointed out, 'They're not models' names, Dad, and I don't care how many Debras there are, there will only ever be one Debra Chase.' To which Babs said good-humoredly, 'All right, Debra it is if we can remember, but you're never going to become a model stuffing profiteroles into your face.'

Babs was right as always. As I was saying, I was shaped like a tub of lard in those days but I never gave it a thought, Babs had always said it was just puppy fat and it would wear off as I got older. Maybe it would of but one day shortly after our celebration dinner (I got those ear-rings by the way!) something happened which precipiced me, with Babs's help and encouragement, into doing something about it instead of just letting nature take its course.

There was a boy I fancied called Simon, he was nearly sixteen and *very* sexy with black wavy hair, he lived just a few doors from us and on my way home from school or wherever I would dawdle outside his home hoping for a glimpse of him at the living room window, or better still bumping into him and saying, 'Oh, hello Simon' or whatever came into my head. I reely had it bad.

Well, on this particlar day I was hanging about Sowerby Crescent hoping for him to put in an appearance, cos it was a Wednesday and I knew that on this day he always went for a kickabout with the Seathorpe Wanderers junior supporters club, when my patients was rewarded by seeing him coming down the path of his bungalow with his mate. My heart leaped, I didn't know where to put myself, I couldn't be discovered just standing out in the street and staring, so I dropped my school duffel bag accidently on purpose style of thing and started stuffing my books and things back into it where they had spilled out. So Simon did not see me until he had opened the gate, when what did his mate say but, 'Well well well, your little dumpling's waiting for you, Simon!' I went scarlet and ran home where I threw myself on the bed and cried and cried and cried, knowing that it must of been Simon who had called me that in the first place. (For the record, just before I made it as Miss South-east Coast in after life, Simon wanted to date me but I told him he had had his chance, I would not of gone out with him in any case, because he only rose to become a British Telecom repairman and although I am not a snob I am afraid that is not good enough for Debra Chase.)

I would not come down for my tea which did not concern Dad much as I was always having sulks and tantrums at that time, it was just my age, but when Babs got home and came up to my room with a chutney sandwich she saw I had been crying, still was in fact. I sobbed out my story and the upshot was that she said to Dad, 'Right, that girl goes on a slimming diet from this day forward', and that is exactly what I did, no messing about.

Now you might think it is difficult for a growing girl to give up chocs, sweeties, crisps, fizzy drinks, chips and other treats but I did not find it so at all, I found it dead easy tell the truth, I spose cos I had been stuffing myself with so much junk food that my body was glad to have a rest from it. Then again I was much helped by Babs who added to her historical pronouncement, 'And as both you and me could do with losing a few pounds before we go on that holiday in Spain, Eric, I suggest we give Marjory I beg her pardon Debra some much-needed backup by going on a diet with her.' The result of this was that cakes and sweet stuffs were banned from Oceanview forsooth.

That was it so far as Dad's slimming regiment went and I don't think he ever lost an ounce, not that he needed to, but Babs and me went on proper scientific diets. First she put us on the carrot and tomato diet, that's all you're allowed to have, just carrots and tomatoes plus carrot juice, tomato juice, and tomato soup with or without grated carrot. This reely worked, we were shedding pounds at a rate of knots but we both started to go yellow so Babs switched us to the orange and peanut diet and that reely did the trick.

I was totally hooked on diets by now, to the extension that slimming became my hobby, I used to cut every diet I could find out of my mags and stick them in a scrap-book, I tried them all in between staying rigidly on the orange and peanut diet, and the one that gave the best results although I should say it is not healthful to stay on it for long, see your doctor, was the Stodge Diet, whereat you eat a big slab of say carob cake or date and nut slice just ten minutes before you sit down to your meal, and this makes you lose your appetite so you just peck at your food. I admit that this is what gave me and my business advisers the idea for the Debra Chase Diet Nibble Muffin but we have never said, as certain so-called exposals in the media have said we said, that you can take off fourteen pounds in a fortnight simply by stuffing yourself with Debra Chase Diet Nibble Muffins, I wouldn't be so stupid.

But I will answer that charge once and for all in a later Chap.

I got so hooked on slimming diets that Dad grew quite concerned, I don't think he knew what dyslexia was but he thought I had got it. 'Look at her,' he would say. 'It can't be right to lose all that weight at her age, she is as thin as a rake.' If he had been more observable he would of noticed what Babs and me had noticed, though in fairness he had not of course seen me with my clothes off. Yes, I was growing boobs! To parodize the astronauts, a short step for womanhood but a big one for Debra Chase.

3

I Lose Some of My Innocence

My first ever holiday abroad was an unquantified success.
We went to the sun-drenched Costa Dorada, Spanish for
'golden coast' and famous for its shimmering beaches of
soft white sand, deep blue sea, shopping areas, old towns
and villages with numerable open-air restaurants,
bars and nitespots in their cobbled streets and squares,
and for its international cuisine. We rented an ultra-
modern apartment near the beach with its own sun
terrace overlooking one of the brand-new complex's two
pools. Unfortunately this was drained for repairs during
our stay but the other one was open, and we were very
handy for the Beachcomber disco which was just below
us, meaning it was all right for me to go down there
without Dad and Babs as they knew I was not far away.
It was close to all the local immunities as there was a
shuttle coach into the town where we went each evening
to sample the fantastic nightlife after a day spent
sunbathing, swimming and sipping erotic drinks at the
poolside bar. So we had a reely fab time.

It was not only my first holiday abroad but my first in
a lot of other things. My first Pina Colada. My first
proper disco. My first nightclub, the Miami Palms, where
I danced for the first time with Dad who taught me all I
shall ever need to know about the Magenta Waltz. My
first visit to an English pub, the Willywarmers Arms, even
though it did have to be in Spain for me to be allowed

in. My first paella. My first proper kiss. My first taste of heavy petting, but only above the waist.

When I say we spent our days by the pool, Dad wouldn't go near it, he said he didn't want a bushman's holiday thank you very much. So off he would go to the video room or for his windsurfing lessons whilst Babs and me lounged by the pool. Babs has always had a good figure and I had one by now, so we were quite the centre of attractiveness. One day this reely hunky guy called Ken swims up to where we were lying sunbathing at the edge of the pool and starts chatting Babs up. He was from Bradford and spoke with a northerly accent. He was in the apartment above us and so he used this to break the ice by saying, 'Excuse me luv, but you're in No 12, aren't you? I thought so, only we're in No 22 right on top of you, so if our Darren disturbs you with his cassette player you'll be sure to let us know, won't you, he drives us crackers with the flaming thing, I've told him I'll chuck it in the sea before I've finished.'

Ken's wife was very much present so although I know Babs fancied him there was no way she was going to enjoy a holiday romance, even if she would of dared under Dad's nose (I think she would of if she had got the chance, Dad doesn't mind her flirting so long as it doesn't go too far, in fact between you and me I think he finds it a turn-on). But through meeting Ken I also met his son Darren and so it came about that it was all systems go for a holiday romance of my very own.

Darren was over seventeen, taller than I (I am 5ft 8½in) with a lean bod as brown as his rippling hair. I was attracted to him at once, he was a near-lookalike of multo-macho Late Late Late Show star Gary Gibbs of South Coast Television, who I had always fancied like mad. Don't get me wrong when I say I never saw Darren with his clothes on!! All he ever wore was either skinny bathing trunks or day-glo beach shorts and baseball boots, with sometimes a sweatshirt if it was somewhere formal like the disco where they wouldn't let you in unless you were proply dressed.

At first Darren had no time for me, I guess he thought I was too young and anyway he had a pash for one of the Spanish maids, I got reely jealous when I saw him chatting her up. Luckily she did not speak any English so he was getting nowhere fast, specially after I told Pietro the barman, who regarded all the maids as his own personal property, that he would be losing one of his harem if he did not watch out!

But then came the day when there was yet another first in my life – my first ever Beauty Contest. It was a Miss Wet T-shirt comp held in the luxuriant Hotel Oasis down near the beach as one of the events of its Bumper Fun Day, and both Babs and me went in for it. We had no hope of winning, for the very simple reason that the judges were the three travel reps looking after the Hotel Oasis's different lots of package tours, so naturally they voted for their own clients, you cannot blame them. But it was all a great giggle and though I was a bit self-conscientous about displaying myself in public like that, I like to think that for my age I carried it off well, I did a reely slinky shimmy along that catwalk, it sure got some wolf whistles. Luckily Dad had not quite reelised just how revealing a wet T-shirt can be on a developing figure, otherwise he would not of let me go in for it! I was disappointed not to of come in even third – quite frankly although the winner was a reel stunna the other two looked as ordinary as Tesco checkout girls which I guess is what they probly were, and with no bosoms to speak of – but it was all made up for when Darren, who had dropped into the Hotel Oasis for the Bumper Fun Day crisp-eating comp, came up to me and said, 'Well I don't care what way they voted, you should have won, they must be blind them judges, either that else mad.' It was the nicest compliment I had ever heard and I could feel myself going even more the colour of a tomato than I already was through sunbathing. But there was even more, cos Darren went on to say, 'Are you going down to the disco tonight, because if you are, you don't dance with nobody else, you dance with me, all right?'

So began my holiday romance. I couldn't wait for night-fall to come, but alas for well made plans I was so excited by Darren's preposition that I ran all the way back along the beach towards Apartments Eva where we were staying, and not looking where I was going I tripped over a bloke who was sunbathing and went sprawling into the sand. When he kindly helped me to my feet I found I had twisted my ankle. I hobbled back to our apartment and bathed it in cold water then sat for an hour dangling my foot in the pool but it was no good, come disco time my ankle was all swollen and bopping was out. Even so, wild geese could not of kept me from my disco date although Dad did his level best to, rattling on about what was the point of going to a disco when you were not able to dance, to which I said it was to listen to the music, to which he said you could hear the blessed music coming up through the blessed floor, to which I said it was the atmospherics I went for and that he did not understand. At the death I trotted or rather limped off with Dad's famous last words ringing in my ears: 'Now don't forget, if you're not back on the stroke of eleven, the stroke of eleven do you hear,

I shall come down there and drag you out.' I said, 'Oh, Dad, even Cinderella didn't have to be home till midnight!' whereupon which Dad said something ever so funnee, he said, 'Ah, but Spanish time is an hour behind us, so their eleven is our midnight, I've caught you there, haven't I, I've caught you there!' Actually I'm pretty sure that Spanish time was an hour in front of us, I think, but it would of been pushing my luck to point this out and say, Oh in that case, why can't I stay out till one? So I just said good-night.

True to his word Darren was waiting for me down in the Beachcomber disco. He was not dancing with anybody else so I knew that even if he was not smitten with the love-bug as much as me he must be serious. I was wearing a silver lurex top handed down by Babs and a reely hip-hugging white cotton skirt, I looked good even if I do say it myself, plus I had sprinkled glitter in my hair which I should say by now had begun to grow to the length it is now, though in those days to give away my trade secrets I was mousy brown not honey blonde!

Darren was very understanding about my ankle, as soon as he saw me limping he asked considerably how I had been stupid enough to do it, then said, 'Well, you don't want to stop down here and risk it getting trodden on Debra, do you think you could make it down to the beach if I put my arm round you and you put your weight on me?' I was thrilled, I did not need to be asked twice I can tell you. I knew that Dad and Babs were going out to the Hotel Nacional dinner dance catering for older people so Babs would not be popping down to the disco to see if I was all right as she usually did. I had been given strict instructions by Dad not to go off with anyone I chanced to meet at the disco but Darren was diffrent, he was practicly a friend of the family and anyway there were so many couples lying about on the beach when we got there it was like Piccadilly Circus. I nearly stubbed my toe again as we picked our way round them, it was so dark that the only way you could tell there was no room to sit down was voices saying, 'Keep going pal' or 'Sorry mate, we're already double parked in this bit.' But Darren finally locationed a spot and we sank into the sand which was still warm from daytime and gazed up at the stars, and it was all so romantic with the sound of the critics I think they were called and all the cigarette ends glowing in the dark, that it seemed the most natural thing in the world to envelope one another in our arms.

I will pull a veil over what happened next, except to say it was not much, just the kind of scene a girl is liable to get into if you find yourself lying on a romantic beach with a good-looking guy. Heedless to say Darren wanted to go further but when I wouldn't he took it in good part, he just said, 'Well if you won't you won't, come on, we're losing valuable drinking time' and off we went to the Willywarmers where I am afraid I drank too much keg lager. Darren was reely considerable, he said, 'What you need is some fresh air, come on, I'll walk you back down to the beach', but all I wanted was to throw up and after that get back to the apartment and lie down.

It was later than I thought when I got back and Dad and Babs were already back from their dinner dance, having left in disgust over the raw chicken they were served. At first I was afraid they might of dropped in on the disco looking for me, but my luck was in, they hadn't. But what I had forgotten was that the bib fastening of my silver lurex top had come undone with a little help from Darren during our beach session, and he had tied it again but in a granny knot which was the only knot he could do. Babs followed me into my bedroom saying quietly as she refastened it properly, 'I won't ask who re-tied this top for you after it must have worked its way undone, but if you want your Dad to enjoy his holiday, next time you go to the disco don't come back with sand on your back.' Some hopes – when I went down to the pool next morning Darren was chatting up two tarty-looking girls from Swindon. He hardly gave me a look, this being a lesson to me, never to throw yourself at any man or you will end up getting hurt, not that I ever threw myself at Sir Monty Pratt so maybe what I mean is that a girl just can't win.

Once back home, from there on in I began to think differently about boys, I don't mean I had never reely thought about boys up until then, in fact Babs sometimes used to say I never thought about anything else, but I had never thought of them in this particlar way, although of course I had read about it. I think those fumblings on the beach with Darren must of awakened me to my body, cos now I became aware that I was attractive to boys and that they were attractive to me, not just to be chatted up by but to make me feel reely feminine, if not all the way at that time then enough for Babs to say 'I can see you're going to be a handful' when someone, it must of been the nosy neighbours at Balmoral or Rosedene, told her about me snogging in the bus shelter at the top of Sowerby Crescent with a boy I was sweet on at the time, I cannot remember his name as those years are a blur.

I do remember going home one night with lovebites on my neck and Dad getting all uptight, he wouldn't say anything direct to me except, 'What have you done to your neck, what have you done to your neck, have a look in the mirror, what have you been doing with yourself?' but when I said thinking on my feet style of thing, 'Midges', he turned to Babs saying, 'Look, you've got to have a word with her, Babs, she'll take notice of you where she won't take notice of me.' Dad then took himself off to do some tile-laying in the Spanish patio he was building on to the side of the bungalow in his spare time when not out tripping the light fantastic with Babs, so as to leave me alone with my big sister stepmother for one of our little talks. I can remember what Babs said as if it was tomorrow, it was the best advice a girl could ever have in that particlar direction, she just said, 'Look flower, much as your Dad would like it I'm not going to tell you what to do and what not to do, because in the first place you'd just ignore it and in the second you know and I know it's sometimes difficult to control your feelings. All I ask is you don't make yourself cheap, don't be, you know, familiar with boys just for the sake of it or to make yourself popular, not unless it's somebody special even though you know it might not last, and for God's sake love, and I'm being serious now, if you can't be good be careful by which I mean be sure the fella's careful because there's no way I'm putting you on the pill at your age, your Dad'd divorce me.' I would give that advice to any girl who is feeling her feet in life.

By the way, just for the record, I may of done crazy things in my teens but one thing I did not do was lose my virginity till I was over seventeen, and apart from a few puffs on a joint at parties just so as not to be the oddball out, I am a complete stranger to the drugs scene, in fact I have a horror of that sort of thing, I have seen too many livelihoods ruined by it. Also, although I have made some mistakes in my life I have never slept with anyone I didn't like, and whilst I may seem outwardly friendly being the egregrious type, I have liked fewer blokes in that direction than many people seem to think. I just wanted to say that.

I have said how I hated school, one thing I did not mind about it was that the boys' school was in the same building, they were in A Wing and we were in B Wing and if that makes it sound like a prison that is exactly what it was. But with a corridor between the two wings where they had the staff rooms and that, if you went off to the loo during lessons or were sent on some errand by the teacher and happened to stray into this corridor, you had a good chance of meeting a handsome boy, in fact I met sevral of my boy friends this way. One in particlar took my fancy, a boy named Alan Sands who is now coincidally a ticket collector at Seathorpe Parkway Station. I often used to see him when I went down to visit Dad and Babs unless I drove down, so it is a small world. Alan was tall with fair hair and though he had given me admiring looks we had never had the oppotential to take it any further until one glorious morning we both found ourselves in the stationery cupboard at the same time! All right, be honest Debra – I was on my way back from the look when I saw Alan going into the stationery cupboard, it was called a cupboard but it was more of a room reely. I could not pass up a chance like that so in I trolled, pretending I had been sent by Roz to get some ballpoint pens.

I must say Alan had a good line in chat-up patter, he said in a Humphrey Bogart voice, it was a reely good imitation, 'My my, of all the girls in all the world, who should walk into the stationery cupboard but you, what brings you here, sweetheart, don't tell me, you've come for some stationery because this is the stationery cupboard, aren't I a great detective?' I can't remember what I said in reply, nothing anywhere so clever or witty, and I cannot remember either how I came to be in Alan's arms a few minutes later when who should walk into the stationery cupboard but the headteacher herself, Miss Mold-Nixon, known to one and all as Miss Mouldy-knickers! I wished the floor could of swallowed me up.

After taking Alan's name she marched me straight to her office where she reely put me through the hoop about my non-existential sex life, it was like Southampton police station all over again, with once more my Dad being sent for and me having to wait in the secrety's room while Miss Mouldy-knickers had a long talk with him. I reely grew to hate that secrety while I was sitting there, she was not what you usually think of when you think of secreties, she looked more like a teacher herself, and although I had to sit there for ages she just would not look at me. I tried to catch her eye and give her a smile just to show I had not done anything that bad, but she kept on busying herself with files and papers and not looking at me till I began to feel reely ashamed. So was Dad when he came out, ashamed of me I mean.

My punishment was that I was suspendered for a month, and at first I thought I was going to be put to the humilification of going back to the classroom to collect my things with all the other girls staring and tittering, but to my relieval Miss Mouldy-knickers came to the door and said to the secrety, 'Mrs Lamb, would you be kind enough to go along to Miss Heseltine's class and collect Marjory's things?' She would not call me Debra. Then I had to go into her room to hear the sentence. After telling me I was suspendended she went on, 'As end of term is only three weeks away, when you'll be leaving anyway, this means in effect that you won't be coming back to John Pennywick Upper School. I'm sorry we've not been able to do enough for you, Marjory, sorry too that we couldn't persuade you to put your back into your work and become a credit to the school, all I can hope is that you'll become a credit to us now you're going out into the world, what would you like to do, have you any idea or perhaps you haven't thought about it yet?'

'Take up modelling, miss,' I said, to which she replied, 'Yes, well I shouldn't raise your hopes too highly in that direction, it's a very overcrowded field and much harder work than it looks.' As if I didn't know, I had been reading models' life stories in my mags since I was ten. But aren't teachers discourageful, though? I seem to remember that when the Beatles were at school their teacher did his level best to stop them becoming Beatles, saying they would never make a go of it. I read the selfsame thing in *TV Times* about soap star Den Dobbs, his teacher said the only way he could become an actor was by going to Radar, and look at him now.

'Very well, go and sit with your father until Mrs Lamb comes back with your things,' said Miss Mouldy-knickers in finality and that was that, my wonderful school career over with. By the way, all that happened to Alan Sands for his part in the Great Stationery Cupboard Scandal was that he was kept in during breaks for a week so I was told, don't anyone ever talk to Debra Chase about sex equity.

I found Dad sitting with his elbows on his knees, staring down at the floor. He did not speak for a bit but then he began in a low voice without looking up, 'Every time you get in one of these scrapes, Debra, you let me down, you let Babs down, you let yourself down, you let everybody around you down, do you realise that, well do you, just give me the common courtesy of an answer.'

I said, 'Yes, Dad', hoping that would be the end of it but he went banging on and on. 'I despair of you sometimes girl, I really do, what we have done to deserve this kind of thing I just do not know. Anyway, I wash my hands of you, I wash my hands of you.' But of course he didn't reely mean it. As we crossed the school playground he chuntered on, 'And you needn't think you're on holiday because you've been suspended from school. Till the end of term you're going to sit down at that dining table every morning from nine till twelve and every afternoon from whatever time you go back to school after lunch till four, and go on with what you've been studying, and every evening I'm going to test you on what you've learned.'

I tried to tell him that education doesn't work like that in this day and age but he wouldn't listen, so at the death I had to go through the motions. Every morning I would sit down at the table with a book called *Adventures in Reading* and pretend to read it until he had gone to work. In the evening he could come back and ask some of the questions out of the book such as, 'Imagine you are Liza in the story, how would you have handled the situation?' or 'Why does Mark refuse to help the old man in the wood, is he guilty of ageism or is there a reason?' but as he had no idea what the answers should be, he had to let me waffle on from what little I could remember from reading the book in class, and after a couple of days no more was said about me going on with my school work and I was left in peace to celebrate my new found freedom and think about my forthcoming career.

*

My first job, in fact the only job I have ever had as regards having a wage packet put into my hands every Friday, was with the Mr Scissors Unisex Hair-fashioning Boutique on Station Road, appointments not always necessary. It wasn't the main branch, that was in the High Street, so we did not catch many glimpses of Mr Scissors' famous clients such as the Seathorpe Sound and Sparkies disco DJs or our local sports celebs, he kept these for himself. I did not much fancy being a crimper but it was between Mr Scissors and the Seathorpe Snappy 24-hour Foto Developing Service, and much as I love Babs I did not want to be tied to her apron strings, not that I have ever seen her wear one, even serving breakfast she looks as if she is just setting off for a night on the town.

I cannot say I was happy working at Mr Scissors in the nearly two years I was there but I was not unhappy, it was better than Woolworth's pick 'n' mix sweeties counter which was where Norma Borridge alias Suzie Dawn found herself working, and I did learn something about hair styling, not a lot but everything to do with glamour and fashion is useful to a model which was what I had set my heart on being, so much so that I would not give Dad or Babs a moment's peace, I must of been a right pain.

Somebody, one of the Seathorpe Polytechnic guys who used to come in to have their hair done on Mondays when it was half price on account of apprentices like yours truly being allowed to have a go, had told me that there was a Referential Library upstairs from the Public Library where you could look up referential books. Such places are not my scene but taking my courageousness in both hands I ventured in and asked the lady if they had such a thing as the Models' Directory which I had read about in the advice columns of mags where girls write in to become models, something I had never done myself because it always seemed to me that if you had to write in to *My Guy* to get yourself started you were in with no chance whatsoever. The lady showed no flicker of sprise or snootiness at such a strange request as it must of seemed to an inteffectual, she just directed me to a shelf where sure enough the Models' Directory was to be found nesting between the Midwives' Directory and the Nurses' Handbook – quite the odd girl out!! After browsing through the glamour pix of all the well-known names in the glittering but tough-at-the-top world of modelling, specially among the Cs where the name of Debra Chase (38–25–35) would figure one of these days, I jotted down the names of about a dozen modelling schools, just the ones who advertised on quarter pages or less as I knew the full page ones would be so pricey that Dad would go out of the window. When I got home I got out the writing pad and sent off for their brochettes which after a day or two began to come trickling in. Course, nosey Dad wants to know what all this mail is that I'm getting, and that was where he made his mistake, cos I said that whilst I was surely to goodness old enough to get private letters if I wanted to by now, I would let him see what was in them if he promised to sit down and read them. Naturally he did no such thing, just flipped through them saying scoffily, 'What a racket, what a racket, do you mean to say there's girls paying good money just to walk round a room with a book on their heads, you could do that at home, here, you can have my sequence dancing manual to practise with.'

But glad to say Babs took it altogether more seriously and went through each of the brochettes carefully, deliminating most of them either because they seemed dodgy in her considerable opinion, or because they were too expensive for what they were, or because we couldn't pronounce their names. The one we both went for after a lot of humming and hawing was Donna Bella Rosa's School of Fashion in Tulse Hill. In the first place the charges were very reasonable or so Babs said, she had once done a two weeks course on skin care when she was toying with the idea of becoming a Mayfair beautician so she knew something about it. In the second place it was very handy for Auntie Doris's in Sydenham where I would be able to stay if she would have me. I myself personly would of liked a flat but no way would Dad of stood for that and anyway where would I find the rent, so Auntie Doris's it would have to be if – and it was a big if – we could talk Dad into it. It was a twelve week course with an exciting syllabub including posture, aerobatics, Yoga, smiling, make-up, hair and fashion, how to handle the media, and a reel live photo session with a professional photographer with Fleet Street credences.

Call me psychopathic but somehow I just knew I was going to get on that course. I knew if I talked to Dad myself I would get the same old answer, 'Modelling course, modelling course, you're working at Mr Scissors', what's wrong with taking a hairdressing course, for one thing you can enrol for nothing at night school, that's if you can spare one evening a week from gadding off to discos and I don't know what.' So I asked Babs to talk to him and she promised she would, sport that she is. They were going in for the South-east Area Cha Cha Cha Finals with a good chance of winning so Babs considered, and she said that with Dad in a good mood she would bring up the subject on the way back from Brighton where they were being held. I waited up crossing my fingers and reading the print off Donna Bella Rosa's brochette. But I am afraid I was out of luck that night. They both came in with long faces and Babs gave me a thumbs down sign. They had come in a humilifying seventh, but even though it was not the most tactile time to ask Dad about me going to modelling school Babs had promised she would so she did, and a right earful she had got in return, they were not speaking to one another by the time they got back home. So my hopes were dashed for the time being.

4

I Lose the Rest of My Innocence

Meantime life went on. Under Mr Gerald, the boss of the Station Road branch of Mr Scissors and his assistant Jessie, I picked up enough about crimping to be allowed to get on with it with the minima of supervisualising if they were anything like busy and the customer was nobody in particular.

Mr Gerald was rather a sad figure. From what I could gather he and Mr Scissors had been live-in companions for ages but it seemed that Mr Scissors had become friendly with Mr Trousers of the leather boutique next door in the High Street, and this was putting Mr Gerald's nose out of joint. I couldn't begin to fathom that kind of relationship in those days, I was still very nave in many ways, all I knew was that Mr Gerald was always nice to me whereas Jessie, who was seprated from her hubby and didn't we know it, was a right cow. She treated me as if I was reely stupid, always having to have her little dig, like when she would ask you to pass a certain kind of comb she would say, 'That's if you know what a cutting comb is by now Debra, oh you do, in that case why are you trying to pass me a wide-toothed comb?' She had me in tears more than once and if it wasn't for Mr Gerald patting my bum and saying comfortable things like, 'Don't take it so hard, pet, we're all sent into this life to suffer' or 'Take no notice, she's just having one of her turns' I would of given in my notice and gone to join the erstwhile

Suzie Dawn as she was by now calling herself on Woolworth's pick'n'mix counter.

But the money was not all that bad considering when you added in the tips, and with a little help from my friends I managed to have quite a good time in Sleepythorpe, all right it was not the pulsating West End where I longed to be but it did have its attractions, most of them with moustaches which I reely had the hots for at that time, I guess it was just a phrase I was going through as now I like my men with designer stubble. As for places to go to, remember I was growing up all the time so I had passed out of the video arcade stage and disco parties at friends' homes (I only ever gave one of these myself, Dad said never again) and was now going to proper discos like Sparkies. We had no fewer than four reel live discos not including the exclusive Bogie's Casablanca which being a Club was out of bounds at that time, plus two five-screen cinecentres plus the prestigeful Wintergard Leisureland, a big pink concrete effigy where the wrinklies' Winter Gardens used to be, with live shows, disco nights, Video Experience and functions, so we did not do too badly considering we were out in the sticks.

Also I was old enough by now (give or take a few months!) not to have to go all the way to the Costa Dorada if I felt like dropping into a pub for a Pina Colada! There was one favrite pub we used to use, it had been called the Builders Arms or something back in the Dark Ages but now it was called Truffles, they had completely re-done it up by pulling out the old musty bar and putting in a chrome bar with high stools, glass dance floor underlit in all different changing colours, and raised seating area with chrome rails and blanquettes, it was all Art Decor style of thing, the only drawback being you had to shout to make yourself heard over the sound system, they must of effected the acrostics when they re-designated it. Everyone who remembered the old place said it was a five hundred per cent improval, I could well believe it having been taken into one or two pubs that had not yet been modernised. Not that I have anything against old pubs, in fact there was one reely ancient one we used to go to quite a lot, Ye Mucky Duck it was called, all right it had been done up too in a way but it had only been Edwardian when it was called something else, the Red Lion I think, but now it was genuine Victorian with coach lamps and cartwheels hanging from the ceiling and everything in dark wood, and everyone knows Victoria was miles older than Edwardia.

Fridays and Saturdays were our big nights out when I used to meet Suzie and maybe one or two others at Ye Mucky Duck, cos it was quite close to where I got off the Shoppa Hoppa at the Shopping Mall. We would have a half of lager then amble down Fish Street to Truffles where usually quite a gang of us would be congregationing, mainly kids I had been at school with or had as boy friends, plus there was always a few fresh faces so it never got in a rut. We would either stay at Truffles all evening, sipping Tequila Sunsets (same as Tequila Sunrises only stronger, so named cos you are sposed to go blind if you have more than one) and bopping a little if we felt like it, then have a McDonald's or Chicken McNugget or sunnink on the way home, or maybe some of us would split and go on to Sparkies or Ravers or one of the other discos, or then again two of you might pair off and go for a Chinese or Indian, you never knew how the evening would turn out, some-times it was great fun, other times it could be dead boring. But this was your life, Debra Chase, before the commencal of your career!

One Friday evening I was sitting with Suzie in Ye Mucky Duck, talking about modelling which was one of our two sole tropics of conversation (you can guess the other one!!) when who should come over but Simon – yes the boy not quite next door who I had fancied when I was a little fatso teenybopper! Nowadays the boot was the other way round, he was always trying to chat me up whilst I could not see what I had ever seen in him. Anyway, after saying 'Is anybody sitting here, girls?' and me saying 'Yes, the invisible man', he sat down and to my mystification raised his Strong Export Brew Lager can to Suzie with the words, 'Well, the best of luck, Suzie, I don't know what the competition's like but if I'm any judge I reckon you're in with a good chance, what say you, Debra?'

I had not the foggiest what he was talking about. Suzie had though, as I could sus from the fact that she was I won't say blushing but I would of loved a dress in that colour. I said snappily, 'I'm sure she's in with a *very* good chance, if only I knew what you were talking about.' Suzie muttered, 'Oh, I didn't want anyone to, I mean I'll feel such a fool if', which loosely transported meant, 'Oh, I didn't want anyone to know, I mean I'll feel such a fool if I come in last', as I quickly reelised as soon as Simon went on to say, 'Do you mean she hasn't told you, Debra? She's only put her name down for the Miss Seathorpe contest.'

No, Simon, since you ask she hadn't told me. Funnee, wasn't it? Because ever since Norma Borridge and me discovered that we both had the same ambition we had been best mates with no secrets barred, or so I had fondly imaginised until now. Suzie knew what I was thinking and began to stammer and bluster about how she'd meant to tell me, it was just that she kept having cold feet about going in for the contest and didn't want me egging her into it. I let her stew in her own goose for a bit and then said sweetly, 'It's quite all right, Suze, cos it just so happens I never told you *I* was going in for it too, I wanted it to be a sprise just like you did.'

This was a forthright lie of course, up until then I had never even thought of going in for the Miss Seathorpe contest, the Miss Wet T-shirt comp on the Costa Dorada back in my early teens had been good fun but since then I had come to think of beauty contests as being degradeful to the female sex, parading yourself in front of a lot of oglers without getting paid for it unless your face (and other parts of your astronomy!) happens to fit and you win. Suzie didn't believe me, natch, didn't believe I had thought of going in for it before hearing she was going in for it that is, but there was nothing she could do except grin and bear it as they say.

As all the world knows, the result of that fatal Miss Seathorpe contest in reverse order was: 3rd, somebody called Tracy whose other name I cannot remember, she was later disqualisised for coming from Brighton. 2nd, Debra Chase. 1st, Suzie Dawn. Well you cannot win them all as the old saying goes but after seeing the smirk on Suzie's face as the sash was put over her head, I determinalised that I would win one of them just to show her, even though I had no reel interest in beauty contests, it is simply not the way to the top of the modelling profession, look at Miss World, how many of them have become Page Three girls, I could not name one, in fact they are barred from going topless. Do not get me wrong, I was still best friends with Suzie, but now we were best rivals too.

Now the next step for Suzie after launching on her new beauty queen career was to enter for the Miss South-east Coast contest, which as the reigning Miss Seathorpe she was fully qualified to do. As a mere runner-up, of course, I was disentitled from going in for it, which was a setback in my ambition to get one over on Suzie as you will have to admit. But as luck would have it I was seeing quite a lot of a photographer from the *Seathorpe Clarion* at the time, matter of fact I met Stan when he was sent to cover the Miss Seathorpe contest, and it was Stan who tipped me the wink that there was still one more beauty contest to go which would qualify the winner for Miss South-east Coast, namely in Portside which sort of runs into the outskirts of Seathorpe, it is a bit of a tip frankly, just caravan sites and factories and old car dumps. No one can call me proud so I was more than ready to have a go but there was just one snag. You had to come from the place whence the contest was being held in, I knew this for certain because it had been in the *Clarion* about Tracy whatever her name was being disqualisised cos she turned out to be from Brighton, she had given her boy friend's address in Seathorpe. Easy easy said Stan, and then he told me a little known fact. Portside may have its own name but for years it has been just a part of Seathorpe, they have the same council. So if you come from Portside you also come from Seathorpe, and since I came from Seathorpe it must thereby mean that I also came from Portside. Not a lot of people know that, as Stan rightly said.

The upshot was that one rainy Saturday Stan drove me over to this run-down Promenade ballroom on what was laughingly called the Front at Portside, the last time a dance had been held there was three years ago according to Babs and they were about to pull it down so I think the Miss Portside contest was the Promenade ballroom's last social engagement. The only homes for miles around were the caravans which were all rented out to holiday-makers who could not care less about a local beauty contest when they had their bingo, so hardly anyone turned up and as for the contesters, there were just five of us, so it was no great credit to Debra Chase's beautiful face, sensational figure and marvlous personality that I won. Being Miss Portside was the next best thing to being Miss Sludge-farm in my book, so I kept very quiet about it and Stan kindly saw that it did not appear in the *Clarion* – this was not so much that I was ashamed of my title as cos I couldn't wait to see Suzie's face when we met on that catwalk!

Unbeknownst to me, going in for that contest just to spite Suzie Dawn was one of the most shrewest things I ever did but without knowing it, since it was because of that move I got involved with sexy soccer star Brian Boffe, and it was my involvement with Brian and the rest of the Seathorpe Wanderers squad that led – but no, there I go again, I must keep that for the next Chap.

There is a certain word which means that when a certain thing happens to you, you could swear black and blue that it has happened before, or maybe someone says something to you and you get the same feeling, or you see a certain place and you think you have been there before even though you couldn't of been. This happened to me, somebody saying something I mean.

The Monday after Suzie carried away the Miss Seathorpe sash, I got to work a bit late to find the Mr Scissors Unisex hair fashioning boutique in an uproar. Mr Gerald was in floods of tears and blubbering, 'I'll kill the bastard, I'll cut his bloody throat with one of his own razors, I will, Jessie, he's pushed me to the effing limit, oh hello, Debra, excuse my French, I'm afraid we're a little fraught this morning, tell you what, why don't you go and make some coffee, I reckon we can all do with some.' All this time he was yanking open drawers and cupboards and throwing his personable belongings into a big Savage and Drawbell carrier bag, that's the big Seathorpe deportment store. I could hear him still banging on whilst I was making the coffee in the little back room, with Jessie trying to pacifize him, saying soothfully, 'Now calm down Gerry, just take it easy, what if a customer walks in, we've Mrs Aspinall coming in at a quarter to and another thing, if you walk out how do you think I'm going to cope, that appointments book's choc-a-bloc for once and I've only got one pair of hands.' Oh, thank you very much, Jessie, I suppose Debra's pair of hands doesn't count.

After a bit more chuntering between the pair of them Mr Gerald came into the back room with his carrier bag and gave me a big hug saying, 'Well ta-ra Debra love, sorry you had to see your Uncle Gerry like this but we're all only human, never mind, I suppose it'll all be the same in a hundred years time, take care, I wish you all the best and try to help Jessie all you can, won't you pet, there's a love, bye bye' and with that he was off without even drinking his coffee.

I didn't get much out of Jessie as to what it was all about, she just said there'd been a row, but one of the girls at the High Street branch who I bumped into later that week at Truffles, Aud her name was, told me that Mr Gerald had caught Mr Scissors and Mr Trousers dancing together in a gay club called Pink Experience and there had been a reel ding-dong fulminating in him slapping Mr Scissors across the face and walking out.

But we are coming to how this effected me and my career. Because of Mr Gerald's walk-out and Jessie having such a full appointments book, there was nothing for it but for her to leave the casuals to me, much though she didn't trust me not to snip their ears. Thus it came about that whilst Jessie had her hands full giving her important client the great Mrs Aspinall of Aspinall's Bun in the Oven Bakeries her henna rinse, it fell to I, Debra Chase, junior hairdresser, to re-touch the highlights in nonesoever than whom's moustache and wavy black hair than of sexy soccer star Brian Boffe, Seathorpe Wanderers' trif transfer find from northern giantkillers Potternewton United!!

Brian was relevantly new to Seathorpe and obviously it was a case of having come to the wrong shop, his mates had just told him they all went to Mr Scissors where they got a discount for being famous faces, and he must of presumed there was only one branch, well I certainly wasn't going to tell him so I had him in that chair with a bib round his neck before Jessie could point out his mistake which she would of done spiteful cat that she is, just to stop me talking to him.

I was so knocked out that my comb trembled in my hand and I heard Brian saying in a northerly accent, 'Do all the fellas affect you like this, luv, or is it my fatal charms?' I giggled pleasantly, thinking he was just making smalltalk, but then he went on to say, 'I know you from somewhere, don't I?' Course, I thought, this has got to be his standard chat-up line, I will go along with it, so I said, 'I don't think so Brian if you don't mind being called Brian, in fact I know so, cos if we had met I'd remember.' Which was true, or so I thought at that moment in time.

So then Brian said, 'Well I know you from somewhere because I never forget a face, do you ever go down to Bogie's Casablanca Club?' I said, 'No, I've never set foot in it worse luck, in fact the only place you could of seen me before is at the Miss Seathorpe beauty contest,' which was true, cos Brian was among the celeb guests, it was the first time I had seen him in the flesh and I thought he was worth every penny of his record (for Seathorpe Wanderers that is) transfer fee.

'That's it!' explained Brian. 'I told you I never forget a face, Debra.' (He knew my name was Debra because it was embroiderised on my smock.) 'Or a figure,' he added cheekily. 'Tough titty, Debra, I think you should have won that contest, honest I do, you would've done if I'd been one of the judges, I mean it.' And that was when I got that I Have Been Here Before feeling for which there is that certain word which is still on the tip of my teeth.

Then suddenly it came back to me what a certain boy had said to me in a certain foreign country after a certain Miss Wet T-shirt contest. But it couldn't be – or could it??? Course, he did not have a moustache in those days which made him look diffrent, but the same resembliance to the heart-throb of my wild child period, Late Late Late Show host Gary Gibbs, was still there now that I reely looked at him. I said, 'Can I ask you a funny question, Brian, have you ever stayed in a place called Costa Dorada, praps in the Apartments Eva?'

Brian gave me a strange look and said, 'Yes, why?' I said, 'And do you remember taking a certain girl to a certain pub called the Willywarmers Arms?' I thought I had better not mention a certain snogging session on the beach with Jessie listening.

'I took a lot of girls to the Willywarmers, why?' said Brian.

'But your name was Darren in those days, wasn't it?' I said.

'It still is,' said Brian. 'But it's my middle name now, I thought Brian was a better name for a soccer player, I think it suits my image better. So you're that Debra are you, yes it all comes back to me now,' he went on unconvictedly. After that we chatted easefully about this and that, me asking him what he thought of Seathorpe and him saying that it was all right, and me saying he'd come a long way in a very short time even if Seathorpe was only in the Third Division, and him saying yes somebody up there must like him and that Seathorpe would not be in the Third Division for ever not if he could help it, and then all too soon it was time to give him the hand mirror and whisk the bib off his shoulders. As he paid the bill minus his Famous Face discount, giving me a generous tip and saying, 'And that's for you, Debra, I'll see you again, eh?', I thought he was going to ask me out, praps hinting 'So you say you've never been to Bogie's Casablanca then, how would you like to go?' but no such luck. Not yet anyway. But luck can change as I was soon to see! His last words were, 'And keep on going in for them beauty contests because you'll win one of these days, take it from me, I'm an expert.' I didn't like to say I was already Miss Portside. I just hoped he would be among the VIP guests for the Miss South-east Coast contest.

But before that day of predestiny came along the Mr Scissors Station Road branch, appointments not always necessary, was to receive another star customer across its porchals.

When you are a beauty queen, that is a beauty queen from anywhere except a dump like Portside, your social life completely changes, you start meeting a different class of fella such as local celebs and well-to-do businessmen, and being taken to a different class of place like Bogie's Casablanca or the Three Seasons or Midgeley's Oyster Divan where some king or other used to take chorus girls in the olden days. So it was that I was not seeing much of the famous Miss Seathorpe, Suzie Dawn, these days, that is not until the morning before the Miss South-east Coast contest, when who should troll in but she herself, Aud at the High Street branch having forgotten to write down her appointment so they could not fit her in. Once again Jessie had her hands full with a favrite client, so it was down to Miss Seathorpe's runner-up to trim her ends and scrunch-dry her flowing locks.

Now I know what the world is saying: that I, Debra Chase, deliberately hacked off most of Suzie's hair in a jealous rage so as to spoil her chances in the Miss South-east Coast comp. This is a wicked liable. Suzie was still my best friend even though we had become bitter rivals and she had grown what some people called big-headed with success, so knowing how proud she was of her lovely long pink hair I could not of brought myself to do such a thing. In any case, as anyone who knows about beauty contests can tell you, it is not your hair which is your crowning glory.

No, what happened was a conurbation of not keeping my mind on my work and sheer inexperience. I guess it was daydreaming about the approaching contest and thinking of the look on Suzie's face when she reelised I was an unexpectant contendant that caused me to hack off more of one side of her hair than I should of done. Short of glueing it back on, the only thing I could do was lop off an extra bit from the other side to even it up, but being nervous because of my silly mistake I once again took too much off, and so it went on. Suzie was reading a mag and it wasn't till she felt the scissors touch her ear that she scented something was wrong and said worryingly, 'I hope you're not taking too much off, Debra, I want to keep it shoulder length.' But then she caught sight of this mass of hair on the floor, it looked as if a pink sheep had been sheared, and she lets out this pierceful scream. Jessie went raging mad of course and Suzie rushed out in tears before I could even explain that there would be a reduction in the bill for any inconvenience caused. Jessie could not fire me with being short-staffed, otherwise she would of. I rang Suzie that evening to apologise but her Mum said she was in her room crying, which I can well believe cos when the word went round next morning that Suzie had pulled out of the contest, I heard it on the grapevine that it was because she had woken up with her face all swollen and blotchy, also with a nervous rash on her neck.

So although I would not of had it happen for all the world, and whilst it was the cause of a long rift between Suzie and I, that was my first piece of luck as regards my chances of winning the Miss South-east Coast sash. The next piece of luck was by way of the contest being held in the Seathorpe Leisure Pool and Fitness Centre. Yes, the very pool where Dad was manager, so being as how he had a big hand in the seating arrangements, supervisionalising the building of the catwalk etc and so forth, he could not very well turn round and say, 'Beauty contests, beauty contests, why do you want to bother your head with that sort of thing, you get some very dodgy types hanging round these events, very dodgy indeed', which is what he said when I went in for the Miss Seathorpe comp at the Corn Exchange. In fact I think he was secretly proud to see his own daughter in the line-up, so was Babs who came along to see the fun. I would like to thank them both publicly for their loyal support at this time, they were a reel moral booster, as they have been all through my career.

But the best stroke of luck of all was in guess who was one of the judges? The judges are not announced till the very day of the contest in case any of the girls try to get round them, such things have been known but I am here to say that they have never been known as regards Debra Chase, so that puts the lie to the veiled insinuendoes in the *Sunday Shocker* about my relationships with certain judges. The same statement I made about the Miss Seathorpe judges, namely that if I gave them sex favours why didn't I win, equally implies to the Miss South-east Coast judges even though this time the results were rather diffrent, in what way we shall soon see. I had never even met four out of five of them, they were the director of the Aqualand Theme Park, the owner of the South Coast House of Waffles chain, a man from the County Council, and the presenter of the South Coast TV Mid-morning Magazine prog who I'd never heard of cos I didn't watch it, the only time I'd ever seen him was on the South Coast Newsround sitting in a bath of custard for the spastics. But how my heart leapt when the fifth judge took his place on the rostern and the MC announced, 'And last but not least will you welcome Seathorpe Wanderers' new rising star Brian Boffe, fresh from this afternoon's triumphant nil–nil draw against Southdown Rangers!' Us girls were lined up on the catwalk as the judges trooped on and it was when Brian winked at me as he sat down that I knew Debra Chase was in with a chance.

It was all so exciting, it was in a complete daze that I heard the MC pronouncing, 'Entrant No 7 is the reigning Miss Portside, delightful Debra Chase, a local hairdresser's assistant whose ambition is to become a model, Debra's hobbies are disco dancing, meeting people and swimming in Daddy's pool, no no he's not a millionaire ladies and gentlemen, Debra's father happens to be manager of the Seathorpe Leisure Pool and Fitness Centre where this Miss South-east Coast final is taking place, so a big hand for Debra if you please!' I suppose I must of made all the right moves and managed not to fall off the catwalk, but truth to tell it was all like a dream, and I was still in such a complete tizz when it came to pronouncing the winners that I could barely take it in.

The owner of the House of Waffles chain was the chief judge so he got to read out the names which he did in a stumbling voice, he could not read properly, he was nearly illiteral. Miss Hove was in fourth place, Miss Rottingdean third and Miss Worthing second, and I can remember I was just thinking 'Oh well it's all or nothing then, most probly nothing knowing my luck' when I heard the chief judge yammering into the microphone, 'But this year's great House of Waffles South-east Coast Beauty Queen is wait for it quiet ladies and gentlemen Miss Debra Cheese I beg her pardon Debra Chase congratulations Debra and will you please step forward to receive your award from Seathorpe's newest soccer star Brian Boffee is it yes Brian Boffee over to you Brian.' I nearly had to pinch myself as Brian put the royal blue sash over my head and kissed me on both cheeks, then did it again for the benefice of Stan of the *Seathorpe Clarion* whose camera had got jammed, then presented me with my very first earnings for being fortuitous enough to be a sex object, namely a cheque for one hundred pounds!

The rest of the afternoon is a delicious blur – Dad, Babs and various VIPs and celebs congratulating me as we sipped pink champagne, a lovely big kiss from Brian Boffe lookalike Late Late Late Show host Gary Gibbs and a slobbering one from the boss of the House of Waffles, and Seathorpe Community Centre Calypso Steel Band playing 'Congratulations' over and over out of tune. But what I most remember is Brian murmuring in my ear as we posed for a photograph enjoying a glass of bubbly together, 'I reckon this calls for a proper celebration, believe me when I tell you the champagne at Bogie's Casablanca is a great improvement on this muck, well it could hardly be worse could it, I'll pick you up about half eight, where do you live?'

So it was I was plunged into the glamour world of fame and fun that has been my life ever since that fatal day. It was the first time I had ever been picked up in a car of any kind let alone a powder-blue Ford Escort XR3i and I could see that Dad was impressed, as for Babs she was goodheartedly envious, saying, 'There'll be no holding her now, Eric,' as it drew up outside Oceanview with Brian tooting impatiently at his Colonel Bogey horn for me to go out and get in.

Except for the Miami Palms on the Costa Dorada with Dad and Babs I had never been to a night club before, but Bogie's Casablanca was all I imagined a swish nitespot to be with tartan-carpeted walls, piano bar if you wanted to sit at it, waitresses in skimpy little French maid dresses and fishnet tights, candles flickring in glass pineapple holders, strobe-lit dance floor, reel live DJ and everything you could wish to eat and drink from champagne and Moscow Roscoes to toasted sandwiches. For ambilence even now that I have sampled night life from London to New York and back again I would rate it if not as high as the West End's exclusive Bonks then a lot higher than some of the places I have been to such as trend-setting Ciro's in Sydenham. Brian was a Status Member so that meant we got a ringside table. Although it was too dark to see much, in my frequent trips to the little girls' room (I was feeling very nervous, and the tight little black number Babs had lent me for the evening kept coming unpinned at the back where she had taken it in for me) I spotted inumerous celebs, from sitcom and bread commercial star Lenny Lyons who has a flat in Seathorpe to ex-*Brummies* star Rita Wren then touring at the Seathorpe Theatre Royal in the West End comedy thriller *Just a Minute Inspector*. Plus, of course, just about the whole of the Seathorpe Wanderers squad who were drifting in with their girl friends or in some cases not, as Brian put it 'Why bring coals to Newcastle, luv?' I did see what he meant, there were some reel stunnas sitting in pairs around the room, I didn't reconise any of them but course people used to come in from miles around for a night out at Bogie's Casablanca, all I can say is I was glad some of those glamour pussies did not go in for the Miss South-east Coast comp, I would of come in last with all that talent.

That night as the champagne and banana daiquiris flowed I came to meet most of the Wanderers team, particly macho six-foot-four striker Sylvester Stallone lookalike Kevin Keene. The Wanderers were celebrating their manager Jock Jarvis, the only one present who was there with his wife so far as I could see, being voted Glacier Double Glazing Manager of the Month, so everyone was on a high. Brian was very attentful, pulling a chair out for me to sit down when we first entered and saying, 'I won't ask you what you're going to have Debra, because it's banana daiquiris for openers then champagne all the way, though come to think of it I might just let you pay the bill because if it hadn't been for my vote you might not have won.' But after that he did not say a lot, just looked around relaxfully whilst banging his arm on the top of our blanquette in rhythm to the music and waggling his fingers at his mates as they came in.

Seeing as I was with Brian it would of been out of order for me to give any come-on glances to Kevin Keene but I have to confess that I felt strangely attractful towards him, so I was more than glad when he sauntered up to our table and said to Brian, 'You don't mind if Miss Seathorpe and me have a bit of a shuffle do you cock, only I've got itchy feet but I'm a very strange person, I just hate dancing by myself.' Brian said he didn't mind a bit, help yourself style of thing, so we took the floor, where to my secret delight Kevin wasted no time in chatting me up, saying, 'I must say Brian's a good picker, how long have you known him, what I mean is does anyone else stand a chance or are you spoken for?'

Now whilst I had been brought to the Club by Brian and fully intended to leave with him as he was entitled to expect of the lady he was entertaining for the evening, he did not own me so I said, 'I'm not a piece of furniture in Savage and Drawbell's with a sold label on it you know, just cos I happen to be with somebody.'

Kevin rolled his eyes and said, 'Good, so shall I spread

it round to the rest of the lads it's every man for himself or shall I keep the good news to myself, you tell me, Miss Seathorpe.'

I said, 'You can do what you think best so long as you stop calling me Miss Seathorpe, the name's Debra,' and he said, 'Got it. Debra.'

I must say we were getting on famelessly. After we had been bopping for about twenty minutes I began to feel a bit guilty about neglecting Brian but then I saw that our table was empty and that he was dancing with this honey blonde number in the slinky gold chain dress (and not very much else) I had noticed him blowing a kiss to when she came in with Wanderers wild man defender Don Dobson. So when Kevin declared, 'Well I don't know about you Debra, but I wouldn't mind conserving my strength for later on', it seemed only natural to go back with him to his table rather than sit on my own like a spare lemon waiting for Brian to come back. He ordered a single malt whisky for himself and a Long Slow Screw Against The Wall for me, then taking his drink with him went over to chat with some of his mates for a few minutes. When he came back Kevin said, 'We're all going on to a place called Henry's Hideaway to celebrate Jock's Manager of the Month award with a bit of nosh, you'd better tag along with me because according to what I've just been told Brian's got himself saddled with some of the lads who don't have transport.'

All right all right, it is easy to see with houndsight what Kevin's game was. Truth to tell I had a pretty good idea at the time but I guess I just went along with it, he was a reel Jack the lad and I liked him a lot, and as for Brian he didn't seem all that bothered about letting me slip through his fingers otherwise he would not of let me dance with Kevin in the first place. As it turned out, in this belief I was wrong but that is how it seemed at the time. And I must say Kevin's white Mercedes coop was definitely one up on Brian's Ford Escort XR3i.

Henry's Hideaway was the first floor of a big terrace house in Regency Crescent overlooking the sea, the other floors being conversionalised into offices all with their brass plates above the entryphone. It was just like a country house living room with plushy green armchairs with tassels, glass-topped coffee tables, old paintings of hunting scenes and a satin quilted bar in the corner in the same material as Babs's duvet at home. If there was a dining room I never saw it, so where we were going to have this promised nosh I shall never know, maybe on trays on our knees. Needful to say none of Kevin's mates from the Wanderers had arrived, much less Brian, and they did not arrive all the time we were there, in fact the club was empty except for the foreign barman whose name was Carlo. Kevin seemed to know him quite well because after he had asked us what we would like to drink and Kevin had said, 'No no Carlo, off you go and ring up the missus in Barcelona which is what we all know you do when the big boss isn't here, because me and this young lady have got something to celebrate and in her honour I am going to concoct a drink known as the Debra Chase Chaser', he let him go behind the bar and fix it.

I don't know exactly what Kevin put in that cocktail shaker, I know there was five-star brandy and that liquor with a cocoa base and cream de menthe but there were other things as well and some of them must of been quite strong, cos as soon as I had knocked it back upon Kevin's command, 'Down the hatch and no heeltaps or you have to drink another one standing on your head', I felt quite ill and needed some air. Remember it had been a long exciting day and I had had nothing to eat since some corn on the cob and a glass of V–8 juice for lunch. Kevin said if it was air I needed he had an electric fan back at his flat so off we went, his pad was only round the corner in Regency Terrace and the little walk in the fresh air made me feel better, I guess I should not of gone in but should of gone back to Bogie's Casablanca to find Brian, but by now I was hungry and Kevin said he would fix me a fried egg sandwich. His flat was three flights up and climbing the stairs I began to feel all wobbly again so as soon as we got in I had to have a quiet lie down when I at once passed out.

I do not know how long I slept but when I woke it was to find myself responding against my will to the wayward Wanderer's hungry embrasures. It must of been four in the morning when Kevin nicely rang for a mini-cab and sent me home. Babs and Dad were out for the count thank goodness. I could not sleep because everything that had happened to me on that eventful day kept swimming round in my head. To get myself settled I unearthed from my chest of drawers the lockable five year diary which Babs had given me for my sixteenth birthday but which I had never got round to starting, and then sitting down at my dressing table I chewed my ballpoint pen for a while and then started the first page of Debra Chase's Sex Romps Diary.

5

Bright Lights Here We Come

As I said, once you are a beauty queen you are in a different world to the one when you were not. Not that I reely thought of myself as a beauty queen, having got one jump ahead of Suzie Dawn that was it so far as Debra Chase was concerned, as Miss South-east Coast I was contentful to leave it at that, I had no intrest in going in for Miss Whole of the South Coast or whatever the next rung on the ladder to Miss World might be. No, I had one driving ambition and that was to be Miss Page Three.

Still, eat, drink and be merry for tomorrow is another day has always been my motto, and so as the reigning Miss South-east Coast I throughly enjoyed basking in the limelight while it lasted. I became a regular habitual of Bogie's Casablanca where Brian had me made an honourable member. I am glad to say there were no hard feelings over my little fling with sexy striker Kevin Keene. I just told Brian what had happened, some of it anyway, and he just said, 'And you fell for that did you? Either you're greener than you look Debra, or Kevin has a very persuasive way with him, I know he's a fast worker but I didn't think even he was that fast, you've got to admire the crafty bugger in a way.'

This was after Brian had rung me up to invite me to make up a foursome with his mate wonder winger Robby Roberts and Robby's current girl friend, vivacious redhead Cindy who worked on the perfume counter at Savage and

Drawbell's, the programme being a Chinese nosh first then all out to this raunchy pub called Squires where they had strip acts, both male and feminine. I did not think this would be my scene but it was a lot of fun, though I must say it did get a bit rowdy when they started fooling around with jelly and cucumbers. One of the fellas was reely funny, he stripped down to his leopardskin jockstrap and then putting a balloon between his bottom cheeks he somehow managed to blow it up, I would love to know how he did it. It was amateur night and I think the guys were secretly hoping that curvy Cindy and yours truly were going to bare all, but I am afraid they were out of luck. Some of the girls were reely good, you could tell they had been practising and what a turn-on it must of been for their boy friends, but the fellas were frankly just embarrassing, they had no idea and as for their vital specifics if you know what I mean, as Brian said, 'If that was all I had to show for myself I'd keep it covered up.' It was a reely good night out and although I am not turned on by that kind of thing I liked Brian a lot so afterwards I went back with him to his seafront pad and it was another sizzling page for Debra Chase's Sex Romps Diary.

But in no way was I beholdened to Brian, we were just good mates who happened to fancy one another if ther was no one else around at the time, it was all relaxed and easy. I guess I went out with most of the Wanderers squad during my year as Miss South-east Coast, though never the substitutes. I also got on good terms with sevral business types such as the under-boss of Seathorpe Car Mart, the chief rep of Glacier Double Glazing who I had met through Jock Jarvis when he was anointed Manager of the Month, and the manager of the Rex cine-complex. I even had a date with a reel typhoon, Mr Lionel Ashe OBE or some such letters after his name, the owner of Ashe Construction who were building the new Conference Centre. It was the first time I had been out with an older man, well I spose they were all older but I mean there was a generative gap of about thirty years in his case but he was reely sweet at first. He took me out to the Three Seasons in his Roller then back to the Royal Talbot where he had booked a suit, I had to pretend to be going to the Ladies and then sneak up to his room by the fire stairs in case the press got to hear of it, it was the first time I had ever done that sort of thing and it was a reel giggle. But then it turned out he wanted to have his way with me in a certain way, no way was I having that so I went on my way, leaving him alone in a luxuriant £100-a-night hotel suit when he could of driven home to his 12-bedroom Jamesian manor house set in its own acres. That experience taught me a lesson in life, always to find out by tactile questioning whether a guy is in any way kinky, cos I am not into those kind of fun and games whatever you may of read in the *Sunday Shocker*.

Like me, Suzie Dawn was also enjoying the high life as the reigning Miss Seathorpe, and sometimes our swords would cross at Bogie's Casablanca or some four star restaurant or other when we would exchange galactic smiles. Suzie had by now given up her job on Woolworth's pick'n'mix counter as being incomparable with her title, there were rumours that she was thinking of trying her luck in London once her year was up but in what line I did not know.

As for my own job, it suited my book to keep it on for the time being. Although Jessie hated my guts and would love to of fired me, I had her over a barrow. In the first place she was too short-staffed and in the second there is a certain catch in having a beauty queen working in your saloon, I mean to say the punters were getting their hair done by Miss South-east Coast herself, how bad as the footballers say? Mr Scissors was dead chuffed at my winning the title and he sent for me to congratulate me himself personly. I hoped he was going to transpose me to the High Street but he said no, he wanted to build up the Station Road business and I was just the star attraction they needed. But he upped my wages by quite a bit which was very nice and came in useful, and very nicely said that any time I wanted to take time off to open a fete or a supermarket or any of that kind of stuff, I only had to give him a bell. I did do a few personable appearances as it so happens, such as starting off a charity fun run also a donkey derby, posing on the bonnet of a Nissen Bluebird at the South Coast Motor Show and opening a new video centre, but no supermarkets I am afraid so no big fees, but it was always nice to put Jessie's nose out of joint when I told her Mr Scissors had given me permittal to take the afternoon off, also it was useful training for when I became a Page Three Girl when I would be commandeering astronautical sums for personable appearances.

As regards my home life at that time I think Dad finally came to terms with the fact that his little girl was a big girl now! He and Babs had their dancing intrests to peruse and now I was grown up they could travel farther afield to enter their various ballroom dancing comps, often staying overnight if it was a weekend, or otherwise not getting back till three or four in the morning, which suited stopout Debra fine! So they led their lives and I led mine, quite frankly we saw very little of one another during

86

this period, I think Dad was quite glad if anything, it must of been a relief to him not to have me banging on about a modelling career every time he sat down to watch the telly. Not that I was letting up on that front but just at the moment I was enjoying myself too much to think about my next step up the ladder. What I thought was, I will get near the end of my year as Miss South-east Coast and then I will put my foot down, I will say Right Dad, I have got a few bob saved and I am not afraid of hard work, I can always get a nights and weekends job in a McDonald's, Spud-U-Like, sunnink like that, so I am off to modelling school and there is nothing you can do about it although of course I would prefer to go with your blessing.

But then suddenly something happened to precipice my long-term plans. I knew from various snide remarks Dad was in the habit of passing – such as frinstance 'And what time does her ladyship intend coming back tonight, that's if she intends coming back at all, I know it's none of my business I'm only your father, but I would seriously like to know as we've got the Latin American quarter finals in East Croydon then supper with Yvette and Max Butterfield to thrash out the new guidelines for the south-east coast area novelty dance knockout, so seeing as we'll be back quite late I just want to know whether it's worth keeping the central heating on maximum' – that he must of been vaguely aware of my exploitations with the majority of the Seathorpe Wanderers and other blokes, in a small place like Seathorpe a little gossip goes a long way.

What I did not bargain for was Dad reading my Sex Romps Diary, I so much never thought he would that I had grown careless about locking it and on this particlar occasion had left it open on my dressing table in my rush to get off to work being late as per usual. The first I knew that the balloon had gone down with a bump was when Babs called me at Mr Scissors and asked me to meet her for lunch, this was most unusual for her, like me she always made do with an apple and a couple of crispbreads. So I knew there was something wrong but she wouldn't say what over the phone, only that Dad had gone beresk when he had found sunnink of mine, so of course I put two and four together and remembered I had left my Sex Romps Diary out unlocked.

I met Babs at the Pizza Per Favore, not the best avenue for a quiet talk as the music was even louder than Truffles, but it was handy for both of us. No sooner had we ordered a ten-inch Siciliana Hawaii to share (my favrite, black and green olives and pineapple) than Babs lunged straight in. I couldn't make out the first part of what she was saying because she was speaking low so as not to be overheard by the adjoinful tables which were only a one-inch gap away, but as the voice of Madonna I think it was faded out between tapes, I heard her going on, '. . . why you have to write that kind of stuff down at all God only knows Debra, but if you had the brains you were born with as your Dad's so fond of saying you might at least have kept it out of sight, he went spare, he really did, he was still frothing at the mouth when we both left half an hour late for work, I tried to persuade him it was just fantasy probably because you were frustrated living in a little place like this when you want to get up to Town to try your hand at modelling but he was having none of it, he just kept saying What gets into her, what gets into her, is there something wrong with her or what . . .?'

Then the Madonna tape started up again and I didn't reely hear much more till we were leaving, even though Babs went on non-stop in between forkfuls of Siciliana Hawaii, but from what I could make out she lived in high hopes of making the best of a bad job by persuadifying Dad that as there was no way he was going to stop me being a right handful short of keeping me locked up like a fairytale bad princess in a tureen, he might as well save himself grey hairs by turning me loose on Auntie Doris in Sydenham and letting me have a crack at modelling, who knows but what I could become a big earner and finish up supporting Dad and Babs in luxury (that was a joke). I had my doubts about this scene personly, but Babs thought touch wood and crossing fingers that she might just be able to swing it.

As we went dutch on the bill and walked out of the pizzery she was saying, 'Now don't go rushing off because there's something I want to say to you private.' So we went up this cobbled alley where we stood in the back doorway of the Friends Meeting House, I think it's a kind of church, and Babs said, I could tell it was difficult for her as she started ever so slowly and was looking down at her shoes, 'Look, I don't know how to put this Debra without you taking it the wrong way, but your Dad's only human, now I wouldn't dream of saying that stuff might have turned him on not for a minute, I mean for God's sake you are his daughter after all, but it might just have jolted him into thinking about what he's been missing in life, do you know what I'm saying to you? I mean with you being there in the next bedroom all these years and these bungalows having wafer-thin walls, I mean all right so you're out a good deal these days but we never know what time you're going to be back and it's a bit difficult to relax if you think someone might come bursting in on you, are you following me?'

Yes, I most certainly was. With anyone else I would of been embarrassed but with Babs it was somehow just girl-talk, even though she was talking about my own father, so I let her go on, not that I could of stopped her now she was in full flow. 'I mean I don't want to spell it out but some of the things you've jotted down in that diary, I mean I don't know whether they're all in the mind or what and I don't want to know, I beg you not to tell me, but where you've put about, you know, experimenting, now I know it's difficult for you to think about your own Dad in that way and I wouldn't expect you to but if it makes it any easier look at me Debra, I mean I'm an active woman, I'm sure you can sense that, I'm like you in a lot of ways and I haven't got one foot in the grave yet, are you taking in what I'm trying to say to you, to be perfectly candid there's a way in which we'd both be glad to get shut of you if you were flying the nest and I can't put it more plainer than that, now I'm sure you know what I'm driving at.'

Again the answer was yes, and whilst as Babs quite crectly interpolated I did not want to think of my Dad in that way, I had often seen them giving one another glances and of course it had crossed my mind to wonder why they sometimes had to spend the night in a hotel after one of their dancing comps when they had only gone as far off as say Brighton, so I understood what she was saying, after all I was fully adulterated by now and had got the vote, not that I have ever used it, I take after Dad in that way, he does not believe in policies.

Babs finished off by saying, 'Well I'm glad we've had this chat and cleared the air, flower, we've both got to dash back to work now at least I know I have, but I'm going to tackle your Dad the minute he gets home tonight, so I want you to do me a favour and do yourself a favour, just make yourself scarce for an hour before you come home, go for a drink with your mates or go for a walk or look round the shops or whatever you want to do but for God's sake just leave it to me to calm him down and break the ice.'

Remembering my social obligement for that evening I said, 'But I've got to get home and change because I'm going out at seven for drinks at Henry's Hideaway with twice-married south coast Karfone King Len Gates, then on to a candlelit supper at the Three Seasons.'

To this Babs only said, 'If you know what's good for you petal, you'll ditch him, say you've got a headache or something, because you, me and your father have a lot to talk about tonight.'

In one way this was the worst advice I ever listened to, because I heard later that after me ringing up to say I had flu, typhoon Len Gates dated petite, attractive Cindy, ex-girl friend of Brian's mate Robby Roberts, and after two whirlwind months they were married and she will be set up for life when the divorce comes through. But in another way it was the best advice I ever had, cos like the good fairy she was for me, everything Babs had predelicted came true.

Doing exactly what Babs had told me to, I whiled away an hour just walking around looking in shoe shops and sipping a frozen daiquiri at Tarzan's, a new bar which had opened in the basement of the Royal Talbot Hotel but it was completely empty, I have never been so bored in my life as during that hour not to say depressed, instead of a glam evening out at the Three Seasons I was going to finish up with a plate of Lean Cuisine in front of Terry Wogan.

I did hope Dad ranting and raving about my Sex Romps Diary would turn out to be a storm in a teabag as was often the case when he got the bite between his teeth over something I had done or not done, but no such luck, he was still banging on about it when I got home.

When Dad was in this kind of mood he had a nasty habit of talking about me as if I wasn't there and this is what he did now, I might as well of still be sitting in Tarzan's staring at the jungle muriel on the wall for all the notice he took of his own daughter. As I walked into the living room he was saying, 'You're not wrong, Babs, you're not wrong, something's definitely got to be done about that girl but what, answer me that, answer me that.' I plonked myself in an armchair where he could not help but see me but he just went on as if I was invincible. 'Have I done my best for her or have I done my best for her, yet this is how she repays us, she's nothing but worry, God almighty I shudder to think of the consequences if she'd left that diary lying around in one of these fancy bars she goes to, we'd've all finished up in the *News of the World*.'

At least Babs made some recognisal that I was among those presence by winking at me as she said, 'It's what I keep telling you Eric, she needs a release for her energies, I mean I know she's bored us all rigid over that modelling course she wants to go on but honestly I reckon it bears thinking about, I really do, oh hello Debra we were just talking about you surprise surprise.'

I said, 'Yes, I somehow thought you were Babs, that must be why my ears are burning,' but for all the notice

Dad took I could still of not been in the room, because without so much as a glance in my direction he went on, 'Modelling course, modelling course, what's wrong with her job at Mr Scissors in Station Road for God's sake?'

To this Babs responded, reely banging the drum for me, I was ever so grateful, 'She's ambitious Eric, she doesn't want to be stuck in Station Road all her life.'

Too true Babs, but all Dad had to say to that was, 'They've a branch in the High Street, haven't they, she could be manageress of that establishment in the fullness of time if she played her cards right!'

Now talking of cards I had already marked Babs's card on Mrs Scissors as she had come to call him, not that it needed marking cos Babs was on to all the local gossip, so I was not sprised to hear her say with another wink at her darling stepdaughter, 'I'm afraid it's be a waste of time playing cards with Mrs Scissors, she's already got a very interesting poker game going with Mr Trousers next door if you know what I mean nudge nudge, now there's no need to raise your eyebrows Eric, your daughter's a very grown-up lady these days, has been for some time in case it's escaped your notice, and she's not hearing anything she doesn't know, in fact it was she who told me.' Then she said something which reely tipped the scales my way, 'But what I'm saying to you is she doesn't need to suck up to Mr Scissors or anyone else for that matter, because after a few years modelling she could buy her own unisex hair-fashioning boutique, isn't that right, Debra? If she's at all successful there's a lot of money in modelling, a great deal of money, Eric.'

That mention of money was the first time I ever knew Dad show the slightest glimmer of interest in the object of a career in modelling. Dad has always been I won't say obsessionalised by money but he does like it coming in, he has always had a lot of outgoings such as running the car and building the Spanish patio extension, and course, living with Babs with her pendant for new clothes and the other good things of life like being first in the Crescent with a micro-wave oven has never come cheap. 'Is there indeed, is there indeed?' he said musefully.

'And of course,' went on Babs cunningly, 'she'd need a manager.'

'Well, as to that,' says Dad importantly, 'one doesn't become co-ordinator of the open-air pool and fitness centre without acquiring a certain modicum of managerial skills.'

'Come to that,' says Babs, giving me another wink, 'you don't become supervisor of the Seathorpe Snappy 24-hour Foto Developing Service without learning management either, so whatever problems may await you when you've made it as a model, flower, you won't have to worry about your invoicing and VAT returns and as for your portfolio I can whistle that through the dark room at cost price for openers.'

'Hold your horses, hold your horses, we haven't said she's going to be a model yet, it requires thought, it requires thought,' chuntered Dad, beginning to walk up and down the room to show he was thinking.

'What is there to think about?' says Babs coaxfully. 'Just imagine, Eric, what with our success with the light fantastic and hers with her figure, we could become quite the local celebrities, it's all grist to the mill if we ever get round to starting our own dance studio.' Starting a dance school was something Dad and Babs had been talking about for years, it was their dream, and as it turned out Debra Chase was to be the good fairy that waved the magic wand for them. But I must not get ahead of myself, we are still a long way off that particlar Chap in my life story – or rather in theirs, if Dad ever gets round to writing Page Three Girl's Long Suffering Father as he sometimes good-humorously threatenises he will!

'It's becoming the local notorieties that I worry about,' he grumbled. 'What would the neighbours at Rosedene and Balmoral make of it if they knew one tenth of what she's put down in that so-called diary, you've not heard the last of that young lady, in fact if I didn't believe it was all in the mind as Babs said you'd be out on that front doorstep tonight, bags packed, never mind going on modelling courses.' This was a great relief to hear, cos whenever Dad said you had not heard the last of something, it meant you had. But in any case Babs came to my rescue by saying, 'Now it's no use going over old ground Eric, there's nothing else to be said on the matter, she's said she's sorry, to me if not to you,' (actually I hadn't) 'but what it boils down to is she's grown out of this town and it's time for her to do her own thing so what do you say?'

If Dad's next words did not exactly convict me that Debra Chase was at long last on her way to fame, fortune and fabulous fun, at least I knew it was the beginning of the tunnel when he said grumblingly, 'We'll have to see, we'll have to see, it's not as simple as you both seem to think, there's the money end to be worked out for one thing, I'll tell you what Debra, just take yourself off upstairs while Babs and your father discuss the whys and wherefors, there's a hell of a lot of things to be considered, a hell of a lot.'

So up I went to my room, scarcely able to congeal my jublification, and so sure it was now just a question of crossing the i's and q's that I very nearly started to pack my suitcase there and then. Instead I just put on my sound system and started going through my collection of cola bears, Bambis and other soft toys which I had accumulised over the years going right back to my bendy giraffe, to decide on which of them would accomplice me on my travails through life.

After what seemed an age Babs came up to give me a big hug and say excitingly, 'Right, I've got some bad news and some good news, the bad news is you're going back to your Auntie Doris's in Sydenham, no way will he let you have your own bed-sitter, that's cloud cuckoo land for the time being.' Big pause, just to keep me on tenderhooks. 'But the good news is I've just called the Donna Bella Rosa School of Fashion in Tulse Hill and you're in luck, they've got a vacancy and if she likes the look of you then you can start a week on Monday at the start of a new course, it's very fortunate everything's panned out how it has because another few days and you'd have missed the enrolment deadline and then God knows what we'd have done, it would have been a case of waiting another three months and you know how he waffles and chops and changes his mind, we could have been back to square one.' Babs was almost as thrilled as me, she would of prattled on like this all night but after a bit Dad called up the stairs, 'Are you coming down then or what the pair of you, or do you want me to drink this dry sherry on my own?'

So over a celebrational sherry we threshed out the details. Dad was more than generous considering his limited resourcefulness, but to save me from having to be grateful he wanted everything putting on a business baseness. He was agreeful to paying Donna Bella Rosa's fees, plus my board at Auntie Doris's, plus a small allowability for myself to stretch out my couple of hundred pounds savings as he did not want me working at the Pizza Palace or wherever and having to get back on my own late at night (or get back not on my own, which I could guess was at the back of his mind after reading my Sex Romps Diary!!), but being as how he was not made of money this was only a loan, came the day when I started making any money from modelling he would take call it twenty-five per cent till it was all paid off plus interest.

I would of agreed to anything to get out of Mr Scissors and into the magical world of modelling but as it happened I knew from what I had read in the biographs of some famous models that twenty-five per cent was chickenfeed when it came to what you could pay out, some of them were paying a quarter of their earnings to their agents. So throwing my arms round Dad's neck I cried out loud enough for the whole world or at least Rosedene and Balmoral to hear, 'Ooh, thank you thank you thank you, I can just see it now, Debra Chase Page Three Girl, wait till you see that caption Dad, Dishy Debra is the seaside stunner you'll be seeing more of, since waving goodbye to a life on the ocean wave at sandy Seathorpe the buxom beachcomber has reely come out of her shell. But though delectable Debra just loves deep sea fishing, here's a catch who'll never have to fish for compliments . . .'

I had rehearsalised this in my head a hundred times but of course Dad had to go and take it liberally, saying, 'What's she on about, what's she on about, you've never been fishing in your life, when I wanted to take you fishing that time you moaned on you'd rather go round the Dolphinarium.'

I said, 'Oh, Dad, it's poetic licentiousness, sillee! . . . Here's a catch who'll never have to fish for compliments, Seathorpe's smasher reely knows how to hook the fellas, with net assets like hers she's sure to stay in the swim.'

I thought it was a trific caption but Dad started looking all hot and bothered, muttering to Babs, 'Are we doing the right thing, Babs?'

Giving me a warning look, Babs said to mollycoddle him, 'I think Debra knows the modelling life isn't all champagne cocktails, Eric.'

I said mischiefly, 'No, it's Debra Chase Chasers as well!'

'What the thump is a Debra Chase Chaser?' asked Dad, to which I replied instantaneously, 'Same as a Suzie Dawn Sizzler without the blackcurrant.' So then of course Dad has to ask who Suzie Dawn is when she's at home, and upon being told Norma Borridge he started raving, 'Oh, that flibbertigibbet, that flibbertigibbet, well at least you'll be away from her influence in Sydenham, oh and another thing Debra, if you're going to be a model you'd better learn to stop slumping and put your shoulders back.'

Still full of mischief I did exactly what Dad was requestful of, asking impiously, 'Like this?' Bless him, I reely think it was the first time he got round to noticing that his darling daughter no longer wore a bra.

He was ever so funnee. 'On second thoughts,' he said quite serious, 'there must be quite a secure future in modelling cardigans.'

Knowing that modelling is a hard egg to crack, and not wishing to come home with that same egg all over my face and my tail between my ears, I did not tell anyone I was going on the Donna Bella Rosa course, just put it about that I was staying with my Auntie Doris in London for a few weeks to look around and make a few contracts. Course I had to give in my notice at Mr Scissors. Jessie was very put out sighing, 'Oh well now that is considerate, the time you've taken off this last year and then you give me less than a week to find a replacement well frankly I don't think he'll stand for it, you're supposed to give a full week's notice and technically as it's half way into Monday I could keep you here till a week on Saturday.' I did no more than put on my coat again and go straight round to Mr Scissors and put it on a plate what I was doing, making him the one acceptance to my rule of not telling anybody. Mr Scissors had the gracefulness to wish me good luck saying as we hugged each other goodbye, 'And don't forget when you're rich and famous to come back and have your picture taken giving the fella who gave you your first break a big French kiss.' I said I would and I am glad to say I kept that promise when I went down to Dad's farewell dance when owing to circumferences beyond his control he moved on from the Leisure Pool and Fitness Centre to a certain business venture which belongs in another Chap, it was not quite a French kiss I should say and course Mr Scissors being nobody outside Seathorpe and district bless his heart, the picture was only used in the *Seathorpe Clarion* with the headline, RESORT'S P3 DEBRA STILL QUITE A SNIP! Still, I am sure it was good for trade and I know he still has it framed in the window, if he knew what some businesses would pay for a personal endorsal of that kind from Debra Chase he would have three kinds of kittens!

I still wasn't seeing anything of Suzie Dawn. For all Dad's misgifts about her leading me astray I think we were both too busy leading ourselves astray if the truth be known, we still waved to one another across a crowded room style of thing but that was about it. So she did not know anything about my big break as it would turn out to be and come to that I did not know anything about her plans either. Not until fate bought us together on Seathorpe Parkway Station, the day I was leaving for Auntie Doris's in Sydenham.

Natch, Dad and Babs came to see me off. I thought for one wild moment as we got to the ticket barrier that I was going to make it on the train without a lecture from Dad but no such luck. Looking pointfully at his watch he said to Babs, 'Why don't you pop into Smith's and get her something to read and a snack of some kind for the journey, we've got a few minutes and there's no buffet car, you wouldn't eat lunch Debra so you'll be famished by the time the train reaches Victoria.'

I knew exactly what I was in for and as soon as Babs trolled off he started. 'Now listen Debra, I don't want to lecture you,' which course meant he did, 'but you've got to remember what it is you're going to London for, it's not to have a good time, that comes later if and when you've proved yourself, it's to work at what you say you want to do, are you listening to me? So that means no stopping out all night, it means no gadding about till all hours, it means no taking people back with you, now you know what I mean by that, your Auntie Doris I won't call her narrow-minded but she takes more of a dim view of that sort of thing than Babs does and well I'll be damned what's that one doing here all dolled up like the dog's dinner?'

'That one' as he called her was none other than Suzie

Dawn, dragging a big suitcase on wheels up to the ticket barrier and as Dad said reely got up to the nines.

Being only a couple of feet apart there was no way we could just exchange our usual frostful smiles, and in any case Suzie knew Dad who having caught her eye felt obligated to say something, namely, 'Hello Norma, don't say you're gallivanting off to London too, what are you doing, staying with relatives for a few days or what?'

'Oh, hello Mr Chase, oh hello Debra, no I'm,' pipes up Suzie, as per usual not finishing her sentience so we were still no wiser. 'So what are you two doing, going up to see a show or?' She could be reely stupid sometimes, Suzie could. There we are with two zonking great suitcases and she wants to know if we're going up to see a show. Yes Suze, and the suitcases are full of cabbages and rotten eggs in case we don't like it.

Now that we had met face to face I couldn't resist giving Suzie my news, even though I knew it would boomerang back on me if I failed the course or didn't get my foot on the slippery modelling ladder. I blurted out, 'Keep it to yourself Suzie cos I don't want the whole world to know just yet, but at long last I'm taking the plunge, I'm off on a modelling course!'

You could of heard Suzie all over the station concorde. 'You're not!' shrieked she.

'I am!'

'You're not!'

'I am!'

'You're not!'

'She is!' snapped Dad irritationally, just as Babs returned from W. H. Smith's with *My Guy*, a *Blue Jeans* photo-novel, a packet of Opal fruits and a Lemon Fizz from the machine. Having gathered that I had told Suzie the news Babs said proudly, 'Hello Norma, no it's Suzie now isn't it, fancy bumping into you, yes it's quite true, she starts on Monday – the Donna Bella Rosa School of Fashion in Tulse Hill, I don't know whether you've heard of it at all.'

'She doesn't!' squeaked Suzie.

'She does!' shouted Dad.

'So what takes you up to Town, Suzie?' I inquired politely with a pointful glance at her suitcase.

Suzie burst into a fit of the giggles, and in that moment I knew that whatever our past rivalhoods we were going to bury our differentials, cos somehow I knew what she was going to say next, even though she didn't say it.

'You'll never guess – I'm going on a,' she started.

'What – a modelling course?' I asked gaspingly.

'Yes!!! At the Donna Bella Rosa hee hee hee hee!'

'You're not!' echoed Babs. Well praps echoed is not the right word as no one had said it before yet.

'I am!' cried Suzie, hugging herself.

'You're not!' This being from me it reely was an echo this time as Babs had said it first.

'I am, I am!'

'You're not, you're not!' moaned Dad like a man possessionised.

'She is, she is!' I cried, not knowing who to hug next. 'I hugged Suzie then I hugged Babs then I hugged Dad who I then saw had a face as long as a fiddler as he moaned, 'Oh, my Gawd!'

6

The Commencal of My Career

So began my new life as a glamour model, and my first step up the golden ladder to fame, fun and fortune. And thusly it was that I found myself, at the age of getting on for nineteen, in the bosoms of Auntie Doris just around the corner from No 23 (Garden Flat) Dunkley Road, Sydenham, where I started my livelihood. Whilst Auntie Doris had been a frequent visitor to Oceanview in the interfering years so she had not become a stranger, I had not set foot in her council flat since leaving London must of been fourteen years ago. It was darker and pokier than I remembered it, which was not very much as I had it all jumbled up with our own garden flat in my memorising, but the spare room where I used to sleep when I stayed with Auntie Doris was as big as my room back at Oceanview and Auntie Doris had made it reely nice for me with a new duvet and her own dressing table which she said she didn't reely use, all it needed was a few night club teddy bears and it would begin to look like home.

To start with I was very happy at Auntie Doris's. Sydenham was so different from Seathorpe and the glittering West End was only a bus ride away, not to mention Sydenham's very own nitespot, Ciro's where South London car dealers wine and dine. But after the first two hours I began to grow bored. How I endured that long weekend I shall never know, it was like being in a Benedictine nunnery.

Suzie, typified, had forgotten to give me her number where she had got herself fixed up, and the thought of her out on the toot without me drove me wild.

Auntie Doris was very sweet but all she seemed to do with her life was sit there and sit there sucking mint imperials and watching telly. When she at long last cottoned on that I was bored she offered to give me a game of draughts, I don't think she reelised she had a fullgrown young lady on her hands. I tried remarking very casually, 'I wouldn't mind popping up West for an hour Auntie Doris, start finding my way about,' but it was a case of 'Now you know what your Dad said Marjory, you've to take it easy and get settled in, there'll be plenty of time for all that sort of thing later.'

I said, 'I'm sure he didn't leave instructions for me to be cooped up all weekend and anyway my name's not Marjory it's Debra,' but that's just where I was wrong because Auntie Doris said, 'Well as a matter of fact that's exactly what he did do since you ask Marjory, Debra I should say, I'll try to remember but why you want to change the name you were born with I do not know.' So all I could do was grit my teeth and think about my fantastic career as a career girl, commencalising Monday.

When the fatalistic day came round at last I was so exciteable that I could not so much as look at my break-fast, specially when it turned out that unbeknownst tome Auntie Doris had prepared me a big fry-up whilst I was getting ready. I could no more of eaten it than I could of swum to the moon and I am afraid Auntie Doris and me nearly had our first row, with her getting on my goat by saying, 'You don't leave this flat without something inside you, if you don't eat fried stuff these days you can have corn flakes with a chopped-up banana, you can have Sugar

Puffs, you can have Weetabix and prunes but you are not going off on an empty stomach.'

I said, 'Look Auntie Doris, if we're going to be friends we've got to get a few things clear. I'm not a little girl any more so if you don't mind I'll be the one to decide what I have for breakfast, if anything, for your information I usually have an apple, sometimes not even that. And while we're about it it's for me to decide if I go out in the evening, who I go out with if anybody and what time I come back, that's if I do come back, and if you don't like it,' I said, 'I'm very sorry but it'll be the best thing all round if I just move in with Suzie, she'd like nothing better but Dad wanted me to come and stay with you.'

Actually that was a little white lie about Suzie. The flatlet she had got for herself in Tulse Hill was rented to her by a trumpeter with the Roseland Big Band Sound called Vince who used to date her sometimes when the band played the Seathorpe Pavilion, he owned the house with his wife but reading between the lines I don't think he was going to be adverse to popping in to see Suzie sometimes whilst his wife was looking the other way, so no way did she want me anywhere near her flatlet, not that I would of come between her and Vince, he was forty if he was a day. (Before I met The Sir I used to think forty was reely old.)

Auntie Doris didn't say much in responsal to my ulti-mation, just 'I'm only trying to do what I used to do when you were little and what Babs has had to do since you left Dunkley Road, and that's stand in for your mother, you might think you're grown up Marjory, Debra, but there's such a thing as being young in years.'

But I could see she was upset so I put my arms round her and said, 'Sorree Auntie Doris, I've got a fit of the jitters I guess with starting my modelling course, and don't think I'm not grateful for the cooked breakfast but honestlee, if I touched one bite it wouldn't be a fry-up, it'd be a throw-up, all right?' So as Auntie Doris is not very demonstrable that was as good as kiss and make up in her eyes, I was glad to of cleared the air though cos things could of got very awkward later on if I had not put my foot down.

Strange to retail, I had never set eyes on Donna Bella Rosa, no auditions or anything, it had all been arranged by post, I had just sent off my photos taken by Stan of the *Seathorpe Clarion* and back by return of post came the application form and the bill for the first month's lessons. So much for Babs's warning, 'If she likes the look of you.' Much later when we had become good friends, Rosa confidentialised to me her politics as regards new enterants. This was quite simply that she never turned anyone away if they had the fees, it did not matter if they weighed fifteen stone and looked like a heavyweight boxer with a moustache, as she said to me, 'Who am I to decide who's got it in them to become a successful model, that's for fate to decide, I'd a girl through the course two years ago, she had a hare lip, but she never stops working, it just so happens that God has made it up to her with a pair of the most fabulous legs going right up to her shoulders which means she's always in demand for modelling stockings, so as I say you never know.' Rosa I should mention is a great believer in the tallow cards, she has always read the fortune of every girl passing through her hands, but she only tells them if the news is good. Needles to say Debra Chase's reading could not of been better although Rosa did say the cards held a warning that I should not be too trusting, well the world now knows what they were driving at.

But as I was saying I had not yet met Donna Bella Rosa so what I told Auntie Doris about feeling nervous was true, I was having kittens by the time I got off the bus at Tulse Hill and followed the directives which had been sent by the School Secrety (who turned out to be none other than Donna Bella Rosa herself, sprise sprise!) on how to get to the Donna Bella Rosa School of Fashion. These led me to a big four-storey house in a leafy avenue, or it would of been a leafy avenue if all the trees hadn't had all their branches sawn off, something to do with their being a traffic hazard I believe. The School of Fashion did not occupationalise the whole house, just the basement, this being consistent of a big studio where the classes were held, plus the hallway where you hung up your coats and changed into your leotards, plus the loo at the end of the hallway, and the office which was just a desk and a filing cabinet under the stairs. Tell the truth, compared with what we had been led to expect by the brochette which spoke of studios meaning sevral, changing felicities and makeup suit (this turned out to be the loo!), it struck me as a bit of a dump quite frankly, glam it defnitely was not – but then I remembered reading how all the big stars like in *The Brummies* have to rehearse in reely grotty bare rooms in barrackses, so this made me feel professional and I did not mind so much after that.

Another disappointal at first was Donna Bella Rosa herself, despise her name she was no more Italian than I was, in fact she came from Clapham. With a fag dangling out of her mouth, it was a fixture, I have never seen Rosa without a fag on the go and ash all over her frontage, and with her bright orange hair, dyed of course, and matching lipstick that looked as if she must of put it on in front of the cracked mirrow in the so-called makeup suit, it made you see double, she looked more like a pub landlady than queen of the modelling courses. But although she could be quite a tartare Rosa reely knew her stuff. She was a retired hoofer, she had been in the chorus of all the big musicals, *West Side Story, Brigadier*, you name it, and she knew everything there was to know about poising and moving your body and stuff like that.

As far as the class was concerned there were twelve of us, eleven if we don't count a girl called Kim who left in the lunch break and didn't come back, saying she wanted to be a flipping model not a flipping dancer so where was the point of spending half the morning doing flipping aerobatics? Aerobatics is where you do exercises to one of Rosa's old LPs, I don't think she had anything later than the Beach Boys, you have to sit crosslegged and rotissorise your pelvis and shoulders, then lie on your back and do scissors and bicycling with your legs, you reely ache all over the next morning till you get used to it, in fact I ached so much I tried to remember who on earth I must of finished up with the night before after being temptationalised into Bonks Club by Suzie, but then I remembered it was nobody special, at least not special in that particlar way – but there I go again, jumping ahead of myself.

Besides Suzie and me, only about half the girls looked as if they could make the grade as models. The rest of the class, well I don't want to be unkind but they were either dead plain or they were just too old in my consi-derate view, which just goes to show how much I knew about modelling at that time because apart from Debra Chase and in her own way Suzie Dawn, the only ones that *did* make it were the ones I wouldn't of given a second chance to. Viv was thirty at least but she is now inconstantly in demand for knitting mags modelling cardigans and that (what Dad would of liked me to do if you remember!), whilst Margot who was even older does that TV commercial for Take 'n' Bake Thinna Dinnas where scatty sitcom star Jilly Jenkins of *Oh No It's Miss Friday* fame plays this greedy housewife – Margot is the supermarket customer who you see looking as if daggers could kill after Jilly has taken the last twelve packs. So it just goes to show that Donna Bella Rosa was right in saying it was not for her to judge who to have on her course and who not so long as their money was good, I have often wondered what would of happened to me if Dad had been in poor circumferences, cos without the Donna Bella Rosa School of Fashion I could never of made it as time will tell. As to the fatality of everyone else on the course, all will be revealed.

So Donna Bella Rosa welcomed us all to the course and told us it was going to be work work work and whatever fancy ideas we might of had we could knock them on the head straight away as there were no short cuts, the road to stardom was paved with heartbreaks and blood, perspirant and tears so if anyone thought it was going to be an easy ride they could forget it, then we changed into our leotards and got down to the nitty-gritty. No coffee, no chit chat, it was straight into ten minutes lumbering up exercises finishing with push-ups which I had not done since getting excused PE at school after Babs got me a doctor's note to say it made me dizzy, actually that was a little white lie but the doctor owed her a favour cos she had once printed up some saucy snaps he brought in to the Seathorpe Snappy 24-hour

Foto Developing Service, defnitely not one of his patients so he said and defnitely not hard porn but defnitely near the knuckle style of thing. I wished it had of occurred to me to bring a sick note with me to Donna Bella Rosa's School of Fashion cos by the time I had finished those push-ups I was just one big ache both in my arms and in my limbs, you could not take a rest because Rosa kept banging on at you saying, 'And push and push and up and down and push and push and Debra's sticking her bottom in the air again and up and down and one more thrust and stop there, now I want you all to sit cross-legged, backs straight.'

So then we go into the aerobatics, and after must of been half an hour of that it was time for our first department class, where you walk round and round the room with a book on your head, with Donna Bella Rosa thumping away at the piano and calling, 'And one and two and shoulders back and one and two and chins well up and one and two and Debra looks as if she's carrying a sack of coal on her head,' which was not fair as my book was longer than everyone else's. 'And what are you looking so miserable about, child?' she chunters on.

Suzie made everyone laugh by saying quite wittily for her I thought, 'Praps it's a sad book.' Course, the books drop off our heads and we were all falling about till Donna Bella Rosa said, 'All right girls, that'll do, joke over, put your books back on your heads, shoulders back now and Debra, pay no attention to what you're carrying *on* your head, just concentrate on what's inside it, you're going to be a model child, cheer up, think beautiful thoughts.'

As I said to Suzie, 'Honestlee, it's like being back at flipping school!', but then as Suzie said to me, 'But we *are* at flipping' which was true enough I spose. So I did try to be good but when it came to thinking beautiful thoughts, all I could think about was going back to Auntie Doris's to play draughts whilst Suzie went on the razzle, cos although I had given Auntie Doris a piece of my mind I did not reely have the courage to stay out without a good excuse.

Luckily for me Suzie was up to every kind of dodge, she was just like she was when we reely were back at John Pennywick Upper School when she would do things like saying she had got the curse to get out of swimming which she hated (unless you count splashing about in Dad's Leisure Pool with lots of boys in attendants), misfortunately she came a cropper when the teacher began to notice she was in the habit of having the curse about once a fortnight and took her to the school nurse who rumbled her in one.

It was in the afternoon, whilst we were doing catwalk practice with Donna Bella Rosa going 'And strut and sway and thrust and shoulders forward and pelvises rotating and don't overdo it Debra, you're catwalking not streetwalking', that Suzie murmured to me, 'Do you reely have to go back to?'

I muttered back without my lips moving, like they do in those old George Raft prison movies on the box, 'Play draughts with my Auntie Doris? No, it's not compulsive, she likes doing jigsaws too.'

'I mean do you have to go back at all, sillee, I mean spose you?' This was Suzie shorthand for 'Suppose you make up a story?' Yes, but what?

Suzie had the answer to that too. Quick as a flash she said, 'Well, as you said yourself.'

'Said what, Suzie?' I said, completely mysterised.

'It's a flipping school, isn't it? So.'

'So what?'

'Well, what happens to schoolgirls when they're naughty?' asked Suzie, speaking a whole sentience for once.

'I dunno, I spose they get on the front page of the *Sunday Shocker* after steamy spanking sessions with sexy sir,' I said.

'No, sillee – they get kept in!'

'Which makes them late home! Suzie you're a genii!'

At this point Donna Bella Rosa called out, 'Debra and Suzie, if you want to chatter please go and chatter outside!' and for a minute I thought we reely were going to be kept in. But it was all right, after our last lesson which was pouting practice we finished pronto at five o'clock. So ended my first strenual day as a trainee model.

The general idea was to sample the razzle-dazzle of famed nitespot Bonks off plush Piccadilly, where megastars, superstuds and their sex kittens go to unwind, but course it was not even dark yet, most of them would only just of got out of bed. So after ringing Auntie Doris and telling a little white lie – namely that Suzie and me had to stay on to practise our pouting as Donna Bella Rosa had not found our exercises very satisfying, and after that she had very kindly invited us to a late supper at her favrite French bisto in Dulwich to discuss our careers as she had already got us marked down as her two star pupils, and she would be sending us home in her brother's minicab so Auntie Doris had nothing to worry about and needn't stay up – we tootled up West for a look at the bright lights and a pizza, salad bowl, sunnink like that, before Bonks beckoned.

As for myself personly, all I knew about the West End was what I had seen on telly plus dimly rembering being taken by Dad to see the *Jungle Book* one Christmas and disgracing myself after having three orange drinks cos I did not like to tell Dad I wanted to go in the middle of the show, I knew how he would bang on, 'Oh for heaven's sake, how many times have I told you to go before we get settled down, now we've got to disturb everyone and find an usherette to take you into the Ladies, I asked you if you wanted to go before the film started and you said no, honestly Marjory you can be a real pain sometimes.' Suzie though knew her way around, because of coming up to visit her disgraced dad in Pentonville, I never reely knew what he was in for, Dad said it was something to do with VAT offensives in his cowboy 24-hour emergency plumbing business, that might well of been so knowing Mr Borridge but Suzie and me had never talked about it owing to our rift, and by the time we came to London together the shamed swindler was out with remittance for good behaviour so it seemed tactile to let sleeping wolves lie.

So once we got off the bus at Piccadilly Circus or near enough I let Suzie take charge, first we went round the Trocadero Centre and looked at the boutiques, I must say it made the Seathorpe Shopping Mall look like a lot of tat, there were belts, posters, Sock Shop, everything you could wish for, then we went through Chinatown with its Chinese phone boxes and all the shop signs in Chinese writing, it looked reely metropolitan. But after that it was still only half past six and we had run out of sights to see, we had done the West End. We wandered around as far as Trafalgar Square which was dead boring, nothing to do except stare at the fountains and keep out of the way of the pigeons, I hate pigeons, always have done, they are even worse than gulls, and after that it was between trotting off to look at Buckingham Palace which I cannot say would of been a thrill a minute, or going back to the Trocadero Centre. This we decided to do as there was a handbag I wanted to have another look at, but then Suzie remembered this pub a guy had once invited her to, she had got talking to him on the train up from Seathorpe on a SuperSava day return and from what I managed to drag out of her the guy had apparently said, 'If you happen to have a bit of time to kill when you get back to Victoria tonight, say you miss your train who knows these things do happen, try dropping in the Chequered Flag Doubles Bar, it is a giggle a minute especially in the Happy Hour, Happy Hour they call it Happy Six Hours more like it goes on all night, you'll like it, it is a really mad boozer, the landlord is a real nut case.'

Suzie had seemingly never gone to the pub cos she had got to get back to Seathorpe to keep a date with a T-bone steak and all the trimmings, but she had the address so we thought we might as well give it a whirl before going on to Bonks. We could not afford to splash out on cabs and we had no idea what buses went to Victoria so we asked a policeman who after saying, 'The Chequered Flag, you don't want to go there girls, if you're looking for a nice cosy pub there's one not far from here in St Martins Lane, I always call in for a bev with one of my mates when we go off duty which is at eight o'clock as luck would have it,' at last told us the way. It turned out to be not far but we must of looked a sight tottering down Pell Mell on our stiletto heels, neither Suzie or me have ever been what you would call big walkers.

The Chequered Flag Doubles Bar was all Suzie's unbeknown friend said it was, with foreign money stuck to the walls and notices saying things like 'Please Do Not Ask For Credit As A Fat Lip Often Offend's' and 'No Farting Area'. But zaniest of all, and this being the main attraction and the reason the joint was already jumping as they say even though it was still early, was all these dozens of knickers hanging from the ceiling on rows of clotheslines, every colour of the rainbow including the Union Jack and every type you can think of from the skimpy little Knickerbox sort which I personly usually wear (there I go giving my secrets away!!) to a pair of huge flapping camiknickers the size of the Goodyear blimp. How they all got up there was like this, it seems that any lady going in during the Happy Hour can have a free Chequered Career which is their house cocktail, peach brandy, Triple Sec, vodka, light rum, orange and lemon juice and Grenadine, but if she cannot finish it she has to present the Guvnor with her knickers, what they don't mention is that they serve it in this zonking great balloon glass holding nearly half a litre as we could see later.

As Suzie and me were still shoving our way towards the bar, and you reely did have to shove, it was like being a sardine in the rush hour, the rules of the game were being shouted out by the Guvnor who wore a straw hat, striped shirt with armbands and big moustache like in a barber's chair quartet. Squeezing this big old-fashioned car horn he was bawling, 'All right, now all you beautiful girls whose first visit this is to Britain's whackiest pub, our speciality cocktail comes with mine host's compliments but there is one condition which I will explain as we go along, now what about you two young ladies?'

Seeing that it was to Suzie and me that he made this referral I was all for having a go, specially as we had to watch the pennies and I had already noticed from the price list that apart from lager and stuff like that the cheapest proper drink was a Pink Pussy at £2.95, but then Suzie giggled into my ear that we had better not as if we lost she was not best placed to keep up her end of the bargain having forgotten to put them on that day, so we ordered two Bloody Shames at £1.50 each, these being Bloody Marys without the vodka.

Just then a mannish voice behind us said to the Guvnor, 'But you forgot to tell these gorgeous girls about our other little tradition Len, which is that the two most ravishing creatures in the bar get Biggles and Gingers bought for them by me and Ian, that's gin, Pernod, tequila, lemon juice and Grenadine girls, it comes highly recommended, mind if I introduce myself well well well, look who it isn't!'

Yes, small world it was no other than the bloke Suzie had met on the Southeast Network Supashuttle that time, Tony his name was, quite a good looker, turned out he was an air extractor engineer from Croydon, whilst Ian was something to do with central heating, I never found out what except that he had a joke about it, 'I pump it in and Tony sucks it out.'

Ian was quite nice, not reely my type as he was too inclinated to treat Suzie and me as two little featherbrains but I was happy to string along with him for Suzie's sake as she seemed to get on with Tony like a horse on fire. In any case I thought we would be just letting them buy us a few drinks till it was time to make tracks for Bonks, but after we had had another Biggles and Ginger Ian said, 'I'm not saying you can't hold your drink Debra, but more than two of these is lethal on an empty tum-tum, how do you feel about a bit of nosh?', so we went across the street to a creeperie for some creeps with savoury filling, after which rubbing his hands Tony said, 'Well the night is young girls, what's next on the menu?' Suzie of course thinks he's asking would she like blueberry creeps or chopped pineapple and cream cheese creeps to follow but I could tell that was not what Tony meant so I blurted out, 'Well we *were* thinking of trying Bonks, weren't we, Suze?'

I could of kicked myself because as soon as I opened my big mouth I knew what Ian was going to say and that is exactly what he did, 'Fancy that, talk about great minds think alike, that's just where we were thinking of going, is that right or is that right, Tone?'

Course Suzie tried to make the excuse that we were already fixed up for the evening and were meeting our boy friends at Bonks by saying, 'Ah but the thing is,' but before I could finish the sentience for her Tony piped up, 'It's a good job we met up then, because you do know it's twelve quid a throw now if you go in by yourselves don't you, only if you go in with us the blokes have to pay but the girls get in for nothing.' I must say this came as a complete shock to me, it had never even crossed my mind that you had to pay to get in, you did not have to in the Seathorpe clubs, they just charged over the odds for the drinks which of course you did not pay for yourself. Suzie and me exchanged meaningless glances and I could tell she was agreeful with me that we had better stick with Tony and Ian as we did not have twelve pounds between us, we could always hopefully lose them once we got inside.

They splashed out on a cab, it was over three pounds

just from Victoria to Piccadilly after crawling through the traffic, it made me wonder how on earth I was going to get back to Sydenham and Suzie to Tulse Hill, still, worry about that when the time comes, for the moment I just wanted to saviour the ambulance of Bonks from the very first moment of arriving.

Actually from the outside it was quite ordinary looking, a bit like the front of a cinema which I believe it once was, in fact it reminded me of the Regal at Seathorpe though of course the pink flashing sign said Bonks instead of Regal, and instead of commissioners in the foyer there were these two big heavy bouncers wearing dinner jackets. There was no queue being too early and only Monday, on Saturday nights I have seen Bonks with queues all round the block, but for this our first ever visit we went straight to the paybox or rather Ian and Tony did.

Then something reely funnee happened, though I spose I shouldn't say funnee, it was very embarrassing reely. Just as Tony pulled back the pink velvet curtains for us to go in, one of the bouncers came over and stuck his arm out between us and the fellas, saying, 'All right tosh, the girls can go in but you two can't, company policy.'

We were all amazed. 'How do you mean company policy, you've just watched us lashing out twenty-four quid, now you're saying we can't come in, why not, give us a reason!' Tony snapped, whilst Ian said, 'I've heard they do this, but I didn't believe it till I saw it with my own eyes, so come on then, as my mate says we're waiting to hear why we can't go in!'

By now the other bouncer had come over, saying officially, 'He doesn't have to give a reason, read what it says on that notice, the management reserves the right to refuse admission right, now why don't you go and find a nice pub, something more your style, there's a very lively bar round the corner called Bubble & Squeak's, say we sent you.'

'So what about the twenty-four quid then, do we get a refund or what?' asked Ian, having reelised that him and Tony had no more chance of getting in than snowballs have of flying, if that's what the bouncers had decided.

The first bouncer said, 'If the girls don't want to go in you can claim a refund but it's up to them, if they decide on going in unescorted that's what you've had the privilege of paying for.' I felt reely bad about it but as Suzie explained to Tony when asked by him what we wanted to do, 'We hate going in without you, Tone, but.' By now there were two other couples lining up behind us and the second bouncer was saying, 'Now come on girls, what's it to be?' so I said hurryingly, 'Look boys, any other time, don't think we're ungrateless but it happens we've come all the way up West specially and we've been traipsing about since five o'clock just waiting for Bonks to open, that's apart from that very nice meal, tell you what give us your numbers and we'll have a reely nice night out sometime next week.' So that's what they did but needles to say we never set foot on either Ian or Tony again, sorree boys.

As I say it was a quiet evening for Bonks but even as we were being shown to a nice table, Suzie and I clocked up four celebs. There was raunchy soap star Den Dobbs of *The Brummies* of who more later. There was super-rat Spud Spicer, mean and moody keyboard kingpin of the Bill Stickers, sharing a joke with fallen snooker idol Mad Mick Martin who I was sprised to see was smaller than in reel life on the telly. There was rock megastar Fanny By Gaslight, with her shocking pillow-box red hairdo and gold lurex bodystocking she made me and Suzie feel reely dowdy, I don't mind saying that though we had dolled ourselves up to the nines for our first day at Donna Bella Rosa's we felt like a couple of auditor typists amidst all this glam, I am only sprised they did not turn us away with Ian and Tony, they must of mistaken us for top models but this was a lesson learned, believe you me it was the first and only time I ever went to Bonks wearing day clothes.

Some of the less than famous faces down at Bonks also looked as if they could be more famous if only we knew who they were, frinstance the bloke at the next table sitting by himself who looked at me smilefully, he reminded me of that actor who makes all those old black and white movies on TV, Clark Grable. Suzie quite agreed, at least she said, 'I know I've seen him somewhere before but I can't just.'

After two Biggles and Gingers and the white wine we had had with our creeps I was perfectly contented to sit there and watch the glass dance floor changing colour, reminded me of Truffles back in Seathorpe, no one was dancing but it was ever so pretty the way it went from pink to red to blue to purple and back again, I could of sat there all night mesmified by it, but one of the Bonks Belles in her pink tutu had come up with a cock-tail menu and Suzie was whispering that we had to order a drink. I was about to order a Sin Twin, that's the same as a Gin Sin except it is so strong it is sposed to make you see double, I did not reely want one but I guessed I could just about pay for one if the worst came to the worst, but then I heard Suzie saying 'Shall we have the house champagne or?' and before I could reply 'Are you out of your brains, how do you think we're going to pay for it, have you seen the price of champagne here, we're going to finish up doing the washing up', the Bonks Belle had said, 'One bottle of house shampoo' and gone to order it at the bar where *Brummies* star Den Dobbs was sitting, I could of sworn he was looking in our direction though it was too dark to be sure. Suzie must of seen my worried look when she ordered the champagne because she said airfully, 'It'll be all right Debs, somebody'll.' This was true as it just so happened but just for that moment I wasn't bothering my little head about who was going to pay for the champagne because I was quite right, he was defnitely staring at us. I was so excited I grabbed Suzie's arm, at the same time crying out, 'Suzie, don't look!'

'Where?' exclaimed Suzie.

'Over there!'

Except he wasn't over there any longer, cos Den Dobbs himself, Terry of *The Brummies* no less, was coming towards us!! I would of swooned, except that no way was I going to miss a second of this dreamy encountenance with one of my favrite soap superstars.

Den was not a bit like he is on the small screen, he acted perfectly naturally, saying 'Hi girls' just as if he had been anybody else. Both Suzie and me scored brownie points straight off by replying 'Hi Den' both together, cos as Den later told Suzie and Suzie told me, he just hates it when fans call him Terry, it is the one thing he cannot stand, that is a tip for anyone mingling with the stars, they like to be known by their reel names not the names of the people they play, that is of course if their reel names are the same as their stage names which of course they are not always, frinstance Fanny By Gaslight is not her reel name.

Both Suzie and me racked our heads for something intresting to say. I am afraid I put my foot in it by saying, 'We watch your long-running hit soap every Thursday.' Even before Suzie had said in that sly way that she has, 'Wednesday' I knew I had made a howler, so I said quickly, 'Ah yes, but I watch it on Thursday on video, because on Wednesday I go disco dancing as you know Suze, it is one of my hobbies.' Den said, 'What's your other one – making all your own clothes?' He just came straight out with it, I spose he has all these lines ready just to say to girls he chats up, probly the *Brummies* scriptwriter dreams them up for him.

Anyway, after we had enjoyed a titter at this it was Suzie's turn to say something intresting so she said, 'Are you on your own Den or?' Den said, 'I don't fetch coals to Newcastle if that's what you mean, chuck. Who'd like to bop?'

Thinking he meant I and was just being polite by including Suzie in the offer, I rose up to my feet when to my sprise he took hold of Suzie's hand and led her off saying to me, 'Another time, eh?' You could of knocked me down with the prudential feather.

Now don't get me wrong, a lot of the fellas go for Suzie in a big way, she's reely attractive and can get any man she likes but I did think it was me he fancied and Suzie knew from the signals I gave her like rolling my eyes that I fancied him likewise, so she was defnitely out of order. But as it turned out I was well out of it cos next morning at Donna Bella Rosa's Suzie nearly got us sent out of smiling lessons she was so full of it, she could hardly wait till lunch break to tell me the whole steamy story of what had happened after she left Bonks with strapping soapster Den Dobbs. Seems that after luring her to his bachelor pad in swanky Belgravia with a curvy Bonks Belle who Suzie could see he was on very friendly terms with but she thought they were just giving her a lift, the sex-mad star waited till the Bonks Belle had gone to powder her nose before asking Suzie how she felt about three in a bed sex romps, he said he knew Jacqui as her name was would be more than willing if Suzie was. Suzie said she felt cheap and used. To make her feel better I said she ought to feel cheap and unused as nothing had happened from what she had told me, but for some strange reason this seemed to make her feel worse.

But getting back to Bonks. Whilst watching Suzie and Den take the floor, I must say Suzie is a trific dancer, she should of been one, I felt these eyes staring at me, it is one of my talents, I can always tell when I am being looked at across a crowded room. Actually it was not across a crowded room but across an uncrowded table, because who should it be looking at me quizfully with his crinkly eyes but the Clark Grable lookalike!

I gave him a big smile as politeness costs nothing, it is the punctility of princesses as Miss Mouldy-knickers used to say at John Pennywick Upper School, whereas he complimented me saying, 'You have a very winning smile, do you mind if I tell you that?'

I said flirtingly as he seemed quite nice though old enough to be my brother, 'I don't mind so long as you don't think it's going to win *you* anything!' after which we got chatting. He kicked the ball rolling by asking, 'Could I interest you in a glass of champagne at all?' Just as I was saying, 'I won't say no' and he was saying, 'Now I like that in a girl,' our Bonks Belle arrived with the champagne that Suzie had ordered, plus to my horror the bill which she put in front of me as if expecting me to pay it out of thin air. Luckily my new friend reached over and took hold of it saying, 'I'll take care of that, do you mind if I join you?' I said, 'I think you'd better, otherwise you won't be able to reach the bottle.' He didn't pay the bill, just scrawled on it, which impressionised me no end, thinking he reely must be a bigwig. Reading his signature I said, 'Egbert Throstle, is that what they call you?'

With a light laugh he said, 'Actually it's Sir, for my sins.'

I wanted to ask, 'Why, what have you done wrong?' but my heart was racing so much I could not speak. Sir Throstle! My first reel live Sir! Course, as I was very quickly to learn you do not reely call them Sir Second Name, you always call them Sir First Name unless they are lords when they only have one, so as he gently correctified me he was Sir Egbert, but he said all his friends called him Eggy and he wanted me to call him Eggy too. From what he said he was a property magnet but he didn't want to talk about that, he said it was boring, he wanted to talk about me so I told him I was a top model, I didn't say a trainee one.

'Really, and what do you model?' asked Eggy, to which I replied truthfully enough, 'What do I model? I model me, sillee!' which he seemed to find amuseful for he then said, 'You know you're quite delightful, Debra. Tell me, would you like something to eat?'

Looking at the little cardboard pyramid listing all the Bonks attractions that they put on every table I said, 'Well since you ask, Eggy, I could just murder the four-star international cuisine of the award-winning Bonks Carvery.'

So finishing off the champagne off we trotted, just in time to bump into Suzie and soap star Den returning to our table. Suzie said, 'Den's feeling peckish, shall we have some smoked salmon sandwiches or?' I could not help getting my revenge on them both by echoing Den's humilifying put-down to me as I waltzed off arm-in-arm with Eggy towards the richly-decorated candlelit ambulance of the Bonks Carvery, 'Another time, eh?'

Sad to say there was an unhappy sequence to that historical evening. I might of known I could not pull the rug over Auntie Doris's eyes and sure enough she was still sitting up in her dressing gown when I tiptoed in at must of been four in the morning. Course, she went rattling on about what time did I call this and where had I been till this hour, I was feeling tired and a bit queazy so I just said, 'It's a long story Auntie Doris and not a very intresting one but my life's my own and all you need to know is I've done nothing to be ashamed of, not that that's any of your business either, good night' and with that I flopped into bed.

What I said about doing nothing to be ashamed of was perfectly true as it just so happened, Eggy was the perfect gent, just put me in a cab and paid off the driver explaining that he could not invite me back to his luxury Docklands flat as he did not have one at the moment, having sold it in a ten million pound property deal, so he was staying at his exclusive gentlemen's club whilst looking around for a London pad, but he did add that tomorrow he would be moving into a discretionary Mayfair hotel for a couple of nights so why didn't we have supper there, to this I was more than agreeful as he had been so nice to me.

So the next evening whilst I was in the bathroom dolling myself up and I heard the doorbell ring, naturally I thought it was Sir Eggy Throstle, as I had asked him to collect me so Auntie Doris could see I was going out with a reel gentleman who I was not ashamed of seeing her humble home, so I thought it would do no harm taking my time in getting ready and let him chat up Auntie Doris a bit. Imagine my sprise when she knocked on the door calling, 'Are you going to be all night in there young lady, your Dad and Babs are here and they've only got a few minutes, they're on their way to one of their dancing comps so just hurry it up.' I ought to of guessed she would of phoned them first thing about my getting in at all hours.

Out I went into the living room to find Dad in what I always called his waiter's uniform, full evening dress complete with white tie, and Babs in yards of pink tiered chiffon decrated with sequins and ostrich feathers, she reely did look a picture straight off a chocolate box. Dad was very agified, he launched straight in, 'Now we can't stay long, we can't stay long, we've got to be treading the Valeta at Forest Hill Baths in thirty-five minutes, what's this I hear about you gallivanting up West and coming home with the milk?'

I said defencefully, 'I'm only doing what Donna Bella Rosa told us to do Dad, she said we had to set about making useful contacts, that's what the modelling game's all about, you've got to get out and meet people.'

'Oh yes,' said Dad, 'and where've you been meeting these useful contacts?'

'At a perfectly respectful club,' I said.

'Which club? What club?'

'Just a club Dad,' I said evadingly. 'Like the darts club or the angling club or the conversative club.'

'What's it called, this club?' he insisted. I knew he would bang on till he got it out of me so I told him.

'Bonks, who the thump's Bonk?' asked my unworldly Dad.

I said blushfully, 'It's not a person, sillee, it's something people do!'

'Oh yes, like what?' Honestlee, you would of thought someone would of told Dad about the bats and the bees, luckily Babs came to my rescue with a wink at me, saying, 'It's a dance.'

'Well it's a new one on me and I thought I knew a thing about dancing,' Dad said. 'In our time Babs, you and I have executed the Cuckoo Waltz, the Latchford Schottiche, the Moonlight Saunter, the Esperano Barn Dance, the On Leave Foxtrot, the Tango Fascination, the Gay Gordons, the Lancers, the Dinky One-step, the Boston Two-step, the Eva Three-step, the Marine Four-step and the Dashing White Sergeant but never to my certain knowledge have we ever performed the Bonk.'

'I think we have poppet, but under another name,' said Babs. The doorbell rang just in time to save Babs and me from breaking up, we were both hooting inside but Dad was so frownful we daren't even look at one another.

'Who's that, who's that?' he snapped as I went to answer the door, Auntie Doris being in the kitchen making a cup of tea.

'It'll be a useful contact, come to pick me up,' I said, and before Dad could finish saying, 'Well send him packing, send him packing, then come back in here because I want words with you young lady, you made a promise to me and you've already broken it, bargains are made to be kept' I had opened the front door and brought in my escort for the evening, complete with a single red rose in a Sellotape box.

Course, as soon as I had introduced my guest of honour as balding, cigar-smoking property typhoon Sir Egbert Throstle, Dad and Babs were all over him, with Babs cooing, 'Do you happen to know *Sir* Monty Pratt, our MP you know, he's quite a friend?' which was true in a way I spose – she met The Sir before I did matter of fact, once when he brought in his snaps of a once-in-a-lifetime dream holiday in sun-drenched Bermuda, and again when he came in to collect them.

'Praps you have met Sir Monty at the House of Sirs, Eggy,' I said just to make conversation, little knowing I was talking about the future man in my life.

'I'm afraid not,' said Eggy, smiling at Babs and Dad. 'Well, if you good people will excuse us . . .'

'By all means, by all means, I expect you two want to get off bonking,' said Dad. Eggy just stared at him open-mouthed. As for Babs and me, once more we were on the verge of falling about, I could see her shoulders shaking, I had to look away before she got me going and in so doing I saw that Eggy was not staring at Dad at all but at Auntie Doris who had just come into the room, and she in turn was staring at him, in fact she looked as if she had seen a goat, I thought she was going to drop her tea tray.

'Well, I'll be blessed, if it isn't Alf Cox!' exclaimed Auntie Doris.

Everyone was so embarrassed, we did not know where to put ourselves. 'No no no, Doris, this is Sir Egbert Throstle!' said Dad, whilst I myself said, 'Your Alf Cox must be a Sir Egbert Throstle lookalike.'

But Auntie Doris stuck to her gums. 'That's Alf Cox

all right, and I'll tell you where he used to work, those big car showrooms on Hyde Park Corner where I was a cleaner, Mayfair Motors, and if you want to know why he doesn't work for them any longer ask him why he was had up in court a few years ago, cashing dud cheques all over London under goodness knows how many names he was, so it's Sir Egbert Throstle now is it, what's he doing in my flat?'

Sir Egbert Throstle as he called himself began to bluster that it was all a case of mistaken indemnity, saying to Dad agitationally, 'Allow me to give you my card,' and I must say that as he did just that I would still of believed him but for something I remembered Suzie saying to me that morning whilst we were talking about our adventures at Bonks, it had just come to her where she thought she had seen him before, it was on visitors' day at Pentonville when she went to see her disgraced dad, but then she said no it couldn't of been him as he did not have a moustache and his hair was brown not black so it must of been a lookalike, and neither of us thought any more about it as all Suzie wanted to talk about was her Night of Shame ordeal with Den Dobbs.

But now as the so-called Eggy gave Dad his card I thought I would just test him out by asking boldly, 'What does it say, Sir Egbert Throstle of Pentonville by any chance?'

He went as white as a sheep. 'I think you'd better leave,' I heard Babs say but I did not even see him go, by now I had thrown myself on the sofa where I sobbed and sobbed with Dad standing over me ranting, 'You're gullible girl, what are you, gullible, well I hope this experience has taught you a lesson,' and so on and so forth till

Babs said, 'Leave her alone, Eric, she's had enough and anyway look at the time, we've got just fifteen minutes to make it to Forest Hill Baths.'

So much for my first acquaintal with the glittering world of Bonks. But despise that cruel setback to my early career I knew that Debra Chase now had lift-off. And that night as I filled in my Sex Romps Diary, even though it was more about Suzie Dawn than about myself, I reelised what it was I reely wanted out of life. Yes – a reel sir or even a lord or duke. And why not? For Debra Chase, the sky was her oyster.

7

Page One Girl

Some people think a model's life is one long romp on a fur-lined bed. There is much more to it than that, believe you me. Those Page Three poses don't just snap themselves, they have to be learned the hard way. Becoming a model is one long grind and not everyone can take it, within the first week we had two more dropouts, we lost a girl called Tiffany to a Live Peepshow in Old Compton Street and Patti to the perfume counter at Selfridge's, they just could not stand the pace.

Every day started with aerobatics, then department, then the catwalk, then something to do with your face like smiling, pouting or just looking sexy which is highly difficult when there are about ten of you trying to do it all at the same time, including our senior citizens as we called them behind their backs, Viv and Margot, who I'm not being unkind they looked like extras in a hard core orgy movie, not that I have ever seen one although when I was a struggling model before my big break I was offered a part in one, needles to say I turned it down, I needed the money but these things return to hunt you.

That took care of most of the morning which would finish up with a different lesson each day such as make-up, hair care, skin care, nails, body-shaping and even how to have a bath, it might sprise some people to know that top models do not just pop into a bubble bath like ordinary morsels even though you may see us advertising them, they have to be very careful what they put on their bodies, also a top model's bathtime is when she does her aroma-therapy which is the art of relaxfulness by the supplication of essenceful oils, and this too had to be learned by sheer hard graft, you had to write it all down in a little notebook as Donna Bella Rosa did not have enough leaflets to go round.

In the afternoons we had more exercises such as how to wiggle properly, how to walk gracefully if for any reason you are wearing flat heels, or slimnastics. Then there would be a talk by Donna Bella Rosa, it could be on dieting, it could be on how important it is to always speak proply, it could be handy tips such as how to make your professional wardrobe go further (the secret is always to buy your sexy undies at Marks & Spencer, then you can take them back after the photo session), it could be on how to be intresting, it could be on anything. One of my favrite lessons was after one of the class, blonde bombshell Beverley, caused a sensation by taking off for Miami or it might of been some other island with this married satellite TV typhoon she had met at Mayfair's luxuriant Ace of Spades international casino. But whilst this came as a great sprise to us it did not come as a great sprise to Donna Bella Rosa who said she had never had a class yet where at least one hadn't gone off to erotic places with a sugar daddy, but she said, 'Since Beverley's night out at the casino has panned out in this particular way we may as well take it as the cue for our next lesson, now has anyone any ideas what that lesson is going to be?'

'Roulette?' asked Suzie all innocent. I think she was serious!

'No, not roulette, Suzie, we're going to learn how to

deal with the gentlemen of the press when they come intruding into our private lives, a model's got to be prepared for the cruel spotlight of publicity, now pay attention because in the kind of modelling some of you will be going into it's very important to know how to sell your exclusive story to the tabloids.'

It was reely intresting, first we had to pretend to have had a mad fling with a VIP called Mr X (except that I called mine Sir X!), then we had to tell our story to the press, little did I know how much I was going to need this training. Donna Bella Rosa first of all told us what we had to say and then she made us learn it, testing us by asking questions as it might be 'What has been said about you since the Mr X Mayfair lovenest scandal erupted?', when we all had to chant in uniform, 'A lot of hurtful things have been said about me.'

'What don't you care about?' Rosa would go on.

'I don't care what people are saying.'

'But what do you want to do now?'

'I want to set the record straight.'

'And what didn't you want to happen?'

'I never wanted any of this to happen.'

'What didn't you dream an innocent night out with Mr X would finish up with?'

'A steamy session in his private sauna.'

After we had learned this off parrot fashion there was another part of the lesson that was just as important, and that was what to say to the other papers when they come round wanting a quote after you have sold your exclusive story to one of their rivals, you have to be very careful cos they will take anything and turn it into a quote, like Donna Bella Rosa said she had one girl who said to the reporter for the *Daily Stunner* through the letter box, 'If you don't stop pestering me I will set my pit bull terrier on you', and this came out as 'Since my steamy nights of illicit love were made public, I have had so many propositions from complete strangers that I have had to buy a pit bull terrier to warn them off.' So you can't be too careful, what you have to say is, 'I have no statement to make' and then when they go on to ask all crafty like, 'But can you confirm that the story is true?' you have to say, 'I have been advised to say nothing, you will have to speak to my manager,' it only needs one little word and they have got you, if you say Yes it is 'Debra admits steamy sex sessions' and if you say No it is 'I lied about steamy sex sessions says Debra.' I must say that afternoon of coaching was worth the price of the whole course to me, considering the number of times I have crossed wires with the press.

Another good day at the Donna Bella Rosa School of Fashion was when Colin came down to give us a practical demonstrance on how to sit for the camera. Colin and me became firm friends for a while, no not in that way, in fact when I first clapped eyes on his fairisle pully and blue shiny suit, I mean not meant to be shiny just shiny with being worn day in day out, I thought he was a 22-carat plonker tell the truth. But whilst no one could call Colin another David Bailey, he reely knew his peas and onions when it came to photography, I learned a lot from him even if he did only work for the local rag. It was Colin frinstance who showed me how to put on the famous Debra Chase wet look pout which has been comparisised with Marilyn's, as well as which he gave me a piece of advice which has been worth its weight in gold to me all through my glittering career, namely just be yourself and act natural. I also owe my first big break to Colin – pity it all had to end in tears but there I go, jumping ahead again.

Colin was great fun to work with. What he did was, he took each of us through a mock photo session in turn, dressing us up in different gear such as in a nurse's uniform with black stockings and suspenders or as a librarian with big glasses standing on some steps in black stockings and suspenders, or a cowgirl out of a Western wearing stetson, cowboy boots and yes you've guessed it, black stockings and suspenders. Whilst he was shooting off his pix (though without film, cos Donna Bella Rosa couldn't run to the cost) he would make up Page Three captions for them like 'Lovely, keep it like that, nice big smile, When dishy Debra rides into town no wonder the West goes wild,' or 'And another one, wet your lips a bit more, big sexy pout now, After a day's modelling delightful Debra likes to curl up with a good book, specially if it's a bedtime story.' Some of his captions were reely witty, he reely had the knack for them, frinstance my traffic warden one, 'Dazzling Debra's just the ticket, no wonder all the guys queue up to *meter*,' course, this was a play on wordage. Then there was the schoolteacher one, 'When it comes to glamour, decorative Debra's in a class of her own, yes she's *really* top of the form!' I don't know how he thought them up, I spose you have to have a special brain.

I must say Colin and I got on like chalk and cheese from the start, I liked him a lot and I guess he must of liked me too cos at the end of that first session he asked me for a date. I didn't reely want to go out with him cos you couldn't get away from it he reely was a complete wally, sorry Colin I mean it in the nicest possible way, but he reely had helped me a lot so I said Oh all right then so long as we go somewhere nice and he took me to a place called the Polo Sorpresa which he said was the San Lorenzo of Sydenham, actually it was quite nice and I love Italian food always have done, I had prawn cocktail, chicken Kiev without the garlic butter and a mixed salad with French dressing, nothing to follow, I've forgotten what Colin had but I know he made me giggle by saying very grandly to the waiter, 'And we'll have a full bottle of whatever's been in the table lamp,' it was red Shanty which I don't reely like, my preferral is either for white or champagne but I didn't like to say.

I don't think Colin was used to eating out much cos he tried to cut his breadstick with a fish knife, but after I had put him at his easement by breaking bits of my own breadstick and popping them into his mouth he began to relax, and at last over the main course he said whilst playing toyfully with his wine glass, 'Perhaps you're wondering why I've asked you out this evening, Debra, well I can assure you it's purely professional, I mean don't get me wrong I think you're a lovely girl and it makes me feel really bigheaded being seen out with you but if I do have an ulterior motive it's not what you might be thinking, the fact is I'll put my cards on the table, I think you and me could go places, Debra.'

At first I thought he meant sunnink like going on to Bonks for a nightcap after our Tia Maria calypso coffee, and I was about to say gently, 'Better not Colin, Auntie Doris'll be waiting up with a mug of cocoa and it doesn't mix awfly well with champagne, besides I've got an early start tomorrow, we've all got to go in dressed and made up as if we were going for an interview so Donna Bella Rosa can criticalise how we look,' but Colin plodded on, 'It's your career I'm talking about, I've been watching you

136

Debra, you have something the other girls at Donna Bella Rosa's don't have, do you know that, of course you do.'

Even though my date with Colin was strictly plutonic it is always nice to hear nice things said about you so I said, 'Thank you kind sir, and what is this certain something if that's not fishing for compliments?'

'Bones,' said Colin.

'Pardon?' I said. I thought for a sec he'd gone bonkers, either that or that he was not used to drink and that the Shanty and the Mutiny on the Bounty I had got the wine waiter to mix for him as an appetitif (that's Malibu, creme de cocoa and pineapple juice) must of gone to his head. (No, it went to his tum cos he went to the little boys' room later and came back looking ever so white.)

'You have good bones,' Colin said. 'That's what makes you different from the pack.'

I was reely disappointed. I said, 'I don't think so Colin, it's not my bones that my forthcoming public will be intrested in, we've all got bones, it's what's on them that counts.'

But Colin went on to say that what he was trying to say was that I was photographic, which of course I now know I am but he was the first person ever to say as much in black and white, honestlee I was so ignorant in those days but the truth is that if you are to get anywhere as a model you have to be photographic, you have either got it or you haven't, being beautiful is not enough, I mean look at Suzie, sorree kid, she reely is a stunner with trific boobs and a lovely bod but she is just not photographic, she has not got the bone stricture, I don't like saying this but when Suzie has her picture taken her head comes out like a melon. So Colin was right and once more taught me an invalued lesson.

'So what it comes down to Debra,' said Colin after explaining all this, 'is that with my contacts and believe you me I really do have contacts all over the place I can get you on Page Three in any paper I like just like that, on top of which I'm not a bad smudger though I say it as shouldn't, anyway good enough to put together a nice portfolio which you're going to need for showing around whoever's handling you, but what I'm saying is if you'll take me on as your manager I'll throw in the portfolio for nothing.'

So that was what it was all in aid of. Now what I thought Colin wasn't awareful of was that when you sign up with the Donna Bella School of Fashion you also sign up with Rosa as your agent for your future career, I tried telling her Dad and Babs were my managers but she said she would sort all that out, I would have to sign as it is one of the conditions that you have an exclusive contract with her, that is why the course is so much cheaper than many others, you get your training at a bargain basement price but Rosa gets it back in commission once your career is unlaunched.

But it turns out that Colin knows all that and that he is craftier than he looks, 'In fact,' he said grinningly, 'I have a contract with Rosa myself, she handles all the commercial stuff and the personal appearances and that but when it comes to press work, Page Three, bingo promotions, that kind of thing, she relies on me and that's where Rosa and me go fifty fifty on the commission.'

'You mean fifty per cent each?' I was clever enough to ask, wanting to know where I stood.

'No no no, nowhere near that, Debra, but forty per cent rather than the thirty you'll be paying Rosa on the commercial side, otherwise it wouldn't be worth my while after splitting it with her but let's face it, Rosa bless her can get you all sorts and manner of jobs but when it comes to getting you on Page Three she simply does not have the contacts so it will pay you in the long run, believe you me Debra, with me managing the press side, Page Three, *Stud Mag*, things like that, I can see you as the next Samantha Fox.'

Now I know a lot of people think us top models have nothing between our heads but I am here to tell you that in this game you reely have to know about the business side, otherwise you get taken to the mender's, there are some reely unscrupeful agents and managers around. Still, in spite of not doing very well at school or maybe because of it, Debra Chase has always been able to take care of herself thank you very much. It made sense to agree to Colin's deposition and I have never regretted signing up with him, well that's not strictly true I did regret it at first as we shall see and I regretted it at the last as we shall also see, but I am the only one out of our modelling class that Colin took on and I am the only Page Three girl out of the class unless you count page three of Paton & Baldwin's Knitting Patterns.

But I did think Colin was pushing his luck a bit when he went on suggestively, 'So what do you say Debra, as soon as we've had our calypso coffee why don't we go back to my studio and get to work on your portfolio right away?'

To clear the air I said, 'There's one thing we've got to get straight, Colin, if it's my body you're after I'm afraid you're barking up the wrong dog.' But Colin said, 'Never fear Debra, if you've any reservations on account of, well, on account of having reservations, let me just tell you I live with my mother, say no more, in fact if it would help you to feel more easy in your mind I'd like you to think of me as a brother.'

'Oh Colin,' I said gratefly, 'would you settle for uncle?'

True to his promise, Colin was the perfect gentleman, considerable in every way. I cannot say I was impressed by his so-called studio, I thought it might be reely flash with lights and a big white screen and umbrellas and Bruce Springsteen compact discs but it turned out to be just the boxroom of his mother's house with an old bedsheet hanging up off of a clothesline, the only umbrellas were of the folding kind of which he did have quite a collection as he said he was always being caught in the rain whilst covering local weddings, and as for background music forget it, would you believe Peter, Paul and Mary? The portfolio was not much cop either, nothing like the saucy snaps I posed for when he came round to Donna Bella Rosa's except then there was no film in the camera, he would not let me take any of my clothes off in case his Mum came in which in fact she did with hot cocoa, she was a replicate of Auntie Doris!

After his Mum had gone to bed, I think she only popped in to see that I was not traducing her darling son, I said to Colin in no disconcerting terms that looking at what he had snapped so far no Page Three talent scout was going to be impressed, I said they had to know what they were buying, and with that I unbuttoned my blouse and put on a sailor hat which belonged to his sea cadet days. Breathing heavily Colin took a few quick snaps then said, 'Quick, make yourself decent, I think my mother's coming down, if she sees you like that she'll wreck the studio, she's quite capable of it you know.'

Later when he showed me the prints this last pose was

the only one worth looking at, Colin himself was quite pleased with it, he said, 'Not too much cleavage and not too little, you've got to be very careful not to go over the top.' I didn't like to tell him I had seen more revealing pix on cornflakes adverts, but I spose it did show my possibilities style of thing although I must say I was having second thoughts about Colin, still I did not worry as I had not signed up with him yet, he said, 'There's no hurry Debra, you trust me and I'll trust you, anyway you don't want to sign anything until you know I can produce results, wait till I get you on Page Three then you can sign on the dotted line.' Quite frankly I thought that day would never come and I must say I quite forgot about Colin until the night Suzie and me went back to Bonks to at last celebrate passing out as fully-fledged top models.

This was something we had been looking forward to after our long long weeks of training and I am glad to say it was quite a memorial ceremonial, or would of been if there had been anyone else at it besides Donna Bella Rosa, Suzie and me, I cannot explain this situation better than in Rosa's speech: 'Now girls, the time has come when you can call yourself professional models, and it is my happy duty as usual to award merit diplomas to my three top students which I shall do in reverse order, but first my end of term remarks. We've travelled a very long hard road together, at least you survivors have, as usual on this gruelling course there have been dropouts, some of you have fallen for the blandishments of the Oxford Street perfume counters, others alas fell behind with their fees.'

Donna Bella Rosa went on to say how she would miss some of her lost lambs as she called them, frinstance Lyndy who she said would have made a very good model if only she'd been able to resist a certain temptationalising offer from the Middle East, and Sharon who she said we all wished her well in her marriage to such a distinguishable-looking property developer, if and when it took place. 'As for Kim,' said Donna Bella Rosa, 'I can only say that what she's doing for a living is a waste of a perfect figure, after all you don't need a 36 inch bust to read out Experiences of a Saucy Schoolma'am on the Dial-a-Thrill Hot Line, so what with Viv having to leave because she's got so many knitting patterns lined up and Margot because she's too grand for us now she's doing her commercials that leaves you two Suzie and Debra, put your shoulders back, you look as if you're trudging uphill with a couple of pails of water each.'

So the upshot was that the three Best Student diplomats had to be divided between Suzie and I. Because Suzie much to her sprise had lost fewer points for giggling in class than me, I can only imagine Donna Bella Rosa couldn't count, she was rewarded third place, but because she had chalked up more absences than I on account of her headaches, some call them hangovers, she missed getting first place and was only rewarded second place. Therefore it was with much pride and pleasure that Donna Bella Rosa announced that I Debra Chase was top model of the Donna Bella Rosa School of Fashion for that particular term. So saying Donna Bella Rosa handed over my parchment scroll saying, 'Congratulations, Debra, and we all look forward to seeing you on Page Three.'

To this I made a speech saying, 'Thank you, Donna Bella Rosa, but however high I rise on my way to the stars I hope I shall always be a credit to the Donna Bella Rosa School of Fashion.' Then we all kissed each other and that was that. Pleased though I was to be top model I had a flat sort of feeling, anti-climate I spose, also I was a bit frightened, I had been saying for so long that I was going to be a model and now I just had to get out there and be one. Suzie was looking rather forlorn too so I said, 'Sorree we couldn't both be top Suze, but look at it this way, I've only got one certification, you've got two, tell you what, I reckon we've earned a night on the town, what do you say?'

'Bonks here we come,' said Suzie.

For every glamour model that ever breathed, Page Three is the gateway to the top. But it is as hard to climb through that gateway as for a camel to pass through a haystack. First you need experience – of modelling, I mean – then you need contacts, and then you need a break.

Well, if twelve weeks of slog at Donna Bella Rosa's wasn't experience I didn't know what was, on the contact front I had Colin and Donna Bella Rosa herself though Colin had yet to come up with the goods, so now all I was waiting for was my big break. This came about in ever such a weird way, it was reely funnee though it didn't seem so at the time.

That evening I was just getting ready to meet Suzie down at Bonks when who should turn up but Dad and Babs, likewise dressed up for a night on the town. 'We just popped in, we just popped in,' said Dad. 'We're on our way to a dinner dance at the Masonic Rooms in honour of Yvette and Max Butterfield, go on, say who are Yvette and Max, they've only won more prizes for their Astoria Samba than anyone else alive or dead, that's all.'

'But now they're retiring, Yvette's sprained her back, poor thing,' said Babs.

'Ooh dear,' said Auntie Doris, 'what was she doing to bring that on?'

'The Astoria Samba,' I said with a giggle, it was meant to be a joke but it turned out to be true, at least Dad and Babs didn't laugh. Dad went on, 'Still, you know what they say, you know what they say, one person's bad luck is another's good fortune, with Yvette and Max out of the way we're in with a very good chance of Latin Close Hold forward-swivelling ourselves to the top as regards the Astoria Samba championship.'

'So we've got something to celebrate,' Babs said.

Oh, and I spose dear Debra didn't have? I love Dad and Babs very much but when it comes to their precious ballroom dancing they can be reely self-central, honestlee you would think sometimes the world was just one big dance floor according to them. So I picked up my parchment scroll and said pointfully to Auntie Doris, 'Shall I tell them what *I've* got to celebrate?' to which Auntie Doris said proudly, 'She passed out today.'

Dad got hold of the wrong end of the stick as usual. 'There, you see, how many times have I told you to eat a cooked breakfast, you won't listen, you just won't listen!' he stormed.

'Not that kind of passing out, sillee!' I said, unfurling my diplomat. 'Dreamboat Debra Chase was today declared top model out of hundreds of other contendants at the exclusive Bella Donna Rosa School of Fashion passing out ceremonial!'

To do Dad and Babs justice they did then offer effuse congratulations, with Babs saying, 'Well done Debra, that'll count for a lot when you start looking for work, what a pity we've got a date Eric, we could have taken her out to celebrate,' and Dad saying, 'She could have tagged along with us to the Masonic Rooms but we've only got two tickets Debra, unfortunately.'

I didn't think it would of gone down too well if I'd said there was nothing I wanted to do less so I just said, 'Shame, still, I wouldn't of been able to come in any case, cos I'm meeting Suzie down at Bonks.'

Dad said, 'Oh yes, that West End disco named after a dance so you say, do you know Debra, I've asked several people in the ballroom dancing fraternity if they could demonstrate the bonk and I've got some very curious reactions, very curious, is it like the Black Bottom at all?'

Trying to keep a straight face I had to go and land myself right in it, I said, 'Not quite Dad, if only you didn't have to go to Yvette and Max Butterfield's dinner dance you could of come and seen for yourself.'

I knew as soon as I said it what I had let myself in for, because after saying 'Any other night, Debra,' Dad turned frownfully to Babs and said, 'Unless . . . You know, Babs, I'm still smarting at not being on the top table tonight, I mean the more I think about it the more it smacks of a downright snub.'

'You know why, don't you?' Babs said. 'Yvette and Max have never forgiven us for the Babs and Eric Chase Astoria Samba variation, I don't think I mentioned it Doris and Debra, it was trying out our new steps that strained Yvette's back, are you thinking what I'm thinking, Eric?'

'Well, we don't owe Yvette and Max Butterfield any favours, do we?' said Dad, and that was that, off the three of us trundled to Bonks, I'm only surprised they didn't ask Auntie Doris along and make a night of it.

Suzie of course was furious but she couldn't say anything, at least not until to my horror Dad took one look at the few couples who were bopping on the dance floor inclusive of purple-haired punk poppet Jailbait and said, 'So that's bonking is it, good God will you look at that girl's hair, now let's see it's one and two and one and two, half reverse and slightly forward, gentleman leading in promenade position, you know Babs, it's not unlike the Doris Waddington Cha Cha Cha refinement, what do you say, shall we give it a whirl?'

I cried, 'Oh, Dad, no!' but they were already minnying their way on to the dance floor, with Babs giving me a wink and saying, 'As I've had occasion to remark before petal, we haven't got one foot in the grave yet!'

As soon as they were out of earsight Suzie said with a heavy sigh, 'Well, if your Dad and Babs are going to show us up.' She meant why didn't we give them the slip and move on to Peppermint Alley, Tinkerbell's, somewhere like that. I said, 'No, Bonks is where the famous faces foregather Suzie, talking of which, look who's looking us over, I think we've struck double top!'

Yes – it was only All English darts ace Len Lipton!!! As he lumbered up to our table, he is even more overweight in the flesh than on the box, both Suzie and me shrieked, 'One hundred and eightee!'

Len seemed quite pleased to be reconised, he said modestfully in that northerly accent of his, 'You don't really know who I am lasses, do you?'

I said flutteringly, 'Well let's see now, I spose you couldn't possibly be All English darts ace Len Lipton who snatched last week's championship game with a devastating spot-on series of treble twenties could you, you were trif, I'm Debra and this is Suzie.'

'Would you like to dance Len or?' asked Suzie, but Len just said, 'Only wallies dance, look at that berk over there.'

'That's my Dad,' I said. Actually, considering they were a couple of wrinklies when comparisised with the kind of guys and gals that get down Bonks, Dad and Babs were not doing too badly, I mean they can reely dance even though they did seem to be doing something like the tango whilst everyone else on the floor was bopping.

Len sat down, helping himself to the champagne which Dad had bought to celebrate, and began to chat us up, saying, 'So what do you two do, then?' and upon being told we were top models, 'I do a bit of modelling myself.' This I knew, he does that advert for Sizzlers, the savoury sausage that bites back. 'Money for old rope, isn't it?' added Len.

'I think it's very hard work,' said Suzie defencefully.

'You should try grafting in a steel mill hen, that's what I had to do before I made it,' said Len. This also I knew, but now he owns a six-bedroom luxury mansion in Croydon complete with jacuzzi and billiard room, it is a dream come true.

We were getting on reely well and Len had just put his big brawny arms around both of us, mine had an anchor tattooed on its wrist as he used to be in the merchant navy, when of all people who should walk in but Brian Boffe! Course, Auntie Doris had told him where I was, Seathorpe Wanderers were playing Forest Hill Rangers next day and he thought he would look me up. Brian did not look best pleased to see me in a comprehensive situation with chubby champ Len Lipton, but then he could not expect to of found me in a nunnery, I was not his personal property. In fact although I followed Brian's career with intrest, always reading the Wanderers result in the *Sunday Shocker*, I had only spoken to him once on the phone since leaving Seathorpe, that was to ask if he could get hold of Cup Final tickets for this reely nice barman I had got chatting to in Ciro's of Sydenham one night, not that I go out with barmen I was just doing him a favour, but Brian seemed reely annoyed for some reason, he said he could not even get hold of Cup Final tickets for himself never mind every flipping Tom Dick and Harry who chatted me up.

Tell the truth, whilst I was pleased to see Brian and could not wait to hear all the news from Seathorpe, I thought without being snobby he was a bit out of his class coming into Bonks, I mean the Wanderers were only Third Division whilst arrows ace Len was world class. Still, he did make all the right noises to Len, saying admirefully after I had introduced them, 'You played a brilliant game last week Len, a real blinder, you really saw that Welsh pratt off, you were terrific.'

'He's not a pratt, he's a big mate as it just so happens,' said Len. Typified of Brian to of said that, why couldn't he just of said Len was brill and left it at that, he ought to of known that all these darts players are big mates, it is just like soccer, the darts world is one big club.

Luckily Suzie changed the subject by asking, 'And how did the Wanderers?'

'We lost two one,' said Brian ruthfully. I said to back him up, having read it in the *Sunday Shocker*, 'But only because of a last minute fluke goal by the visiting team's no more than average striker Tom Tipper.'

'Seathorpe Wanderers, you're Third Division aren't you?' said Len, a bit sneerfully I thought. Brian had asked for it though, as I say he was out of his depth, but still trying to help him I said, 'But you're third from the top, aren't you Brian?'

Then Len said something really nasty, he said, 'Being third isn't good enough in this life, pal.' He needn't of said that, but Brian gave him as good as he got, coming back with, 'Scoring goals is a bit harder than scoring in some other games, mate, anyway don't let me keep you.'

'You're not keeping me, I was here first,' said Len. I thought Hello, trouble, but just then lo and be blowed if Colin doesn't walk in with his camera round his neck, I guess that's how he managed to get past the bouncers in his shiny suit, they must of thought he was one of the papa ritzy, they let them in when the club needs publicitee. He too had been round to Auntie Doris's, honestlee I don't know why she didn't put a pronouncement out on Capital Radio saying where we were, luckily Dad and Babs were still enjoying their ballroom-style bopping, otherwise there would not of been enough room for everyone to sit down at our table, it was getting reely crowded.

Colin was in ever such an exciteful mood, he plonked down the newspaper he was carrying under his arm and said triumphally, 'Right, I said I'd get you on Page Three didn't I, there you are girl, it's an advance copy of tomorrow's paper, hot from the press.'

Course, I grabbed the paper as if my life depended on it which I spose it did in a way. Although it was dark and you couldn't see proply, I could make out that it was open at a big picture of yes you've guessed it, yours truly!! It was the snap I had made Colin take with my blouse unbuttoned and a sailor hat on, and it was accompanified by this zonking great headline that said SAUCY!

I threw my arms round Colin, crying, 'Colin, wheeeeeee! Look everybodee, I'm in the *Daily Stunner*, isn't it fantastic!'

'Lovelee!' said Suzie with a glassful smile. Then picking up the paper and peering at it, she always was short-sighted, she said, 'Just a minute though, what's?', whilst Brian who was looking over her shoulder read out,

'Woodwork teacher's dog fouled pavement, this doesn't look like the *Daily Stunner* to me, mate.'

'*Daily Stunner*, who said anything about the *Daily Stunner*, this is the *Forest Hill & Catford Free Advertiser*!' said Colin spiritfully.

I just wished the floor could of swallowed me up, I was so humilified. '*The Forest Hill & Catford Free Advertiser*, you mean that paper that gets pushed through people's doors full of adverts and nobody reads it, you said you could get me in any paper you liked, you said you had contacts!' I cried.

'I do Debra, but the picture editor of the *Sydenham Free Press* is on holiday and *What's On In South-east London* has just adopted a no-cheesecake policy, so that left us with the *Free Advertiser*.'

To make matters worst Len Lipton had picked up the Forest Hill free rag and was laughing to himself and shaking his head from side to side.

'Something amusing you, mate?' asked Brian.

Chucklingly Len wheezed, 'Oh, it's one for the lads is this, it is definitely one for the lads.'

I must say Brian was marvlous. 'It's not all that funny, she's got to start somewhere,' he snapped all angry.

'We've all got to start somewhere pal, but not next to a pile of doggy's doings!'

I'm not too clear what happened next, I know Brian said something about Len looking for a knuckle sandwich then started talking about coming outside, and Len said something about it was lucky for Brian he had an exposition match the next night and didn't want to hurt his throwing arm, and then Brian said something I couldn't catch and bopped him one, so of course throwing arm or no throwing arm Len had to repatriate and within split seconds they were on their feet going at it hammer and thongs. Meanwhile Colin was snapping merrily away with his flash camera, I was reely impressed, he was as good as the papa ritzy, lucky for him they had all gone to Swamps that night where wild child chart topper Virgin Mary was having her sixteenth birthday party, so he had got a scoop. Meanwhile Dad came charging over from the dance floor to see what all the commotion was about, with Babs tugging at his sleeve and crying warningly, 'Don't do anything silly, Eric, you know we've got the South-east Area Rumba finals on Tuesday.' Meanwhile the two big bouncers were shoving their way through the crowd – one of them gets hold of Brian, the other gets hold of Len and Dad who was foolishly trying to break up the fight, and frogmarches them out, with Len shouting 'Get off my throwing arm, you'll sprain it!' and Babs going 'Don't stand on his foot, he's a ballroom dancer!' Talk about an exciting evening. But I did not know just how exciting until the next morning.

The *Daily Stunner* reely did us proud. There all over page one, under a big headline saying DOUBLE BOP! was one of Colin's pics showing Brian thumping Len, Len thumping Brian, Dad trying to separate them and me looking startling in the foreground. There was another pic on page five and I was in that too, so was Dad, he was furious, I had to face him at breakfast on account of he and Babs had stayed over at Auntie Doris's as he was in too much of a state to drive back to Seathorpe after being mishandled by the Bonks bouncers, they don't mess about when they throw you out believe you me.

Dad kept going on about what the neighbours at Rosedene and Balmoral would make of seeing us all involved in a common brawl as he put it. I tried to tell him it was all good publicitee, but as Babs said looking at it from their point of view, 'For you maybe Debra but not for us, we've the Seathorpe and District Ballroom Dancing Association to think of, your father *was* in with a chance of becoming President this year and another thing, what are Yvette and Max Butterfield going to think after me ringing the Masonic Rooms and saying we can't get the car to start yet here we are large as life in a London night club, I shan't know where to put myself at the next function we go to.'

They kept chuntering on like this till the doorbell rang and with Dad shouting after her, 'If it's the Press, tell them we've no statement to make!' Auntie Doris went off to answer it. I heard voices and then she came back with this reely dishy young guy, I'm not kidding he looked like a young Robert Redford, reely handsome and ever so smartly dressed, which is more than can be said for the bloke he was with who all I can say is he looked a complete dickhead. Even though he was only about five feet tall, weighed fourteen stone at least and was a good ten years too old for this type of gear even if he had the figure for it, he was wearing a silver bomber jacket complete with Day-glo decorations, dark glasses, black ruffled silk shirt open to the waist revealing gold medallions and hairy chest, and tight designer jeans tucked into cowboy boots. I took one look and cried, 'It can't be!' but it was, it was Colin!

I said astoundfully, 'Colin, what have you done to your-self?' he said, 'Only cracked it, baby, I really cleaned up last night and not only that, I've been offered a freelance contract by the *Daily Stunner* so how about that?'

Dad snorted, 'That scandal sheet, that scandal sheet,

there should be a privacy law, you didn't think to ask our permission before getting us splashed all over that rag did you, oh no, still so long as there's a fat cheque in it for you I suppose other people's feelings don't matter.'

It was only when the dishy guy with Colin said, 'We don't invent that stuff Mr Chase, we just embellish it a bit and print it, the moral is if you don't want to get into the newspapers you shouldn't make news' which I thought was fair enough, that I put two and two together and reelised not only that he must work for the *Daily Stunner* but also that I had a pretty good idea who he was cos I remembered now, I had seen his pic so I said to Colin, 'Don't tell me this is Mike Mooney, Tishubi Instant Throwaway Camera Glamour Photographer Of The Year!' which of course it was! Mike is only the *Daily Stunner*'s top smudger who takes all those sizzling pix of the Page Three Popsies, I couldn't wait to tell Suzie, I knew she would go bananas green with envy. I was just thinking that very thought when I heard him say something that would make her even greener, 'You've got it in one Debra so I think you know why I'm here, as soon as I saw your fabulous figure in Colin's snaps of that punch-up last night I said to myself, The big search is over Moono, that's our next Page Three Popsy definitely!'

I could of fainted, in fact I nearly did, the room was going round like a seesaw, I just threw myself into Mike's arms, kissing and hugging him and sobbing with reel tears in my eyes, 'Oh thank you thank you thank you thank you thank you thank you!'

Dad was scandletised, he was going, 'Get off him, girl, he's from the gutter press, you don't know where he's been!' I still couldn't take it in, I cried, 'Oh, my lifetime ambition reelised at last after that cruel early setback with the *Forest Hill and Catford Free Advertiser*, pinch me somebody it's a dream come true!'

Then Colin and Dad started talking business, with Colin saying, 'It all worked out for the best though, didn't it Debra?' and Dad saying, 'You think so, do you?' and Colin saying, 'Speaking as her manager—' and Dad saying, 'Speaking as her manager, speaking as her manager, but *we're* her managers, tell him Babs, tell him Debra.' They would have to of picked a time like this to start squabbling, poor Mike Mooney didn't know where to put himself, he just picked up the *Daily Stunner* and pretended to be reading the horrorscopes.

'You can't be, she's got an exclusive contract with Donna Bella Rosa and through Rosa with me,' pointed out Colin which I spose was true enough, so in answer to Dad's question which was 'Is that true Debra?' I replied 'Yes Dad,' wishing they could just talk about something else. Then Babs had to chip in with her twopennorth saying, 'But you've got an exclusive contract with your Dad and me, flower, you can't have two exclusive contracts.'

I said, 'Sorree, I thought two exclusives made a negative,' though truth to tell I didn't reely know what I was talking about, I was a bit out of my depth. Luckily Colin came to the rescue suggesting we got compromised by increasing the commission a smidgeon as he put it then splitting it three ways between Donna Bella Rosa, himself and Dad and Babs, that sounded like four ways to me so I was a bit dubient, but as Babs explained, 'It's to your advantage, poppet, instead of getting twenty-five per cent your Dad and I will only be taking twenty per cent and so will Rosa and so will Colin, so we're taking a cut in our commission whereas you'll be getting double twenty per cent, that's forty per cent, think about it.'

That seemed all right to me but in any case I could see that Mike was looking at his watch, you could tell he was a busy man, he just wanted to get this business talk over with and be on his way to his next appointment with some luscious lovely, strictly business you understand. So it was the clincher when Mike added to what Babs had just said, '*And* appearing on Page Three.'

For the first time it reely hit me. Throwing out my arms triumphally so that a button popped off my blouse I crowed, 'Page Three! Top model ravenous Debra Chase was a Page One girl when darts demon Len Lipton and soccer star Brian Boffe fought over her tooth and nails at superstuds' hangout Bonks in London's glitzy Mayfair, but devastating Debra's a Page Three girl now, like to see more of her, fellas, wheeeeee, eat your heart out Suzie Dawn!'

All Dad said in reply to my heartfelt speech was 'Button that blouse!'

8

I Go Topless

Just because the name of Debra Chase was on everybody's lips before I was nineteen it does not mean to say I became a star overnight, far from it. Until you have made the grade there are a lot of ups and downs in this business and some days it feels like there are more downs than ups. All right, I had got my break, award-winning top photographer Mike Mooney had promised to make me a Page Three Popsy but I was not out of my neck of the woods yet. You do not just have a topless photo session and then lo and hey presto next day you are in the *Daily Stunner*, you have to get in the queue. Mike's studio diary was completely chokky block for weeks ahead so I just had to impatently wait my turn. Then to top it all, just as it was at long last coming up to Debra's day in front of the camera he was unexpectantly sent off to the Virginal Isles to snatch pix of a certain Princess on holiday, the *Daily Stunner*'s reglar royal snapper Harry Hawke being off ill with teethmark poisoning off of a police dog which bit him for treading on its paw in the skirmish to snap one of the royal kiddies feeding a duck in St James's Park. This meant that Mike was going to be away for quite a while, so although I could not wait to get my clothes off, for the camera I mean, I just had to be patent.

But a girl has to eat and as my allowability from Dad stopped when I finished my modelling course – he seemed to think that now I had had my fling as he put it I ought to go back into hairdressing and just be a model part time as and when jobs came up, you just couldn't get him to understand that it doesn't work like that – I had a living to earn. I was lucky to have both Colin and Donna Bella Rosa looking after me and they got me some intresting work such as sitting on a yacht at the Boat Show and handing out sample tea-bags at the Hendon World Trade Centre, I also thanks to Colin got my second appearance in print, namely holding up a giant-sized box of a new line in toasted marshmallows for a mag called the *Catering Journal*, I think it was a two packs for the price of one big saver promotive offer, and then I did a bit of fashion modelling for that big department store in Peckham, what's it called, doesn't matter it was all good experience.

At the same time I was building up some quite useful contacts at Bonks. Thanks to my exposal on the front page of the *Daily Stunner* I had become quite a celeb down there, in fact the very next time Suzie and me dropped in the owner of the place no less, none other than laid-back, medallioned millionaire Ralphy Appleyard, sent over a bottle of champagne on the house, well when I say sent over he wasn't actually in that night but he had left instructions with the Mater Dee and not only that, with the champagne came the Bonks Gold Membership Card which means you are now reconised as a Face, this means you are allowed to sit in the Magic Circle as the in crowd call the bar area, rubbing shoulder blades with the famous and the big spenders. Suzie didn't get one which put her nose out of joint a bit but of course she was always welcome to come into the Magic Circle with me.

Suchlike was how I came to meet screwball chatshow whizzkid Chuck Cheeseman which led to my third appearance in print and Suzie's first much to her delight, this was when he posed for the papa ritzy with his hands looking as if they were down our cleavages though they weren't reely, and we all finished up in Gary Grant's Gossip page in the *Daily Screamer* captionalised as 'Zany chatshow host Chuck Cheeseman whose future plans are in doubt following sex scandal allegations, keeps his hand in chatting up these two busty beauties at London's exclusive Bonks night spot'. I was annoyed they did not print our names, we had spelled them out slowly enough, but anyway it was one for the scrapbook.

As it happened nothing came of our encountenance with Chuck much to my relief. The sex scandal mentioned by Gary Grant involved three in a bed romps with underage bimbettes and wannabees. I thought that after Suzie's misexperience with super-rat soap star Den Dobbs she wouldn't want to know, but when it became plain that Chuck was intrested in us she signalled me to follow her into the little girls' room where she said, 'I know what you're thinking Debs but.' I said, 'But what Suzie, you know what it said about him in the *Sunday Shocker*.' She said, 'Yeah, but they were under age, we're over age so.' I didn't know what she wanted us to do and was getting quite confused, luckily for me when we got back into the Magic Circle Chuck Cheeseman was chatting up two other chicks so it was all water off a duck's back. Whilst this was a weight off my mind Suzie I think was quite miffed, I believe she would of gone along with any plans Chuck might of had for us, she had seen how I was being drawn into the company of the rich and famous and she wanted to be part of the scene, you could not blame her but tell the truth I didn't reely fancy Chuck at the time, sorry Chuck. But I did keep a soft spot for him and was reely glad when the *Sunday Shocker* had to fork out a quarter of a million I think it was for slandering him, but unhappily by then he had taken up a ludicrous job in Australia so our paths never met again.

But what all this is leading up to is the bloke at the next table who I noticed staring at us after Chuck came over and the papa ritzy started snapping away, he was quite good looking in an ugly sort of way, designer stubble, baggy suit you could see your face in practicly, anyway as soon as we got back from the Ladies he is over at our table like a jack out of a rabbit, I spose he wanted to stake his claim before anyone else could get a look in. Bending charmfully over our table he said, 'Excuse me girls, excuse me Debra, I believe you know my friend Kim, you were on a modelling course with her right, she told me all about you when we saw that coverage in the *Daily Stunner*, that was very funny, can I introduce myself, my name's Julian James, I see your glass is empty, how about a drink I don't know whether your friend would like one?'

This of course was a hint to Suzie to make herself scarce while he talked to me, this she was quite happy to do as Julian was quite defnitely not her type, mine neither come to that now that I looked at him close up, on top of which she had spotted an Elvis lookalike sitting at the bar who I knew she was interested in and he her by the looks he was giving her. Actually he reely was Elvis's smitten image, it could of been him, I might even of thought it was him if I didn't know Elvis was alive and well and living in Mexico, yes I truly believe in that, it was all in the *Sunday Shocker* and whilst as I know to my cost you cannot believe everything they print it reely carried convention, they had checked it out and it seems he faked his own death then had himself flown to

Acapuncture in a mink-lined coffin with air holes in it to get himself sorted out, it had all got on top of him, know the feeling. Still, that is another story as they say.

Anyway, after I had ordered a Harvey Wallbanger's Crazier Brother, for the uninitialed that's the same as a Harvey Wallbanger but with three times as much Galliano, Julian asked if I minded if we talked a little business. Turns out he runs a service called Dial-a-Thrill Hot Line among other operations, where the punters ring up to listen to a tape of a sexy-sounding lady rabbiting on about her so-called experiences, course it costs them, 38 pee a minute I think he said peak times and the tape goes on for five minutes so work it out. I already knew from Donna Bella Rosa that Kim was doing this kind of work but from what Julian was telling me she had laryngitis, whether she reely had or not or whether it was just a come-on we shall never know, but the whole point was that these tapes are changed monthly apparently and he had four of Kim's scripts waiting to be taped – Naughty Nurse, Office Affairs, School for Sex and Satin Sheets, course the unsuspicious punter does not know these are all one and the same girl or even that they are made up.

Anyway Julian said the money was good for only a few minutes' work if my voice was right and he was pretty sure it was but he had to put me on tape just to make sure, it was just a question of whether I could sound as if I wasn't reading it out so how about it?

My motto has always been nothing adventured nothing lost and so as I had nothing on the next day, no I don't mean it that way, just on noon found me round at Julian's flat in one of those big mansion blocks in Earls Court, quite a nice pad from what I saw of it which was not much because as soon as he had poured me a Perrier water from his mirrow-plated living room fridge, it was all I wanted, I never drink when I'm working, he led me into a little room off the super-modernistic kitchen which he had got done up as a recording studio with tape decks and all that stuff. Julian sat me down in front of a mike and told me to chat away so he could get what he called voice levels, of course I was nervous and could not think of a thing to say, he tried to relax me by asking what I had had for breakfast but it just so happened that I had not had any breakfast that day, I often don't, so all I could think of to say was 'Nothing'.

Julian then said, 'Don't worry about a thing, Debra, tell you what, let me give you one of the scripts to run over, read it through and when you're ready try reading it out, we'll take the voice level from that.' So then he gave me these two or three scruffy sheets of typewritten paper and after going through the first few sentences, it was a load of old rubbish in my humble opinion but I thought if that's what the punters want it's up to them, so I began to read it out into the mike.

As far as I can remember it went sunnink like, 'Hi, this is your favrite playmate Mandy and I'm so glad you've called, cos this time I've been an even naughtier nurse than usual and that's certainly saying something as you'll agree if you caught my last sizzling instalment, well, even though I somehow seem to have got the nickname Randy Mandy around the wards I'm not reely man-mad until the right man comes along which I'm happy to say seems to happen quite frequently, well, a couple of evenings ago I found myself on night duty with a handsome new doctor called Dr Kildoon . . .'

This was as far as I got, cos Julian switched off his tape deck and taking off his headphones said quite good-humorously, 'All right, let's stop it there for a minute, one thing's for sure, it can only get better, I don't want to discourage you Debra love but I reckon you've a great future announcing the train departures at Victoria.' Seems I was saying it all in a monologue instead of empathising some words to make it sound more intresting, this made it come over as if it was being read out instead of said. So Julian got to work with his ballpoint and marked the words I was sposed to empathise, and then I had another go. Oh yes, and I was sposed to sound more sultry by putting some sexy breathing into my voice. So he switches on the tape and off we go again.

'HI, this is your FAVRITE playmate Mandy and I'm SO glad you've called, MMMMM, cos this time I've been an even NAUGHTIER nurse than usual, MMMMM, and that's certainly saying SOMEthing as you'll agree if you caught my LAST sizzling instalment, MMMMM . . .'

That was no good either, this time I was overdoing it apparently, Julian's verdict was, 'You're not auditioning for the Last of the Red-hot Zombies, darling, put a bit more life in it, a bit more you know *coarrr*, do you know what I mean? All right we know it's not Shakespeare but you can't fake it, it's like stage acting, if you don't believe in the part yourself no one else is going to believe you and the punter really does have to think you're this randy nurse getting herself laid in this empty private ward she happens to have the keys for, and that you're getting a kick out of telling him all about it, right? Otherwise he's going to stop ringing the Dial-a-Thrill Hot Line, he's going to switch to one of my many rivals, so I'm not going to make any money and that means you're not going to make any money.' I didn't know quite what to say so I just nodded wisely. Then Julian looked at his watch and went on, 'Tell you what, maybe I'm being unfair, maybe I'm pushing you too hard too soon, I should've let you sit down quietly with the script on your own, imagine the situation in your own mind, get in the right mood, listen I've got one or two things to do, why don't I leave you on your own for a while, just read the script, really try to put yourself in Mandy's mind and Mandy's body and we'll take it from there and don't get all uptight, it's going to be all right.'

Well, I did my best to contemplate and get it how Julian wanted, for one thing I have always prided myself on being a true pro, if I do a job it gets done proply, and for another I had not been paid yet. But I am a very slow reader as it just so happens, in fact when I was at school Babs used to think I was dyspeptic until Dad pointed out that I was just the same as him, he simply didn't agree with reading, so by the time Julian returned I had not even finished putting in my MMMMs and underlining all the words I reckoned needed empathising, let alone practised reading my script all through. As Julian came back into the room by the way I could not help noticing that he was now wearing a silk dressing gown with nothing underneath it so far as I could see, but being very nave in many ways I thought no more about this, only that he must of been getting changed to go out for lunch when he took it into his head to come back and see how I was getting on, maybe whilst his bath was running.

This time he made me go through the whole script right to the end, but as I came to the last sentience which was 'That was SOME steamy session, MMMMM, but horny Dr Kildoon is STILL panting for MORE and SO am I, MMMMM, uh-uh, that's torn it, HERE comes Ward Sister so we'll just HAVE to wait till NEXT time, MMMMM,' I saw Julian was shaking his head as he switched off the tape.

It was a reel putdown and I was practicly in tears as I said, 'I'm sorree, Julian, I know I've made a reel hash of it but I've just not been trained for this kind of thing, now if you'd asked me to smile down the phone without talking I could of done it on my head, still, there we are, spose we call it a day eh, just give me something for my time and we'll forget the whole deal, all right, sorree it didn't work out, just one of those things.'

So then of course he has to go and make a pass at me, he must of thought I had got turned on by reading his Naughty Nurse load of codswallop, anyway the next thing is that he is sliding his arm around my shoulder whilst murmuring persuadingly, 'Look baby, tell you what, maybe you don't like working from a script no problem, why don't we go into the bedroom, make ourselves comfortable, we'll take in a couple of drinks and a portable tape recorder and then you can just make up your own script as we go along, just say what comes into your little noddle, doesn't matter how blue it is, I'll edit it, what do you say eh?'

What do I say, he wants to know. I said firmly, 'Julian, I wasn't born tomorrow, I want out, OK?' At least I give him Brownie points for knowing when he was beaten, he just threw up his arms and said, 'OK! Forget it baby, there's the door, it's open, it's not locked, you're free to go whenever you like but if you'd like a drink we'll have a drink all right?' Matter of fact I could of done with a stiff glass of champagne or sunnink after my ordeal but I thought it best if I made an excuse and left as they say.

And that would of been that as regards my short-lifed career as a Dial-a-Thrill Hot Line chat lady except that it wasn't, there is an unhappy sequence. But as that was not until I had hit the big time after forgetting all about Mr Julian James Esquire it will have to wait for a later Chap.

That royal holiday in the Virginal Isles seemed to be dragging on forever but Debra Chase still had to pay the rent, not that Auntie Doris very kindly charged me any but even bus fares cost money so I still had to take on any work that was offered – bit more fashion modelling, this time in Luton, holiday release crouper at one of the world's top gambling casinos in swish Tottenham Court Road, and yes it is true what the *Sunday Shocker* made me say, I even did a stint as a suspendergram girl!! It was an eighteenth birthday party for the son of this big industriousist, he was ever so sweet and shy the birthday boy that is! It was over in Dulwich Village, I had to dress up as a policewoman and pretend I had come to arrest him for speeding on the M25 in his Vauxhall Cavalier 1.6GL, course being me I had a fit of the giggles and fluffed my lines so he guessed it was a put-on – but I sometimes wonder if that blushing boy has ever reelised thinking back on it that he had his trousers pulled down and a big lipsticky kiss plonked on his boxer shorts by no other than Page Three Popsy Debra Chase, don't get me wrong it was all good clean fun but they were all snapping away with their Instamatics, some of those candid camera shots could make a fortune if they got into the wrong hands such as *Raunch Mag*, luckily I am protected against such exploits, they have to buy the rights.

Everything comes to a beginning and at long last one morning it was in all the papers that the Royals were back from their holiday so I guessed Mike Mooney must be back too. I must say he does have this regretful habit of keeping perspective Page Three Popsies on tenderhooks – it was over a fortnight before he called me, turns out he had been in Pamplona for the bullfighting, I told him seems to me life's one long holiday for some people, you would of thought he'd had enough of beaches after the Virginal Isles. But at long last one morning just as I was getting ready to go out, I was sposed to be giving out leaflets at the Soft Furnishings Fair at Olympiad but I'm afraid that for the first and only time in her life Debra Chase ducked out of an assignation without giving priority notice, because whilst I was changing my stockings, if the first pair hadn't of laddered I would of been out the door and who knows what would of happened, the phone rings and Auntie Doris passed it to me saying, 'It's for you' and of course it was Mike.

I started babbling down the phone about how I hoped he had had a fab time and did he get to speak to the Royals personably but Mike cut me shortly, saying, 'Yeah, great, fantastic, bloody hard work but yeah, marvellous, yeah they joke with us all the time it's no big deal, listen Debra, tell you why I'm ringing, I've been let down, well not let down she couldn't help it poor cow but Jenny Joy, you've heard of Jenny Joy, she's gone down with food poisoning, dodgy oyster or something, so it leaves me right in it, studio booked for today but no model, if I send a car round do you think you could get here by eleven, I know it's short notice but you see how I'm fixed.'

Had I heard of Jenny Joy? She was only the *Daily Stunner*'s Rear of the Year, wasn't she? And I, Debra Chase, was being asked to stand in for her, I should say sit in for her!! Course, I squealed that I would be ready and waiting. Sorree Soft Furnishings Fair, but you couldn't expect a girl to turn down the biggest break of her lifetime. I have often wondered what would of happened to my career if that stocking had not laddered and I had been half way up the street when that fatal call came, Mike always says he would of caught up with me sooner or later but you never know in this game, he always had his eye open for talent and who knows how many new Page Three Popsies he would of got lined up before he got round to little me, if ever?

Still, no use worrying about what might of happened. The car dutifully arrived as promised and I was whisked off to the *Daily Stunner* plant on Banana Wharf, I don't know what I was expecting but it looked a bit of a dump quite frankly, just a big brick box with barbed wire round it, more like a factry reely and once you got inside it was more brick and bare pipes everywhere, reely depressive. Not to worry though, so long as it was where Page Three got made it did not matter to Debra Chase if the place reassembled Battersea Power Station, so in I sailed and gave my name to a commissioner.

I must say his responsal reely gave me a shock, he stared at me owlfully through these thick glasses saying, 'Mike Mooney, Mike Mooney, there's no Mike Mooney here, no he did work here but he got a better offer from the *Screamer* so I'm afraid you've come on a wild goose chase young lady.' I could of wet myself, but then he gave me a big wink and I could tell he was joking even though he still didn't smile, Cyril his name is and we became good friends, it's how he greets all the new models, we laugh about it now at least I laugh but Cyril doesn't, it's a kind of point of honesty with him, but it was defnitely not funny at the time.

After ringing Mike to say I had arrived, Cyril conductored me to the bowls of the building where the studio
was, it took a long time to get there cos he walked with
a limp, I think he must of fought in the war. I had never
been in a reel camera studio before, it made Colin's
Mum's spare bedroom look like Colin's Mum's spare
bedroom if you know what I mean. It was so big you
could of held one of Dad and Babs's ballroom dancing
comps in it, though I don't think somehow Dad would
of depreciated the music coming out of the sound system,
he doesn't agree with reggae, says it ought to be banned.
Everything was set up for my photo session, big white
screen, big white plastic puff for me to incline on, big
umbrellas all over the place, enough lights to illumine
Wembley Stadium, everything you can think of not forgetting Mike's favrite Nikon 801 camera on its little tripod,
it reely looked so small and insignifical, made you wonder
how he manages to turn out such great pix with such a
titchy little camera but of course as the world knows (and
I do mean the world because Mike's work is syndicalised
to I think it's 600 diffrent countries) he is the best in the
business.

Saying, 'Mike won't be long, that's if he's not forgotten
you're here because he's very absent-minded you know,'
Cyril departured with another wink, leaving me alone in
the Page Three Popsy studio. I felt like Marilyn on the
set at MGN or wherever. I was too exciteable to be nervous
and seeing as I was all alone or so I fondly imaginised I
just could not resist draping myself across the big white
puff and practising some of the poses I had learned at
the Bella Donna Rosa School of Fashion. For some reason
I sposed when Cyril phoned Mike to pronounce my arrival
that he was up in an office somewhere, maybe chatting

to the editor, how do I know, but unbeknownst to me he was in the dark room next to the studio all the time, the first I knew of this was when I was sitting on the puff with my hands pressing down on it behind my back with my boobs sticking out and my mouth doing my Marilyn pout, and I heard Mike's voice behind me saying grinningly, 'Now don't tell me because I happen to be an old movie buff, it's Jane Russell in *The Outlaw*, no it isn't it's Jayne Mansfield in *The Girl Can't Help It*, how are you honey, glad you could make it.'

Course I was terribly embarrassed and when I'm embarrassed I always resolve into giggles, but somehow this broke the ice cos Mike gave me a big hug and with this great dirty laugh of his chortled, 'Right, get them off Debra, don't look so shocked I'm sure it's not the first time you've heard those magic words,' which reely relaxed me, needles to say he was only joking, we had coffee first. This was brought in by Mike's pretty young assistant Linda, she was only a kid, she was on a youth training scheme, she made me feel reely old and for a sec I felt a fit of the blues coming on as I thought of my life fleeting by, then I thought Don't be stupid Debra, your life's only just beginning, you know the old saying, the rest of the world starts here.

Oddly enough I was more embarrassed at the thought of Linda seeing me topless than Mike with who I was not embarrassed at all, maybe this was because she was a little bit flat-chested whereas as the world knows I am the reverse. Fortunately when I stepped out of the little changing cubicle Linda had finished doing whatever she had to do with Mike's lighting equipment and made herself scarce, as I was to learn Mike Mooney likes to work alone, unlike some famous smudgers who always have to have an assistant dancing attendants, passing them rolls of film and all that style of thing.

I am often asked how you feel when posing topless in front of a man photographer, specially when he is all male like Mike Mooney. The answer is you feel exciteable but not in the way my dirtyminded readers are thinking!! You are on a high, I guess it is like being an actress on your first night. And for the record, to answer my next most asked question, no the photographers do not try anything on, not usually anyway although as the saying goes there is one black sheep in every barrel, but with the reel crack snappers like Mike they are too professional. Course, what you might get up to after the session is up to the individualistic model, there is one top model I could name who cannot wait to get her clothes on and hop into bed with her smudger if she fancies him which she usually does, she is noted for it, but suchlike stories will have to keep for another book.

Mike is very good at putting models at your ease while he is setting up, he just chatters on saying relaxful things like, 'Been down to Bonks lately, not got into any more fights I hope, I was down there Friday was it no Thursday, packed it was in fact it was too full, I wouldn't like to be down there if they had a fire,' till pretty soon you forget you are sitting there wearing not much more than a smile above the waist. In fact I was so relaxed I did not even reelise we were into the shoot till I heard Mike saying, 'OK Debs, now I want a nice faraway dreamy look for this one, concentrate on what you're having for supper tonight.' This happened to be Auntie Doris's cod cakes so I thought about a big juicy steak at somewhere like the Kensington International Hotel Britannia Chophouse, which seemed to do the trick as Mike seemed very pleased saying, 'Good, super, just like that, lovely smile, now this might seem corny but I want you to say cheese.'

So there he was snapping merrily away when who should stroll in as bald as brass but Colin, looking a right nana in a Presley-type white cotton suit two sizes too small for him, how he got past the commissioner we will never know, I can only think it must of been while the commissioner was rolling about on the floor laughing. I could tell Mike was annoyed at the intrudal but being as Colin was one of my managers he couldn't say much. Debra Chase could though, and did. Covering my boobs with the kimono style of thing they give you I snapped, 'Charming!'

'Now now, no need to get your knickers in a twist Debra,' said Colin soothfully.

I said, 'If my knickers are in a twist, it's cos I'm not wearing any!'

He said, 'It's only Uncle Colin looking in on his client.'

I said, 'Colin the last time an uncle saw me like this I was in my bath playing with a plastic yellow quack-quack!'

Anyway, after a bit more of this sort of thing it turns out that Colin hasn't just come into the studio to play Peeping Tom Dick and Harry, as my manager he wanted a word with Mike about my hobby and I don't mean stamp collecting.

Now I don't know how many of the punters notice this, not many probly, they're too busy feasting their eyes on the topless charms of the curvaceous cutie on display, but every Page Three Popsy has to have a hobby. This is so that the sub-editor has something to put in his caption, as it might be 'Pouting Petra's hobby is swimming, looks like she's been practising the breast stroke!' or 'Stunning Sue's hobby is cycling, that's why she'll never have a spare tyre'. Course, it's not necessary for these to be reely your hobby, but so long as you're pictured looking through a lifebelt or perched on a bicycle nobody is any the wiser. That's another thing – it has got to be a vidual hobby, one that you can see. I mean to say you could put a model in front of an artist's easel and stick a brush in her hand and the caption would be, 'Bubbly Beth's hobby is painting, no wonder she looks such a picture', but if you were to say that her hobby was meeting people or travel, frinstance, all you would finish up with would be a model just sitting there like a lemon, which believe it or not is not very intresting, I know Mike had just shot off a whole roll of film of me doing nothing but smiling but these were just warm-ups which he could later sell privately to an Australian pin-up mag, one of Mike's perks, seems they like their topless models straightforward naked and unadored down under.

So you can see that there is much more in this business than meets the eyeful. Having explained all this Mike said, 'So we've got to find you a hobby Debra, do you play tennis by any chance, we could put an eyeshade on you and get you holding a racquet over one of your boobs, no? How about cats then?'

'As in Curvaceous Carol keeps cats, so *that's* what keeps Carol kittenish!' said Colin. 'What is your hobby Debra, you must have one?'

'Playing draughts with my Auntie Doris,' I said, it was the only thing I could think of, quite frankly apart from dieting I haven't had what you might call a proper hobby since I used to play the fruit machines on Seathorpe Pier.

'Oh yes, I can just see it,' said Mike, getting all sarky though in a friendly sort of way. 'Dreamy Debra's hobby is playing draughts with her auntie, no wonder she's such a classy mover. There's nothing for it chaps, we'll just have to dream one up.'

Upon which he opens up a kind of dressing-up cupboard full of all sorts of gear like the stuff Colin had me posing in when we had our mock photo session at Donna Bella Rosa's, such as a watering can for if you're sposed to be a gardener so's the caption can say 'Gorgeous Gaye's hobby is gardening, so that means everything in the garden's lovely' or an apron and wooden spoon so it can say 'Lovely Liza's hobby is cooking, so *that's* why she's such a tasty dish'. I would of loved to of posed in some of the erotic undies Mike had stashed away in his cupboard but as he explained, fishing out a string of onions, a berry and one of those striped burglar shirts that French gigglers are sposed to wear, 'No, the editor's off the kinky stuff at prez darling, he's trying to get elected to the Reform Club, here try these on for size.'

I couldn't for the life of me see what I was sposed to do with a string of onions, all I could think of was 'Dazzling Debra likes peeling onions' which didn't seem the most sizzling caption in the world to me, but Mike gave me a big sigh saying, 'Do me a favour, come in darling, Dizzy Debra's hobby is learning French!'

'She's already got six O levels, now she's after those Ooh levels,' chipped in Colin.

Being very green in those early days I said thick as they come, 'But I don't have any O levels at all and I can't speak a word of French!'

Mike and Colin just looked at one another then up at the ceiling and I finely got the message. So after Mike had said, 'I don't know whether you've got anything to do this morning Colin, but if you have now's as good a time as any to be doing it,' thus supplely giving him a

173

hint to leave us to it, Colin took himself off and we got down to business. Putting the berry on my head, draping the striped jersey over my bare shoulders and holding the string of onions in front of my tum I posed for what turned out to be one of the best and most talked-about Page Three Popsy pix ever taken, it was a sensation, Mike only snapped away for five or six minutes to get his best shot but those five minutes were to change my life. Since then of course he has taken enough pix of me to paper an army barracks with, in fact that's exactly what some squaddies in Germany somewhere once started to do and their officer made them take them down again, the *Daily Stunner* took up the case with a big story headlined BRASSHATS BAN OUR DEBRA'S BERLIN WALL, it was great publicitee. But though Mike's consequent Debra Chase snaps have gone round the world winning prizes for him and making me the household name I am today, that first Page Three Popsy pic which they entitled FRENCH DRESSING! remains my firm favrite of all time, I can still quote the caption by heart:

"Allo 'Allo. Dishy Debra really knows her onions when it comes to speaking French. She learned the lingo as a model in gay Paree – so now when those Frog fellas get too fresh she can say Non Non in their own Ooh La language.'

Mike Mooney and me are known to be best mates and there is bound to be gossip but we have both always shrugged it off. Did I have a fling with Mike? Let me put it this way. Every model falls a little in love with her first photographer, sometimes a lot, and I was no acceptance, I am not counting Colin. Mike has done a lot for me, not only as a model but to build up my confidence, he does not just point the camera at you and expect a responsal, he reely coaxes your personalty out of you, it's a gift that not every photographer has however brilliant. So yes, maybe I did begin to think of Mike in that certain way. But Mike has a lovely lady, Tricia, she is a reel knockout who could of been a model herself if only she had been tall enough, as it is she is a *Daily Stunner* secrety, I call her his pocket Venus. But Tricia has flaming red hair and you know what that means, if she even thought there was anything going on between Mike and any of his models the fat would reely be in the frying pan. So as regards Mike Mooney and Debra Chase, as the old saying goes we are just good friends.

9

Page Three Popsy

Course, Dad went mad, though not at first. He never reads the papers and Babs only reads the *Daily Mirrow* and somehow proud as I was of making my debit on Page Three of the *Daily Stunner* I could not think of a way of telling Dad to watch out for his little girl appearing topless without him flipping his lid. I could of told Babs but she would of told Dad and he would still of gone spare. Course, I knew he would hear about it sooner or later from the nosy neighbours at Balmoral and Rosedene but being the coward I am I thought I would face the musical chairs when the time came.

As luck would have it Dad and Babs were in Felixstowe for the Open Tango Championship when Debra Chase hit Page Three, so it was not until they got home next day that the balloon hit the roof. Incidently, if Balmoral and Rosedene chance to be reading this, and I bet they are lapping up every word, I would just like to ask why it is, if certain people are so shocked by what they see on Page Three, that they take the *Daily Stunner* in the first place. Hypercritical isn't the word. But the point I am coming to is that a day is a long time in modelling, and by the time Dad learned that his darling daughter was a Page Three Popsy the offers had started to flow in, which put a different complexity on the situation from his point of view. But there I go, jumping ahead again.

When at long last Mike Mooney phoned to tip me off

that my pic was to appear in tomorrow's *Daily Stunner* I was like a cat on hot toast, I could not wait for the next day to arrive or rather the night before to arrive, cos I don't know how many people know this but you can usually buy tomorrow's *Daily Stunner* in the West End at about 11.30 the previous night, in fact there is an old bloke comes into Bonks every night selling it. So of course that night was going to be gala night at Bonks for Debra Chase, Page Three Popsy.

Suzie, Mike's girl friend Tricia, Colin and me met for a bite of Chinese beforehand, I had to invite Colin even though I knew he would turn up looking as if he was on his way to a fancy dress party which of course he duly did, head to foot in wrinkly leather would you believe, he looked like a giant prune, sorree Colin but you do ask for it mate. Suzie had let her hair go back to its natural pink after a spell being green and she looked reely smashing in her tight red rubber dress and fishnets, I think knowing this was my big night she had pulled out all the socks so as not to be outclassed by me and who can blame her, but I do not think when it came to attention-grabbing that even startling Suzie could beat daring Debra in my confectionery of silvery sateen cobwebs which shimmered tantalisefully so that no one could quite make out whether I was wearing anything underneath or not (for the record I wasn't but don't tell Auntie Doris!!). By the way I mustn't miss out Tricia who looked lovely in her green dress as she always does.

The arrangement was that Mike Mooney was going to meet us at the Peking Experience as soon as the *Daily Stunner* was off the press and he had hotfooted it across town from Banana Wharf, we would then wait till we knew the paper seller must of done his round in Bonks and make our triumphal entrance. I must say I felt physiologically sick waiting for Mike to arrive, though I love Chinese I could only toy with a few spare ribs, some bean curds and a bit of Suzie's crispy duck, I hardly touched anything else, I kept thinking Oh my God, what if the editor doesn't like my pic and he makes them change the Page Three Popsy at the last minute, or Oh my God, what if there is a big air crash and they need Page Three for a picture of the wreckage. Even worse was knowing Suzie was thinking the same or rather hoping for it, I'm not saying Suzie has a jealous streak, just that it is the first time I have ever seen anyone using chopsticks with crossed fingers.

But I need not of worried, Mike duly turned up with half a dozen copies of the paper and there I was on Page Three as large as life in living colour, the reproductiveness was trific. I just sat there feasting my eyes on it and drinking in the compliments which came not only from my friends but even from the waiters, you could tell from their grins how much they liked my Page Three pose.

I must say that though I have seen more than one of the young Royals down at Bonks from time to time I have never seen them treated better than me and my party were that evening. Everyone had seen the next morning's *Daily Stunner* of course and all eyes were upon me as we were conductored to one of the best tables in the Magic Circle while the papa ritzy's flashbulbs popped merrily away. Ralphy Appleyard himself, the guvnor, came over to our table, he knew Mike Mooney who introduced us and he gave me a kiss saying, 'Well done my love, pity he hasn't got your nipples in focus, you ought to get him to give you a session when he's not half pissed, he's really not a bad snapper when he's sober.' Only joking of course,

Ralphy always sends everybody up, it's his style, yet he has gagged his way into a multi-million pound business as the *Sunday Shocker* put it when they exposed him for fixing up rock stars with rentboys, I've since got to know Ralphy quite well and he's ever so nice, always says hello if you are passing his table.

As the champagne flowed that night, except for Colin who even though he can't drink was on Rusty Coffin Nails, that's the same as a reglar Rusty Nail but with Benedictine as well as whisky and Drambuie, all sorts of people came up to congratulate me including soap superstud Den Dobbs, now known after Suzie's experience with him to be soap super-rat Den Dobbs, for Suzie's sake I didn't want him anywhere near our table but it does not do a girl's career any harm to be seen chatting with celebs, you have got to think of these things. Course, I was quite a celeb myself already, you can always tell you are one when blokes come up saying, 'Hello Debra, how's Debra, you're looking gorgeous tonight but then you always do,' when you don't even know them.

It was a wonderful evening except for one small disappointment. As I have said you sometimes saw some of the younger Royals at Bonks and this night was no acceptance so I thought, because standing at the bar talking to top rock guitarist Adam Adam was I was nearly sure he was a certain Royal personalty though I couldn't be absolutely positive as he was wearing a false moustache and dark glasses to remain incongruous. What was even more exciting was that he was looking in my direction!! By now Mike and Tricia were dancing and Colin had reeled off home after one Rusty Coffin Nail too many, so it was just Suzie and me sitting at our table.

In a low voice, squeezing Suzie's arm so hard that she

yelped like a puppy dog, I said excitingly, 'Suzie, you see the guy talking to Adam Adam, I think it's Andrew Lloyd Webber royal teaboy Prince Edward!'

Gawping, Suzie said, 'Reely? *The* Prince Edward?' She can be reely thick sometimes, I said, 'Honestlee! How many Prince Edwards do you think there are?'

'Dunno,' said Suzie, 'but he's coming over.' He was too! We both stumbled to our feet and started curtsying like mad and giggling but of course it wasn't him at all, only an Andrew Lloyd Webber royal teaboy Prince Edward lookalike, just my luck. Turns out his name does happen to be Eddie though and that he is often mistaken for HRH, henceforth the moustache. Eddie just wanted to congratulate me on my Page Three success, he said, 'That's a smashing picture, Debra, I bet the *Daily Stunner* sells like hot cakes tomorrow, hope we'll be seeing more of you.'

Quite taking to Fast Eddie as I already thought of him I answered smilingly, 'There isn't much more to see!'

'And what do you do, Eddie?' chimes in Suzie, fluttering her pink eyelashes to make her presents felt, not that I minded, it can be very hard work being the best friend of a Page Three Popsy, even if you are sitting there half-naked you have to draw attention to yourself before the fellas notice you, they have eyes only for their favrite topless model.

'Oh, nothing exciting, I'm a scaffolder,' said Eddie. I was ever so disappointed, not only was he not Royalty but he wasn't even anybody.

To make polite chitchat I said, 'You must have a good head for heights Eddie, personaly I suffer from vertebrae,' what I reely wanted to ask was how a humile scaffolder could afford a night out at Bonks, just a simple Hawaian

Highball and you are talking about a fiver. Suzie must of been thinking the same thing cos tactile as ever she blurted out, 'And don't you find Bonks pricey Eddie, I mean for?' She meant for a mere scaffolder. I said to smooth the situation over, 'I spect he does a lot of overtime, Suzie.'

'I work hard and play hard Debra and right now I'm playing hard,' said Eddie. 'Fancy a twirl?'

It was the last thing I fancied. For one thing my head was already twirling enough with all the champagne I had had plus the remainder of Colin's last Rusty Coffin Nail so as not to let it go to waste, that's one thing Dad has always drummed into me, and for another as I've said before I am defnitely not a snob but if I couldn't do better for myself on my first evening as a Page Three Popsy than a simple scaffolder then I might as well of stayed at home with a good book. So I told Eddie I was waiting for Seathorpe Wanderers star striker Brian Boffee, and after saying rather cutfully, 'You'll have quite a wait then, they were playing Cardiff today and it's a long ride back,' he went for second best and took the floor with Suzie, and that was the last I saw of them that particlar evening, after they had finished bopping he took her off to his own table to chat her up and pour Moscow Roscoes down her throat. Fast Eddie.

Truth to tell, Debra Chase's Big Night Out was turning into a bit of a damp fizz, cos by this time there I was sitting all on my lonesome. Now the one thing a Page Three girl must never do is be seen sitting by yourself, it is very bad for your imagery and if the papa ritzy chance to snap you at an empty table with a champagne bottle in front of you it is in the gossip columns next day with some made-up story about how you were seen drownding your sorrows after your girl friend sexy Suzie Dawn stole your hunky mystry boy friend from under your nose or some such rubbish. So I took myself off to the little girls' room a bit sharpish as they say.

There was no sign of Mike Mooney and Tricia after I had powdered my nose, seems they had come back to the table and thought I had legged it so Mike had signed the bill (nobody was freeloading, he gets it all back on his exes) and they had called it a night. No way was I going back to that table to sit on my own and no way was I going to muscle in on Suzie and her scaffolder, so I just meandered slowly out making it look as if my escort was following close behind as soon as he came out of the little boys' room, and getting one of the bouncers to call me a cab, off went Debra Chase back to Auntie Doris's council flat in Sydenham, feeling down in the dumps and a bit like Cindrella turning into a pumpkin.

But I perked up soon enough next morning when the phone began to ring, in fact tell the truth I nearly jumped out of my wits cos I thought it was an angry Dad on the line, who else would be ringing at seven in the morning? The answer was Donna Bella Rosa who was reely over the moon, I couldn't stop her, she was gushing away like the bath taps I had left running, very unfortunately I forgot about them while she was babbling on and the water flowed over and through the flat below's ceiling, so out of Debra Chase's first Page Three Popsy fee there was a redecrating job to pay for but we will draw a veil over that.

'You're a credit to the Fashion School and dare I say it you're a credit to me but above all you're a credit to yourself Debra,' Donna Bella Rosa burbled. 'Now there's great things ahead for you, great things, I've already had the *Daily Stunner* switchboard on asking if it's all right to pass on my number, they've had five calls already, of course it could be dirty old men but don't worry your little head, I'll deal with all that, I'll filter the calls, there'll be offer after offer after offer before the day's out, you'll see Debra, now I'm going to ask you a favour.' This was that she wanted me at short notice to come down and give a little talk to her recurrent class about what it is like to be a Page Three girl, they were sposed to be having Colin and his mock photo session that morning but he had phoned Donna Bella Rosa to say he couldn't get out of bed as he must of caught flu. Yes, and we know what kind of flu don't we Colin, it is called Rusty Coffin Nail Runny Nose, isn't it? Apart from my auditionalising for Julian James's Dial-a-Thrill Hot Line I had never given a talk in my life but I had to say yes so I said yes.

This was just one phone call among many that morning. Brian rang and was most complimentful, he said the Wanderers all sent their love and by way of a tribune to me they had pinned my Page Three Popsy pic up in their changing room to use as a dartboard. (This may sound like an insult to the uninitialled but I can insure you that in the strange world of soccer it is the very reversal, when I tell you I replaced the Soaraway *Sun*'s Easter Eggstra Page Three Special in the team's afflictions you will get the general idea.) Mr Scissors rang and said he was reely thrilled for me, then sprise sprise who should he put on the line but Mr Gerald! Yes they were together again, I was so pleased for Mr Gerald, he sounded reely chuffed with life when I asked him how he had been keeping, he was like a dog with two balls saying, 'Well I did have a bad patch as you know pet a while back but everything's fine again now, it's all swings and roundabouts isn't it, sometimes you're up, sometimes you're down.' Story of my life.

And who else should ring out of the blue but my old English teacher Roz, she too was knocked out, she said, 'You know my views on women as sex objects but with that reservation I'm really pleased for you Debra, I won't show your Page Three to Miss Mold-Nixon much as I'd like to, I'm afraid she disapproves of the human form but from a very different standpoint from mine as I'm sure you can imagine, but as it happens I've only just recently started my English class on a How The Media See Women project and your Page Three will be great input, so all my congrats on being a John Pennywick Upper School text!'

No one else in Seathorpe except Dad and Babs had Auntie Doris's number so you could say I got a full house, I was highly flattered. But it was a different story when it came to the girls I was on my modelling course with, sad to say I got one call and one call only and that was from Viv who does the knitting patterns, I spose Beverley, Patti, Tiffany and the rest of the gang were just jealous, probly they thought if only they had stuck with the course they could of been Page Three Popsies too, well maybe they could and maybe they couldn't, all I can say is that Debra Chase got where she is by sheer hard graft and guts and if they couldn't stand the heat they should of come in out of the rain which course come to think of it is what they all did.

Course, when I say there were no other calls from my old Donna Bella Rosa classmates this is not counting Suzie who was on the blower for half an hour, but only to talk about Fast Eddie her steamy scaffolder who she said she had just had breakfast with, I didn't ask where as Auntie Doris does not approve of that sort of thing but I guessed she had not just been out to meet him at the corner caff! Now whilst Suzie had had plenty of boy friends since coming to London including her landlord Vince the big band trumpeter when he could sneak down to her flatlet without his wife knowing, this was her first bed and breakfast relationship so far as I knew. By the sound of it she reely had it bad, she was head over ears in love, I was reely pleased for her but I did wish it could of been someone a bit higher on the socialising scale than a mere scaffolder.

By the time I was ready to go out the only person I was expecting to hear from who still hadn't rung was Dad, touch wood. I was beginning to think I had got away with it but Auntie Doris knew different saying with great sageness, 'Either he's been trying to get through and you've been engaged or he's taken one look at that photo and had a heart attack.'

I said, 'Oh Auntie Doris, do leave off, there's pictures like that in the papers every day!'

She said, 'There's horoscopes in the papers every day but I don't expect to wake up and read Capricorn you are in for a nasty shock, your favourite niece turns out to be a French model!'

That of course would of been Miss Mouldy-knickers' idea of what had become of me if Roz had shown her my pic. With Auntie Doris I knew she was joking in that funny way she has – that is, making a joke of it but not reely joking if you follow me, I mean deep down I think she was quite shocked but she didn't want to show it so instead of saying she was she just tried to make me think she was pretending she was, that doesn't sound right but I know what I mean even if nobody else does. Anyway, just to remove any lingering doubtfulness out of her mind I said, 'Auntie, I am not a French model!'

'You know that and I know that but what must they think at Rosedene and Balmoral?' said Auntie Doris.

I said spiritually, 'I'm sure they'll be green with enviousness cos Dad has a famous daughter, and as for what Dad's going to say, Auntie Doris, my belief is he'll be very proud of his little girl.' Course, I didn't reely believe that for a second and seeing as the phone just at that moment took it into its head to start ringing again I was off out of that flat like a cat out of a bag just in case.

Going back to the Donna Bella Rosa School of Fashion was strange, course I had kept in close touch with Rosa either by phone or going round to her flat which honestlee was a complete tip, full of cats which I cannot stand being near me getting hair all over your clothes and digging their claws into your stockings, I was reely relieved when with the rise and rise of Debra Chase she got herself a proper office in Charing Cross Road. But this was the first time since my passing-out ceremonial that I had ever made a return to the Donna Bella Rosa School of Fashion, it was just like going back to school, course that's exactly what it was but you know what I mean I hope. It was like stepping into the past to tiptoe down into that familial studio and see all the girls in their leotards walking round and round with books on their heads whilst Rosa thumped away on the piano with clouds of fag ash mushrooming up out of the keyboard with every bunch of notes she played. When I say all, fact is there were only four of them. I thought that like the class I was in there must of been a few dropouts to the perfume counters, strip clubs and for the lucky ones millionaires' playgrounds of this world but no, Rosa said it was the quiet season and only these four had enrobed for the course this time round. I must say I'm afraid they were all throwing their money down the spout, they were just puddings with not an ounce of personalty between them and with no more hope of becoming top models than I have of climbing Mount Everton. But a talk on what it is like to be a Page Three Popsy I had promised, and a talk on what it is like to be a Page Three Popsy they were going to get, even though my knees were shaking and I was suffring from a bad attack of stage frightfulness.

But at the death, after Donna Bella Rosa had introduced me and got the girls sitting crosslegged at my feet so I felt like the Chief Brownie, I could not think of anything to say, I just said, 'Well girls, one thing's for sure, if any of you are wondering how Debra Chase managed to get herself on Page Three she sure as hell didn't talk her way on to it, the gift of the gab is defnitely not among my priceless assets,' at which they all giggled, so this encouraged me to go on for a bit longer saying, 'Also I don't think there's any tips I can give you that Rosa won't have given you already, so all I can say reely is that what you need in this job most of all is dedification, you have to want to reach the top so badly that you go out and seize opportunism by the throat, and that's reely all I've got to say about it but if any of you have any questions, any questions at all, I'll be glad to try and answer them.'

Not so much as a dicky-bird did I hear, the four of them just sat there staring up at me with their mouths wide open catching flies, I have never felt such a nana. I was hoping that if they did not have any questions Rosa would come to my rescue but she was answering the phone, I could hear her in her little office under the stairs saying, 'No I'm sorry, even if you offered double we couldn't touch it, she will be opening shops yes but not that kind of establishment, we've got a reputation to think of . . .'

I said, 'Well, say something one of you, even if it's only goodbye' and then broke into a fit of the giggles, which I always do when I am feeling shy. This set them going too, so as Donna Bella Rosa came back into the studio we were all tee-heeing away like hyenas, she gave me ever such a frosty look, I felt like a prefect who has been left in charge of the class and let them run riot.

I knew her phone call must of been about me so just for the sake of something to say I said, 'Who was that you were turning down Donna Bella Rosa, sex boutique, sounded like?'

She said grimfully, 'Worse than that, a silicone transplant centre, it'd give your public a completely false impression.' Course, this got everyone going again, even Donna Bella Rosa herself once she reelised what she had said, but after letting us giggle away for a minute or so she clapped her hands and said, 'All right girls, we've had our fun, it wasn't as hilarious as all that, now who's got a question for Debra, she's made a special effort to come and talk to us today so let's see you make an effort too, come along, one of you must have a question, Candy let's have a question from you.'

Having been put on the spot Candy who I must say her name suited her cos she looked as if she lived off the stuff, went bright red and had another little titter, but in fairness she did come up with an intresting and intelligible question at the death, namely, 'What do you do to relax after a hard day's modelling?'

Course, I could of answered that until the crows came home so right off the top of my head I started prattling away about the wonderful world of Bonks where top models mingle with the stars of soap, soccer, snooker and song. I had just started on listing the raunchy rock kings and sexy soap studs I had so far met within the portholes of the Magic Circle, or if not actually met then seen in the bare flesh, when the phone rings again.

Hurrying off to answer it Rosa said, 'Just hold it for a jiffy Debra, I don't want to miss any of this,' she just loves hearing gossip about the glitterity, it comes of having been a showgirl I spose. But I would of stopped anyway as I wanted to know if her phone call was another offer for Debra Chase, which in a way it was as I heard her saying, 'Donna Bella Rosa School of Fashion, no this is her manager, no I'm afraid we don't give out personal numbers no, and we certainly don't give out details of that kind, I'm very sorry sir I haven't the faintest idea what she wears under her dress, thank you very much I'll tell her you breathed!'

Needles to say this cracked us all up once again, and there we were falling about when who of all people should walk into the studio but Dad, course he'd been told where I was by helpful Auntie Doris. This was just as Donna Bella Rosa slammed down the phone snarling, 'Fifth sex maniac this morning!' Course she'd never met Dad who happened to be wearing a rather grubby raincoat as he always does if the weather is at all undercast, so taking one look at him I'm afraid Rosa jumps to the wrong conclusion. Pointing dramatisingly at Dad she cried, 'Oh my God they're coming round in person now, out, you, before I call the police!'

We laugh about it now but it was highly embarrassing at the time, specially in front of the girls. Anyway, as Dad got bluer and bluer in the face, in trolls Babs who had been parking Maud the Ford as his latest car being an Escort was called, we all cram ourselves into Rosa's office under the stairs where we get things sorted out, though not till after Rosa had mistaken Babs for my Mum which the youthsome Babs was not best pleased about.

Even then, Rosa went on putting her sock in it by saying gushfully to Dad, 'You must be proud of your lovely daughter Mr Chase.' This was defnitely not the right thing to say at this junction, waving the crumpled copy of the *Daily Stunner* he was clutching Dad started ranting, 'Proud, madam, proud, it's a Press Council job is this, a Press Council job!'

I said soothfully, 'Now Dad, don't take on, you knew I'd be going topless sooner or later.' Not that I had told him I would in so many words but I had been living in hopes that Babs would of dropped the hint. If she had it could not have been a highly broad one since Dad raged on, 'Not completely, not the whole hog!'

'Your Dad thinks you could have made more of a feature of the string of onions,' said Babs. Thanks a lot Babs, nice to know someone is on my side.

At least I had Donna Bella Rosa sticking up for me, she said stoutfully, 'All I can say Mr Chase is that since that picture appeared this phone has never stopped ringing.'

'*My* phone's never stopped ringing!' bleated Dad. 'If it wasn't Rosedene it was Balmoral and if it wasn't Balmoral it was the *Seathorpe Clarion* asking what's all this about her having been a model in Paris, you make me a laughing stock Debra, a laughing stock!'

Now it just so happened that Donna Bella Rosa had earlier acquaintalised me of a little bit of news concerning a certain modelling assignation she had just booked for me, so I was able to say with complete confidentiality to Dad, 'Never mind Dad, after the next week the laugh will be on the other foot.'

'What's she mean, what's she mean?' babbles Dad.

'She *is* going to be a model in Paris, Mr Chase,' said Rosa.

Course, Dad being Dad he gets hold of the wrong end of the brick, crying, 'Oh my God it's the slippery slope Babs, now she's baring her chest in front of foreigners!' Even when Donna Bella Rosa reinsured him it would be nothing like that, I would be modelling clothes, he was still not satisfied, asking suspectfully, 'What kind of clothes?'

'Underclothes,' said Donna Bella Rosa quite rightly.

He went mad. 'She is not modelling French knickers!'

I said, 'Dad it's Paris, they don't wear English ones!'

'No knickers of any kind!'

Goodness only knows what Donna Bella Rosa's four star pupils out in the studio were making of all this, course instead of getting on with their department exercises as instructioned by Rosa they were all earwigging like mad.

Anyway Donna Bella Rosa once more comes to the rescue, saying with a big heavy sigh, I'm sure she could of been an actress if she hadn't been a hoofer, 'Ah well, bang goes a thousand pounds.'

Course, Dad pricks up his ears at once, saying sharply, 'How much, how much?'

'A thousand pounds for less than a day's work Mr Chase, that's the kind of fee she can expect to command now she's a Page Three girl.' This was what Donna Bella Rosa had already told me and I still couldn't take it in.

'Is it indeed, is it indeed?' says Dad thoughtfully.

'Still,' Rosa went on all sorrowful, 'I can quite see your point Mr Chase, as Debra's co-managers you wouldn't want to draw commission on anything you didn't approve of.'

At this point Babs says pointfully, 'I'm parked on a double yellow line, Eric' and Dad, taking the hint, stares at his watch, claps his hands briskfully and says, 'Yes, we can't stand here chattering all day, well it's no use crying over spilt milk or locking the stable door after the horse had bolted for that matter, so you just behave yourself in Paris young lady and don't forget to send us a postcard.'

'Yes Dad,' I replied dutiously.

IO

Debra Chase, Business Lady

And what was Debra Chase's impersonation of her first ever visit to Gay Paree? I will give you some idea by just showing you a glimpse of my diary, not my private Sex Romps Diary but the big fat Filofax I had to keep now that I had hit the big time. Any idea I might of had of seeing the sights, malingering over a four-course lunch at a typified boulevardier cafe and having a candlelit supper at a romantic little bisto in Montparnice was knocked on the head as soon as I saw my crowded programme.

Leaving her class in the hands of Colin for their belateful photo session, Donna Bella Rosa came with me to Paris, partly as chafferone so as to satisfy Dad that I was not getting up to mischief, some hopes, and partly to make useful contacts. This was our punishment schedule: 4 am alarm call, plus wet sponge in the face from Auntie Doris who I do not think had even been to bed, she was so terrified I would miss my plane. 5 am, Donna Bella Rosa arrives in minicab, set off for Heathrow. 5.15, return to Auntie Doris's for forgotten passport. 6.30, arrive Heathrow, check in, buy mags and duty free scent. 7.30, flight to Paris, arrive 9.35 losing an hour owing to their time differential. 10.00, depart by waiting limo for studio in Rue St something or other, arriving just after 11.00 to find impatient smudger already there. His name is Jan and he turns out to be gay which suits me fine, you know where you are with gay photographers and they are always good snappers. 11.15–1.00, snap snap snap through twelve changes of very pretty undies, I would not of minded a free sample, they are very French but specially designed for a mail order catalogue to sell in England which is why they wanted an English model, why they could not just of flown over a parcel of knickers and had the pix taken in London we shall never know, it is how the crazy world of fashion operates.

Lunch, forget it. Our break from 1.00–1.30 consists of Jan disappearing to look at his negs and me and Rosa meandering across the Rue for a stand-up ham sandwich or rather picking the ham out of a big wodge of French bread which was all they had, plus a little bottle of white wine we treated ourselves to seeing as after all we were in France. 1.30–4.00, continual of session, finishing with Jan kissing me on both cheeks and saying I was wonderful, but in French. By the way I had no language problems with Jan as he also speaks English. 4.00–5.00, fast car to airport. Check in, buy duty free fags for Babs, duty free Scotch for Dad, duty free model of Awful Tower for Auntie Doris. 6.00, flight to Gatwick, arriving back miracfully at same time owing to having got back the hour we lost going over – Rosa tried to explain it to me but I still cannot understand it to this day and that's after having been to New York where the differential is seven hours I believe, so you have longer to figure it out. 6.30, Gatwick to Victoria shuffle, arriving 7.00. Cab to Kensington International Hotel, Cromwell Road, for cocktails in his suit followed by supper downstairs in the Britannia Chophouse with none other than Mr Jevvons of the Countrywide Car Mart, for business talks. Bed at 11.30 (in Sydenham that is, Rosa was present throughout my teat-a-teat supper and in any case I was too exhausted to be anywhere else but in my own little bed).

So that then is a typified day in the life of Debra Chase, top model. Course it is not always like that – I have been back to Paris sevral times since when things have not been so hectic and being able to relax a little have been taken to all the clubs and discos, so by now I know it like the back of my head. But in those early days it was work first, last and in the middle.

At first no job was too big or too small as they say on the side of removal vans. On the big side, that hotel business meeting with Mr Jevvons resulted in a contract to be the Countrywide Car Mart's next Calendar Girl. Imagine, Debra Chase, Calendar Girl after only a few short weeks in the business! Yes fellas, now you could *all* make a date with dreamy Debra! On the small side, would you believe flying to Newcastle and then being whisked by car to a place called Darlington, just to be seen with other celebs at a new nitespot called Gargles? I didn't have to do anything, just show my face, have my picture taken, sign a few autographs, zonk back a Killer Zombie (that's three kinds of rum, lime, pineapple and apricot liquor) and pick up £500 in readies. Course, when I talk about these jobs being small, the fees certainly were not. Right from the start Donna Bella Rosa laid it down that I would not cross the street for less than £500, and very soon as my pic began to appear all over the place she was able to up this to first £750 then £1,000 an appearance. Mark you, I had to graft for it. It was not so unusual for me to spend all morning at a photo session, grab a sandwich, then have to dash up to Birmingham or over to Swindon to open a new d-i-y centre or kitchen accessories carry-out, then be seen at one of the local nitespots, for a fee of course.

The result of all this fantastic activity was that despise heavy expenses and the commission I was paying to Donna Bella Rosa, Colin and Dad and Babs, I was slowly but surely building up a nice little nest egg for my old age – say when I was 22! Donna Bella Rosa had very shrewishly made me hire her accountant, Mr Cuthbertson, who got it organised for me to have not one bank account but two. Into the Debra Chase No 2 account went a certain percentageful of my earnings which I could not touch, this was for tax, VAT, accountant's fees, stuff like that. But everything in the Debra Chase No 1 account was mine to do as I liked with, I could blow the lot if I wanted, thanks to Mr Cuthbertson's foresense I was never going to find myself in the situation I have seen so many of my friends land themselves into, where they have hit the big time, spent like there was no tomorrow and then found themselves with ginormous tax bills they could not pay.

I had never had much to do with banks and was a bit nervous of them tell the truth, so when these reglar statements started coming through the post I did not open them at first, I knew I must have enough in the bank to pay for new clothes and whatever else I needed but as I was too busy earning money to spend much of it I just tucked my bank statements behind Auntie Doris's mantelpiece clock without looking at them. After a while though Auntie Doris said they were gathering dust so I thought I might as well open them before throwing them away. I could not reely follow all these diffrent columns of figures but luckily Brian had dropped in, Seathorpe Wanderers were away to Hammersmith Rovers and he had sneaked off from the Hammersmith West End Central Continental Hotel where they were staying to enjoy a quick nosh with his childhood sweetheart which is how I now thought of our relationship. Brian understands all about figures, he has a pocket calendator, so he was able to mark my card.

I had two nice sprises, one of them a reel knockout. The first was that they had not charged me intrest on my bank balance (told you I didn't know anything about banking!). But the second, wait for it, was there was no fewer than twelve thousand pounds in the Debra Chase No 1 account. I could not believe it, I kept saying, 'Check it again Brian, they must of added in the date, are you sure they haven't been putting things in the wrong column, you do hear of such things, maybe it's a computer error' but no, there it was in black and white, at the age of not yet nineteen Debra Chase was £12,317 90p underdrawn!!

Course, this called for a celebration. Now a celebration to me means Bonks and Bonks means Suzie so despise Brian grumbling that he had a match next day so he did not want to get plastered and anyway it was me he had come to see not Suzie, I gave her a bell.

To my sprise, instead of leaping at the invite she was I can only say a bit shifty, saying, 'Ooh I'd love to Debs, only I've got to stay in to.'

'Wash your hair?' I suggested. Funnee I thought, I've never known Suzie to stay in on a Friday night since she was nine.

'No, to do my packing,' Suzie said. This could only mean she had got an assignation at long last, I was dead pleased for her, things had not been going all that well for Suzie on the modelling front, in fact her only credit so far was an advert for Ma'mselle's Magic Mud Mask which quite frankly had her looking like a Malteser, in her shoes I would of turned it down but there you go, beggars cannot be choosers. So I said warmfully, 'Don't tell me don't tell me, you've got that job at the Birmingham Motor Show, smashing Suze, you'll look trif draped over the bonnet of a Ford Sierra.'

But no, turns out she wasn't off to the Motor Show. It was a bad line but I thought I heard Suzie mumble that she was off to Barbados.

I shrieked, 'Barbados! You're not!'

'I am,' said Suzie.

'But who's taking you to Barbados? Tell Suzie, tell, before I break your neck!'

'Fast Eddie.'

'Barbados,' said Auntie Doris, sucking on one of her mint imperials. 'I thought that was a bubble bath.'

'No, you're thinking of Bahamas, Auntie,' I said. 'Barbados is a place, it's where they drink coconut juice out of pineapples, or is it pineapple juice out of coconuts, Fast Eddie you say Suzie, but he's a humile scaffolder, only millionaires go to Badedas!'

'Why can't he be both?' asked Suzie.

Yes, come to think of it, why couldn't he? Come in Debra. Course I have to drag it out of Suzie, but it turns out Fast Eddie doesn't climb up scaffolds himself, he has 300 men to do it for him, the only thing he climbs in and out of is his Roller – he was a millionaire at 23, admittedly with a little help from his construction typhoon Dad who by the way was the reason Suzie wasn't too keen on the world knowing about her little jaunt to Badedas, seems Daddy did not approve of Fast Eddie's floozies as he charmingly called the Prince Edward lookalike's inconstant companions. To myself I wondered if he would of minded his son having his picture in all the gossip columns as the escort of Page Three Popsy Debra Chase, just to think I turned Fast Eddie down, ah well you cannot win them all Debra. But aloud I wished Suzie a super trip and then hung up, feeling a fit of the blues coming on you could dye your jeans in. I am not the jealous type, never have been, but the thought of Suzie lolling about on golden sands drinking out of a coconut or pineapple whilst I got to open a home freezer centre in Dollis Hill reely depressed me, don't know why, maybe I got to thinking what is the point of getting to the top when all Suzie has to do is wiggle her pert little bum and off she wings it to Badedas, I guess the top and bottom of it is I must of been working too hard.

But I perked up soon enough down in Bonks with a couple of Zorgan Morgans inside me, that's the same as a Morgan Zorgan except they put the light rum in first. And then I had this wicked idea. I think it was Brian saying, 'Don't take this the wrong way Debra but you're looking a bit tired, I reckon you could do with a holiday, it's getting on to the end of the season and me and Robby Roberts have been thinking of getting up a foursome to spend a couple of weeks on the Costa del Sol, that's me, him, his current lady she's called Jilly you'll like her, and you if you'd like to come and you can get away, I know you like Spain so what do you say?' that put it in my mind.

Or maybe it was the Zorgan Morgans talking. Anyway, I heard myself saying, 'You're right Brian, I am a bit bushed, it comes from working so hard and I do need a rest but I don't fancy Spain, been there, done that as the saying goes.'

'Well we're not dead set on Spain, there's always Portugal.'

'What about where Suzie's going?' I said boldfully. 'If it's good enough for her I'm sure it's good enough for me, it's coming up to my nineteenth birthday so let's kick the boat out, why not Bri?'

'I'm afraid you're way out of my league there Debra,' said Brian. 'It's Seathorpe Wanderers I'm playing for at the moment remember, not the World Cup squad. And I can't speak for Robbo but I reckon he'll say the same thing, he's just bought a four-berth cabin cruiser so I know he's a bit strapped for cash.'

I said, 'We can leave Robby Roberts out of this Brian, it's you and I I'm talking about, and so far as the where without is concerned I've got twelve thousand pounds in the bank tax paid if you remember, so how about it, I'm propositioning you Bri, that's if you've no strong objective to being a top model's kept toyboy!'

I knew I would think worse of my mad idea sooner or later but for the present all I could think of was that if Suzie Dawn could go trolling off to these topical islands staying in a fab hotel suit with sun balcony overlooking the beach on the strength of one mud pack advert, then Debra Chase could go one better, I would rent a beach bungalow with its own fridge and me and Brian would have the dream holiday of a lifetime.

Brian hummed and hawed and said he would think about it, he had to say that cos of his pride but I knew he would come round to it at the death which of course he did. Meanwhile he was so chuffed at the thought of being a kept man for a fortnight that when I asked for another Zorgan Morgan he broke his golden rule of never drinking the night before a match and instead of a Bells of St Clements which is just orange juice and lemon he ordered a Horse's Ass, that's the same as a Horse's Neck but with twice as much brandy and half as much ginger ale, whether that had anything to do with Seathorpe Wanderers losing three nil next day I didn't like to ask.

If Suzie hadn't been going away with Fast Eddie I don't think I would ever of made that suggestion to Brian, in fact I know I wouldn't, but now I had come out with it I began to get quite excited about sharing my dream holiday with him, as he said I did need a break and since I liked Brian a lot, who better to accomplicise me, we would have a few laughs with maybe a little romance thrown in but with no strings, at least not on my part. But you know what they say about many a slip between mice and men. A few evenings later I was staying in for a change as I had to be up at cracko for a session with the *Daily Screamer* who wanted me for their Zingo Bingo promotion, I don't think the *Daily Stunner* were best pleased being a rival paper but there was nothing they could do about it, I was not tied to them. So there I was curled up with my holiday brochettes and sucking one of Auntie Doris's mint imperials when the phone rings and it is Dad, calling from Donna Bella Rosa's School of Fashion of all places, he said he and Babs had just called in on their way to the Walthamstow Latin American Silver Bowl competition and could I spare a few mins right away.

I couldn't think what they were doing at Donna Bella Rosa's, maybe they wanted to look at her books, after all they were partners with Rosa and Colin in a certain very valuable property known as Debra Chase, though why they had not met round at her flat I could not understand unless it turned out that Dad didn't agree with cats, I wouldn't know as I have never discussed the subject with him. Anyway, after calling Sydspeed Minicabs with who I now had an account I slipped a raincoat over my sweater and jeans and set off to solve the mystry. By the way Kanji my reglar driver paid me a wonderful compliment, he said, 'If you don't mind Miss Chase, without all that make-up you have to wear you look really nice you know, I hope you don't mind me saying that to you.' I said, 'Why course not, thank you Kanji,' knowing exactly what he meant, namely that I looked like the girl next door figure that every man is secretly in love with, it is a side of Debra Chase the world never gets to see I am sorry to say, I am raddled with my glam image but reely that evening if you had seen me stepping out of Kanji's minicab outside the Donna Bella Rosa School of Fashion you would of just thought I was a more-than-average attractive nobody.

There was ever such a funnee sound floating up Donna Bella Rosa's basement steps, it was a strict temperance Flamenco being played by Victor Sylvester, I ought to know as I heard it played often enough back at Oceanview, Dad and Babs used to drive me spare with their Victor Sylvester LPs. So more mysterified than ever I tiptoe down into the studio and there's Donna Bella Rosa beating time next to the record player whilst Dad and Babs are grimfully shimmying backwards and forwards and stamping their feet, Babs looking exactly like a Spanish dancer complete with shawl and a rose between her teeth, Dad wearing a bum freezer jacket with a mastador's hat hanging behind his back, plus ruffled shirt, tight dress trousers and Cuban heeled boots, Babs was a picture but Dad honestlee I'm not kidding he looked an even bigger wally than Colin and that's saying something, sorree Dad.

They did not even notice me come in till the music stopped, when me and Rosa dutiously clapped and Babs gave us a deep curtsy whilst Dad bowed saying, 'Thank you Rosa, thank you Debra, now if we can keep up this standard in Walthamstow tonight Babs, I reckon we'll give Madge and Bruno Tackersley a run for their money.'

'They're the reigning Flamenco champions,' kindly explained Babs. Thank you Babs, I didn't think they were rock stars. 'Isn't this a wonderfully springy floor Debra, Rosa's been telling us it was a dance studio at one time.'

'Yes, I was saying, the Ballet Terry et Jimmy,' said Rosa. 'I don't think Tulse Hill was ready for them, either that or they weren't ready for Tulse Hill.'

'I knew it had some such history the minute I set foot on it, it was born to dance on this floor, born to dance on,' said Dad. 'Now Debra, I'm sorry to drag you away from your Auntie Doris's and we know you need your beauty sleep but what we've got to say's just between us four.'

'Your father has a little business proposition for you, Debra,' said Rosa.

'Reely?' I said. 'Fancee!' But I could not of been more in the dark.

'I think it's best if we explain it to Debra, Rosa,' said Babs, taking Rosa's mock-leopard coat down off its hook as she added confidingly, 'We can get through to her easier.'

So letting Babs help her on with her coat Donna Bella Rosa said, 'I'll leave you to it then, you'll find me up the road in the Jubilee Tavern Doubles Bar and I'll be sure to have the champagne waiting.'

'Champagne, goodee, but what are we celebrating?' I asked as Rosa went out.

'Your Dad's been fired,' said Babs bluntfully.

'Congratulations,' I said automatonly, but then taking in what Babs had just said I exclaimed, 'Fired? Oh Dad, you're never being hounded by bluenose bosses because of your daring daughter Debra's Page Three Popsy pose, are you?'

'No, as it happens,' said Dad. 'It could have been that mind, it could have been but it wasn't, no, the Seathorpe Public Baths and Leisure Amenities Committee have decided in their wisdom that I've been spending a disproportionate amount of time away from the Pool on ballroom dancing activities.'

'It was that last tango in Inverness that tipped the scales, if you ask me poppet,' said Babs.

I was reely out of my depth now, I said, 'But if Dad's out of a job what is there to celebrate?'

'Ah, well there we have it,' said Dad, not exactly tapping his nose but he could of been doing. 'You know that saying, as one door closes so another one opens, no I can see you don't, never mind, let it pass, but you do know that all the years Babs and I have been married we've nurtured one burning ambition, to start our own dancing school.'

That I did know, yes, in fact looking back it seems they talked about nothing else, every time some big room in Seathorpe became vacuous, as it might be over Burton's or in some old church, Babs would drool, 'Ooh, if only we had the capital, wouldn't that make a lovely venue for the Babs and Eric Chase Academy of Dance?' and Dad would shake his head regrettably and say, 'You can't expect people to dance on composition tiles no matter how highly polished Babs, and sprung pine costs money,' then Babs would say, 'That's what I'm saying Eric, if only we had the capital.'

So now Dad went on, 'Now the prospects for ballroom dancing were never brighter Debra, it's the up and coming activity.' You could of fooled me, instead of up and coming I thought it had been and gone and said as much but course Dad was not having this at all, he said, 'You wouldn't think that if you'd been dancing the Everglade Waltz at Basildon Civic Centre last Friday, there wasn't room to make a rotary natural turn, was there Babs?'

'So in short we've decided to take the plunge and give it a go,' Babs said. 'Your Dad's got a bit of redundancy to come and we've struck a very good deal with Rosa to take over the lease of this place.'

'The beauty is we've a floor here that's tailor-made for dancing,' said Dad, bending his knees and sort of going sproing-sproing with his feet as if he was on a trampoline, he looked ever so funnee. 'So that's a big saving for a start.'

'Lovelee,' I said, I was reely glad for them, but I didn't see where Donna Bella Rosa came into it or where I came into it either for that matter.

Babs started to spell it all out for me, explaining first of all that Donna Bella Rosa would be giving up her modelling course to spend all her time on her stable. I said it came as news to me that she even had a horse but it seems what Babs meant was Rosa's stable of models, consisting mainly of I, Debra Chase. This did not reely come as a sprise to me, I knew Donna Bella Rosa's classes were getting smaller and smaller, this in spite of her now being able to advertise herself as the teacher who groomed Debra Chase for stardom, fact is would-be models were scared off if anything, they reckoned the modelling school that handled Britain's No 1 Page Three girl must be way out of their reach, so Donna Bella Rosa reasoned it out anyway and I must say I think there was something in it, I remember when Babs and I were looking at modelling course brochettes I was scared stiff of even thinking about signing up with one of the reely famous ones like Lucy Clayton.

Course, Rosa becoming full time manager for me plus the few smallfry models she was already looking after before she struck gold made sense for both of us. But so far as Babs and Dad taking over the studio and turning it into a dancing school, I still couldn't make out what it had to do with I, Debra Chase.

'Financial back-up,' said Dad.

'It's your overheads,' said Babs. 'There's printing, there's post-age, there's electricity, there's business rates to pay, there's advertising, there's a hundred and one things to fork out for, as I say it takes capital and your Dad's redundancy money will only stretch so far, even after we've sold the bungalow there's not going to be much left by the time we've paid off the mortgage and put down a deposit on a flat up here, not at London prices there isn't.'

'So what we're looking for Debra,' said Dad, 'is a sleeping partner, let me explain it to you, that's someone who'd be prepared to invest in the business for a nice little profit without having to do any work, it bears thinking about.'

'The Debra, Babs and Eric Chase Academy of Dance!' pronounced Babs, jabbing her hand in the air as if she was spelling the words out in neon lights.

'Take your time Debra, give it some thought,' said Dad, looking at his watch, 'bearing in mind we've got to be taking the floor in Walthamstow in just over an hour.'

Well, I must say it did need thinking about, when it comes to business you do not just sign on the dotted line, you have to sit down quietly and weigh up the pros and roundabouts.

There were a lot of things to consider. Dad and Babs

buying a flat in London, frinstance. It would obviously have to be on the Tulse Hill side of Town and I didn't reely fancy them living on Auntie Doris's doorstep. Matter of fact now I had a reglar income I was beginning to think about getting a pad of my own, it was not always a conveyance to travel back to Sydenham in the early hours and if I didn't travel back to Sydenham I would get funny looks and pursed lips from Auntie Doris. So maybe Dad and Babs moving to Tulse Hill would be just the spurt I needed to look for a little place in Chelsea. But if I put down a deposition on a little place in Chelsea, would I have the capital as Dad and Babs called it to infest in the Debra, Babs and Eric Chase Academy of Dance? Problems, problems.

One thing was for sure though and that was as for them selling Oceanview, I could not be doing with that. Every successful model I had ever read about had bought a house for their parents and Debra Chase was not going to be the odd girl out, all right so Dad and Babs had a nice bungalow already but I had always meant one day to take over the mortgage and pay it off for them, so now would be as good a time as any, that way they could keep on Oceanview as a weekend and holiday place as well as for their old age when they hung up their dancing pumps and retired from the Debra, Babs and Eric Chase Academy of Dance.

But there was no time to go into all that now, what Dad had to know before they rushed off to Walthamstow was whether I would be wilful to be what he called their sleeping partner or not. Now anyone who knows anything at all about business will tell you that you cannot make a deal until you have looked at the figures, so I said, 'How much?'

'Would say twelve thousand leave you short, petal?' asked Babs.

Ah well, easy come easy go I always say. Dipping into my bag for my cheque book, since Dad said they could do with the money right away so he could settle things with Donna Bella Rosa, I came across one of the travel brochettes I had picked up for Badedas or Barbados, I still can't remember which it's called never having got there at the death. I dropped it in the rubbish bin and there went my dream holiday with Bri. Come to that, bang went any idea of finding a nice little flat in Chelsea for the time being. Still, all in a good cause.

I must of looked a bit glum as I handed over the cheque cos Babs gave me a big hug and said, 'I know it's a lot of money flower but you won't regret it and just think, it's not every model of your tender years who can stand up and call herself a business lady.'

Now that reely did cheer me up. Debra Chase, Business Lady! Delightful Debra may look dizzy but behind those baby blue eyes there's a bubbling business brain, yes fellas, Debra's figures are even more profitable than Debra's figure!!

'Come on,' said Dad, 'we've just time for that glass of bubbly with Rosa before we push on to Walthamstow.'

Don't ask me why but despise being on top of the world on account of being a reel business lady, I heard myself saying wishfully, 'I don't spose I could have coconut juice out of a pineapple, could I?'

'Pardon?' said Babs.

'Or pineapple juice out of a coconut?'

'What's she on about, what's she on about?' went Dad.

'Never mind, Dad,' I said.

11

I Meet Sir Right

You win some, you lose some. Dad and Babs quickly reelised their dream of opening their own dance studio, they were lucky enough to find a nice modern flat in a block that had been built on purpose not very far away, and after a bit of arm-twisting agreed to keep on Oceanview with me paying the mortgage, not that I was doing them any favours cos as Babs pointed out it would come to me in the end after they had gone to the great ballroom in the sky. Rosa set herself up in her office in Charing Cross Road where right from the start she was doing very nicely thank you. Oh yes, and Suzie had the most trif time with Fast Eddie on their island paradise, she came back looking like a bronze statuesque and what's more she and Fast Eddie were by now so much like that (you have to imagine I am crossing my fingers) that he wanted her to move in with him, the only snag being that his luxuriant Marble Arch pad belonged to his Dad who would not of put up with it, so next best thing he moves her into a lovenest over a doner kebab house in Notting Hill Gate, how lucky can you get?

But what, you may be thinking, has Suzie's good fortune got to do with my new way of livelihood as Debra Chase, business lady? Only that if Suzie had not gone away with Fast Eddie I would not of thought of going away with Brian, except maybe to the Costa del Sol where he wanted to go in the first place, and he was not best pleased when he heard that owing to having infested all my savings in the Debra, Babs and Eric Chase Academy of Dance our dream holiday of a lifetime was now a non-starter, in fact he was furious.

Where we had it out was at my old stomping-ground Bogie's Casablanca in Seathorpe, now re-named Thatcher's but it was still the same place except there were now a lot of new drinks with names like Denis the Menace and There Is No Alternative on the cocktail list. What was I doing in Seathorpe you may ask, well, it was just before Dad and Babs moved up to London and as a favour to Dad I had come down to grace his farewell dance with my presents, it was given by the Seathorpe & District Ballroom Dancing Association, strictly members only but as a partner in the Debra, Babs and Eric Chase Academy of Dance Dad told me they had made me an honourable member.

Having put in an appearance and danced the Viennese Waltz with Dad for the benefit of Stan from the *Seathorpe Clarion*, my plan was to leg it down to Thatcher's where I was meeting Brian. This is in actual fact what I did at the death but before that there was brief encountenance at the Corn Exchange where the dance was being held which I ought to tell you something about, as it was to have quite an important affect on me. When I say important it only changed my entire life, didn't it?

But I am getting everything out of sequel now cos before that there was another encountenance and I spose that helped change my life too in the long run, though looking at it another way it would of changed anyway. How this came about was that as I was just sidling off, Babs comes up to me with this big fat woman in tow, I remembered her vaguely from Mr Scissors where she used to come in to have her hair blue-rinsed by that cow Jessie, Mrs Aspinall she was called, she was the owner of Aspinall's Bun in the Oven Bakeries in Station Road and a couple of other avenues and didn't she like you to know it, you would of thought she owned the Royal Talbot Hotel.

When I say fat, I will give it to her that she was not as fat as the last time I'd seen her, she was as fat as a hippodromatus in those days whilst now she was only as fat as a pig. Turns out that's what Babs wants to talk about.

'I know you've got to rush off pet,' she says, 'but you remember Mrs Aspinall don't you, course you do, hasn't she lost weight, tell her how slim she's looking, we hardly recognised her at first.'

'Lovelee,' I said, giving Mrs Aspinall one of my dazzling smiles. All I hoped was she didn't intend dancing the Military Twostep cos she would of gone straight through the floorboards.

'Only she's been telling me all about this diet she's on, haven't you Mrs Aspinall, and talk about great minds think alike, you remember the diets we used to go on when you were a little podge, now see if you can cast your mind back to the one we found most successful, for ten points Debra what name did we give to it?'

'The stodge diet,' I said plitely to Mrs Aspinall. 'We used to eat a date and nut slice before meals and this used to deaden your appetite, by the way talking of dates I've got one waiting for me down at Thatcher's, crikey Moses is that the time, must dash.'

'With me it's bran muffins,' said Mrs Aspinall, plonking herself in front of me so I couldn't get away. 'We've been baking them as a special order for the House of Waffles for this American Breakfast Experience they're pushing at the moment, I don't see it catching on myself, not in this town, anyway though I say it myself Debra they really smelled delicious those bran muffins, now I make it a rule never to eat anything that we bake except outside working hours, Babs will tell you, it's the only way otherwise it'd be shortbread shortbread shortbread, cake cake cake from morn till night but these bran muffins ooh, they were irresistible.'

'So let me guess, you had one little nibble, naughtee!' I said, trying to bang the story on the head so I could get away.

'Let her tell it in her own way because it's important is this,' said Babs. 'She had more than one little nibble, didn't you Mrs Aspinall?'

'I had two!' giggled Mrs Aspinall. Debra Chase's beauty tip for the day: if you have six chins, keep a straight face.

'Two bran muffins that is, not two nibbles,' said Babs.

'Talk about more-ish, they were out of this world,' Mrs Aspinall rambles on. 'They're from an American recipe and honestly Debra I've tasted some bakery lines in my time but those bran muffins left everything else at the starting post so far as I'm concerned, talk about melt in the mouth but of course, what had gone clean out of my mind was I'm due at the Women's Luncheon Club in less than twenty minutes.'

'Couldn't eat a thing,' said Babs.

'I just pushed my roast chicken round the plate Debra, I had a few beans for appearance's sake but that was all I could manage.' I reckon we can skip what else Mrs Aspinall didn't have to eat that lunchtime – just cos I had to put up with a blow by blow account of how she got hooked on bran muffins there's no reason why anyone else should. What it all boils down to is that she o-d's on them, can't keep her podgy hands off them, loses her appetite for proper meals and drops seven pounds in one week and another seven the next, bringing her down to can't of been more than fifteen stone.

'Of course I won't say I wasn't taking laxative pills as well because I was, and all right admitted I'd already cut out the fried stuff at breakfast,' said Mrs Aspinall, 'but it's the bran muffins that's done the trick Debra, I'm convinced of it.'

'So she's thinking of putting them on the market,' said Babs.

'Only you see to launch a product like that from scratch we'd need a name,' said Mrs Aspinall.

'The Debra Chase Diet Nibble Muffin!' sings out Babs as if she was doing a commercial.

'Babs tells me you're always on the lookout for investment opportunities, Debra,' said Mrs Aspinall.

Well, I was and I wasn't style of thing. The Debra Chase Diet Nibble Muffin – yes, liked it, liked it, and I could see my face on all the posters and in the slimming mags and that, but I had already sunk a lot of money into the Debra, Babs and Eric Chase Academy of Dance and being a shrewish business person I wanted to get that on its feet before I expended in other directions. Anyway, just at the moment all I wanted to do was go down Thatcher's, hand Brian his red card and get it over with.

Babs saw me biting my lip so she said, 'I know you're a bit overstretched at the moment, flower, but we're only talking about starting in a small way, try it out locally then if it looks like catching on spread the net wider bit by bit, so no way would it involve large amounts initially, anyway don't give Mrs Aspinall an answer now, we've put the idea in your head, sleep on it and maybe you and me can have a quick chat before you go back to Town in the morning, ooh no peace for the wicked, there's your Dad waving, he'll murder me if I miss this rumba.'

So that was how we left it for the time being. Looking back I wish we'd left it there for good.

There are two halls in the Seathorpe Corn Exchange, the smaller one upstairs where our dance was taking place and the bigger one downstairs where a dinner dance was going on and didn't we know it, every time our band played a quickstep you could hear their band playing a slow foxtrot and every time our band played a slow foxtrot the sound of a waltz came drifting up, so as you can imaginise the Babs and Eric Chase footwork was not quite up to scratch, pity as it was Dad's last night. Anyway, turns out that the dinner dance downstairs that is causing all the racket is the annual thrash of the Seathorpe Consistency Conversative Party, their guest of honourable being the local MP yes you've got it in one, Sir Monty Pratt.

Having at long last torn myself away from Mrs Aspinall I was on my way downstairs to the cloakroom when I spotted a couple of our dancers called Simone and Tony Eglington down in the lobby, chatting to this very distinctful-looking redfaced gentleman with a reel neat thatch of grey hair that looked as if he brushed it for half an hour before going out (he does, with two ivory-backed brushes!), grey militant moustache and reely well-fitting dinner jacket, he made our lot look like penguins out in a gale. I knew that Simone and Tony were big pals of Dad and Babs, or anyway big rivals, so I thought better say good-night, but just as I was about to give them a wave and call out, 'Well ta-ra then,' Tony said loudly, 'Oh Debra, there's a Very Important Person would like to meet

214

you, Sir Monty may I present Seathorpe's celebrated Page Three Popsy Miss Debra Chase, Debra I don't think you've had the pleasure of meeting our distinguished Member of Parliament, Sir Monty Pratt.'

I knew he was someone special from the start, though just how special he was going to be of course at that time I had no idea. I was just conscientous of being fixed by this pair of piercing blue eyes that seemed to look right through my face and into my head, you would of said they were cold eyes except for the good-humorous wrinkles round them, whilst at the same time he took my hand and held it in a grip I knew I could not of got away from if he did not want me to, yet it was so gentle. As the world knows he is an older man but although he looked his age which is 57 on account of his primature grey hair he did not have a spare ounce on him (fifty press-ups every morning would you believe?), being short and stocky with it he could easily of run to fat if he had let himself go.

But what struck me most about The Sir as I began to think of him almost from Day One was that I would of known he was entitled even if Tony Eglington had not let the cat out of the cradle. You could just tell. Looking back on my disasterous encountenance with the so-called Sir Eggy Throstle, it was laughable how I could ever of believed he was a Sir, if only I had met Sir Monty Pratt first he would never of taken me in for a second.

But even though I knew Sir Monty was a genuine Sir I thought at first he must be a foreign one like a Count or a Baron or something, because his very first words to me were in foreign. As I had no idea what he was jabbering on about except that he was onchontay something or other, all I could say in reply was 'Pardon?'

'I beg *your* pardon,' said The Sir swavely in that lovely deep voice of his. 'I thought I'd read in the paper that you were fluent in French, my mistake.'

'Oh, I am fluent but I don't reely speak it,' I said with a pleasant giggle. 'I can just read street signs and that. Are you French then?'

'I believe I'm right in saying Sir Monty learned French at Rugby, isn't that correct Sir Monty?' said Tony Eglington, smirkfully rubbing his hands, he was a right crawler when talking to anyone more important than himself.

'I was taught French at Rugby, which isn't necessarily the same thing,' The Sir murmured modestfully.

'Why do you have to speak French to play rugger?' I asked. Then I reelised I'd asked a silly question. 'Oh, course, for when you play in the International.'

'Isn't she delightful?' beamed The Sir at Simone and Tony Eglington. Simone said, 'She's a love,' looking as if she could scratch my eyes out.

'I must get back to my masters but it's been a very great pleasure meeting you in the flesh so to speak, Miss Chase,' said The Sir. 'I'm about to make a speech on business opportunities in my constituency and I shall make a point of mentioning that I've just had the pleasure of meeting the young lady who has done as much as anybody in this hall to put Seathorpe on the map.'

I knew he was a charmer from Babs who often talked about the time he brought his dream holiday snaps in to be developed, but this was one of the nicest things anyone had ever said to me in my whole life, all the nicer cos I'm not banging my own trumpet but I knew it was true, I kept thinking of those lovely words for the rest of the evening and as soon as I got back to Oceanview where I was spending the night I wrote them down. So that was the first mention of The Sir in my Sex Romps Diary though by no means the last!!

I was so chuffed that all I could do was giggle and mumble a plite thank you. We shook hands again and The Sir said, 'I believe you live in Town now Miss Chase, you must come and have tea with me at the House one day.'

I said, 'I'd love to, where do you live?' but instead of giving me his address The Sir just chuckled and said to Simone and Tony Eglington, 'Look after her, she's very precious.' With this second great compliment, honestlee he could of charmed two birds out of a bush, he gave me a little bow and off he went to the little boys' room. After saying to Simone and Tony what a lovely man he was, hoping if they saw him again they would pass it on, I went and picked up my coat then hung about in the lobby for a minute or two in case I might accidently on purpose bump into him again, but then I heard a booming voice coming out of the big hall where the Conversatives' dinner dance was being held and reelised it was The Sir making his speech, his words being indistinguished through the big closed doors there was no point in listening for his mensh of Debra Chase so off I trotted to meet Brian at Thatcher's but without any feeling of disappointal or let-down, somehow I just knew The Sir and me had not seen the last of one another and that our paths would meet again.

In the meantime there was Brian to be sorted out. I knew there had to be a showdown, as I say he was livid when I broke the news that our dream holiday was off but that was only briefully on the phone so he was sure to want to have a good old moan about it, I was dreading it specially as I had thought it all out and decided it was time for Brian to be given the Big E, the elbow, he was a nice boy, a lot of fun when not banging on about my seeing other men which he was in the habit of so doing, but I had my career to think of and he was getting in the way of it, I could not be doing with that not even from Sylvester Stallone himself.

I had no idea how I was going to tell Brian it was all over between us, I thought I would just play it by ear, but as it turned out I did not have to. Having expected to find him highly frosty I was pleased to see that he was quite friendly, but it was not a question of forgive and forget because as soon as I had ordered a Grantham Gobsmacker, that being the same as what used to be a Between the Sheets when the place was Bogie's Casablanca, he started bellyaching away, whingeing, 'Right, well as I was saying on the phone the other night I can't help feeling a bit pissed off at you giving backword on this Barbados trip, I mean first it's on and then it's off, I mean why bring it up in the first place, you must have known you were going to invest that money, you can't tell me your Dad just sprung it on you out of the blue and you signed away twelve thousand quid just like that . . .' and on and on and on.

I let him chunter on while I drifted into nice thoughts of The Sir and the kind things he had said to me. But after a few minutes it filtered through to me that Brian had changed his tact because he was saying, 'Anyway, as it so happens Debra, no thanks to you it's all worked out for the best because I was never too keen on your forking out for the holiday in the first place, I've got my pride, it made me feel like a kept man, I know we joked about it but that's how I did feel and it's no use saying I didn't, but as luck would have it we can still make it to the Costa del Sol with Robby Roberts and Jilly, I think it's pretty big of them after messing them around like that, they were going to go with Kevin Keene and his bird, you remember Kev yes course you do, anyway they've had to drop out, the bird's up the spout and it's all turned very nasty, she doesn't want to get rid, so at the death it's all worked out for the best, for us anyway.'

Oh yes, and has anyone thought of consorting Debra in all this? I was even madder than Brian had been when I told him the Badedas trip was off. I said, 'How do you mean it's all worked out for the best, who says I want to go to the Costa del Sol?'

Brian quite obviously thought I was playing hard to get, so he said easefully, 'You've got to take a holiday some time, Debra.'

'Yes, I know Brian,' I said, 'but I'll have it when I want to have it, not when someone else decides it for me.'

'I'm not someone else Debra, I'm Brian. You seem to forget you've been going out with me for the best part of two years, even if we can't see so much of one another for the time being.'

I said, 'I'm afraid there's something I've got to put you right on, Brian. I don't go out with you as you put it, all right we have been out a good few times but it doesn't make you anyone special, no forget I said that, you are special but not all that special, I mean we're not engaged, we don't live together, I see other people all the time and so do you, so let's not pretend we've got any big deal going because we haven't.'

'So what you're saying is you don't want to go to the Costa del Sol with Robbo and Jilly?' said Brian. Actually I thought I was saying a good deal more than that but it would do to be going on with so I said, 'I can't, I've got too much on.'

'You don't even know when we're going yet.'

'We're not going Brian, at least I'm not, I haven't got a free day between now and August.'

I think Brian could tell this was a little white lie because he said, 'I'm sorry Debra but I don't believe you.'

'You'll just have to unbelieve me then, won't you?'

I must say I wasn't prepared for what came next, it was like a bolt from the blues when Brian said, 'All right, if you won't come you won't, nobody's twisting your arm, but I'm giving you a day to think it over Debra, and if the answer's still no I think you and me had better call it a day because quite frankly you're becoming a bit of a pain, ever since you took up this modelling lark all right I was proud of you at first but you've just been getting too big for your knickers.'

Funny him saying we'd better call it a day because those were the self-same words I was just about to say to him. 'We've had a lot of laughs Brian,' I was going to say, 'and I'll always be fond of you, but if you think you only need to whistle and I'll come to you I'm afraid you have another think coming, you don't seem to reelise I'm a different lady again from the one you used to take out here in Seathorpe and even then you couldn't tell me what to do and what not to do but I've got my interdependence now Brian and it's something I very much enjoy, I've got a life of my own and I'm very sorry but there's no room in it for someone who tries to keep me chained down so taking it all round I think we'd better call it a day.' Natch, I couldn't say all that now, all I could say was, 'We better had call it a day then because I can tell you here and now the answer is still going to be no.' But I felt cheated out of my farewell speech as well as cross that Brian would go away thinking he had given me the Big E instead of the other way round.

We sat there in a sulk for a while, then all of a sudden a big crowd from the old days zoomed in, when I say old days I mean faces I'd got to know in Thatcher's when it was Bogie's Casablanca after I became Miss South-east Coast, fun people, young estate agents, time-share salesmen, people like that, people who worked hard and played hard, they had been to a twenty-fifth birthday party at the Royal Talbot Hotel and were a bit merry. Anyway, upon spotting Debra Chase it was kiss kiss kiss all round and they all very noisily drew up chairs and pulled round tables until our little table for two had become a big rowdy table of about sixteen. The Grantham Gobsmackers and There Is No Alternatives flowed and everyone laughed a lot and we were having a reely good time. Only Brian was quiet being still in a sulk, and after I came back off the floor after bopping with a bloke called Tim I think, he sold caravans, I must say it made a nice change from doing the Viennese Waltz with Dad, I noticed he wasn't there. At first I thought he had just gone to the little boys' room but as the night wore on I reelised he had gone without even saying good-night. And that was the last I ever saw of Brian Boffe. Sad reely.

Actually he did ring me a couple of days later but by that time I had other things on my mind and didn't want to speak to him right then so I told Auntie Doris to say I'd call him right back, but owing to these same things on my mind I clean forgot. Sorree Brian but it would never of worked out anyway, I do think of you sometimes but us career girls are not cut out for going steady, we have to make sacrificials and you were just one of them.

*

There are a lot of ways in which I do not take after my Dad but none more so than as regards Fate. He does not agree with it whilst I am a great believer in it.

I forgot to mention that by this time I had acquisitionised my first car, just a little turquoise Mini but I loved it, I went everywhere in it till one day I left the hand brake off and it ran into a bus. Well, the morning after Dad and Babs's farewell dance at the Corn Exchange I trolled out of Oceanview bright and early only to find I had a dodgy clutch. This put me in a spot as I had to get back to Town to open a carpet warehouse in Ealing. Luckily Babs came to my rescue saying, 'No problems pet, go up to Town by train, I'll get the car serviced and drive it up Wednesday when we move into the flat, that's if you can manage without it for that long, you'll be doing me a favour because I can load it up with a lot of the stuff like our ballroom dancing trophies that we don't want to trust to the removal van, your Dad was going to make two trips but this'll save him a journey.'

So although I was loathsome to part with my precious Mini even for a day or two I let Babs call a cab and caught the 9.06 from Seathorpe Parkway and that's what I mean by Fate, cos if the clutch hadn't gone on my Mini and I hadn't got to get back to open that carpet warehouse I should never of got that train and I would never of found myself sitting in a first class carriage opposite none other than Sir Monty Pratt himself. Course, you can go back even farther and say that if Dad had not been fired and been having his farewell dance I would not of been back in Seathorpe in the first place, in fact you could go back even farther than that but I can just hear Dad saying, 'What's she on about, what's she on about, you might just as well say none of this would have happened if you hadn't been born, it's all superstitious mumbo-jumbo.'

When I say I found myself sitting opposite The Sir, truth to tell at first I was sitting by myself and hoping no one else would get in the carriage as when you are famous and they get you cornered your public can get a bit exhaustive sometimes. But then just as I was unwrapping a stick of chewing gum and opening the *Daily Stunner* to page three to see if I had any up-and-coming rivals, you have got to keep in touch with world events in this job, there was a rap on the window and who should be standing on the platform raising his hat but you know who.

A moment later he was sliding back my comportment door saying, 'Good morning Miss Chase, may I join you or are you one who prefers her own company at this unearthly hour, now I shall quite understand if you want to read your newspaper.' Actually I had already read my *Daily Stunner* as it had taken him a few seconds to get into the carriage but even if I hadn't there was no way The Sir was going to get away now I had him to myself! Plitely I said, 'Fancy meeting you Sir Pratt, have a piece of chewing gum, are you going up to Town?' – stupid question, there was nowhere else he could of been going except East Croydon and The Sir is defnitely not the East Croydon type. He was ever so smartly dressed in a three-piece pepper-and-salt check suit, you could of mistaken him for a high-class bookie, with a blue shirt and stiff white collar and blue and white striped tie which he told me later was the tie of his regimen, he was once an officer in the army and I guess they let you keep the tie as a momentum.

I found him reely easy to talk to. He asked me what

had brought me down to Seathorpe again and I told him all about Dad and Babs and their intrest in dancing, The Sir said when it came to dancing he had two left feet, actually I have danced with him at the Rainbow Room in New York and he was quite good, you have to be when you are a Sir because you are always going to functionals. Then he asked me who I knew in Seathorpe and I gave him some of the more respectful names, business types mainly and of course he knew them all, so that was a great bondage between us. Then we talked about my modelling career which he said must be very interesting, so by way of paying back the compliment I said it must be intresting being an MP and a Sir too and it turned out that it was. He told me ever so much about his job, you would of thought we had been friends for weeks. Seems when you are an MP you do not have set hours, you do not even have to go to the Houses of Parliament at all unless you feel like it, not unless there is an important debut and you have got to go and vote in it. He said he was what they call a back benchman I think it's called, he could of been the Ministry of something or other if he had wanted to, it was offered to him, but this would of meant giving up his business intrests for some reason.

These he reeled off, he had his finger in all sorts of pies but the ones that he was most involved in were reel pies, that is to say the family business Pratt's Pork Pies Ltd, course I had heard of them as they are also the makers of Sizzlers, the savoury sausage that bites back, as advertised by All English darts ace Len Lipton. This I thought must be another acquaintal we had in common so I said, 'Oh in that case I expect you know Len Lipton, I can't say we are exactly best mates but he was in a ruck with one of my boy friends and we all finished up plastered all over the front page of the *Daily Stunner*, hee hee hee!'

Sir Monty said No, he didn't have much to do with the advertising side, in fact except for board meetings he didn't have much to do with Pratt's Pork Pies Ltd at all, they practicly ran themselves. Then he said in a jokey sort of way but rather worriedly I thought, 'And do you and your friends often finish up plastered all over the front page of the tabloid press?' I knew straight off what he was thinking – spose me and him had a fling, would we end up in the headlines? Call it preposition but I think he knew straight from the start he was playing with fire, it was one of the things that attracted him to me, some men are like that, it is what drives them on, they like to live dangerously.

Not that Debra Chase had any idea of leading anyone up the Swanee River, it is not my style, so to reinsure him I said simperingly, 'No, I prefer to finish up on Page Three, by the way is there a Lady Pratt?'

Course there was, just my luck, but at least he did not try to pretend he was not married like some men I have known in my life, not that you can get away with it when you are a Sir cos as he once explained to me people can always look you up in *Who's Whom* if they are curious about your background, I wish I had known that when so-called Sir Eggy Throstle was giving me the runaround.

To his credential The Sir was perfectly straightforward, did not try to make out his wife did not understand him or anything like that, he just said, 'Oh indeed yes, the delightful Pussy, we've been married for many years in fact you remind me we're fast approaching our silver wedding so something must be done about that, village

225

bonfire I suppose, Pussy's always loved a bonfire, she's very much a country girl, doesn't come up to Town very often and so dividing one's time between the House, the City and one's surgery at Seathorpe. I see little enough of her but she's a very good sport old Pussy, we're the firmest of friends.'

Not knowing the first thing about policies in those days, later he explained them all to me when he took me on a tour of Parliament, I naturally thought a surgery was where you went for a sick note, so nave as they come I said, 'I didn't know you were a doctor on top of all your other achievals.'

The Sir roared with laughter, giving his knee such a great slap that he must of hurt himself, then he said chortlingly, 'Oh dear oh dear oh dear, no I'm not a doctor you delightful young creature but I would certainly prescribe you as a tonic, you're like a ray of sunshine on a gloomy day, now look here Debra if I may call you Debra, we seem to be at Battersea Bridge already, now I'm certainly not going to allow you to escape a second time, when shall I see you again?'

Talk about being swept off your feet, he didn't even ask if I would like to see him again, just went on the assumal that I would and course he was right, he might not of been a doctor but he could of set himself up as a mind reader any day.

I said boldly, 'You did mention having tea at your house, that's if Lady Pratt wouldn't mind but as you say she doesn't come up to Town much so praps she won't know.'

He said with his moustache twitching humourfully, 'No my dear, I don't run to a house in London though I do have rather a nice flat in Brook Street where I should be only too pleased to entertain you to tea, but in point of fact I was thinking of the House of Commons where I really do look forward to showing you off to my friends and enemies both, however in the meantime I'd like you to consult your diary and see if you can't fit me in for lunch.'

For one wild moment I thought of ducking out of opening that carpet warehouse at the very inconventional hour of lunchtime, just not turning up, I could ring up Donna Bella Rosa afterwards and say ever so sorree, I had lost my Filofax and forgotten all about having to be in Ealing. So that shows how badly I wanted to see The Sir again. Course I did not dare do any such thing, Donna Bella Rosa would of roasted me alive, so I said regrettably, 'Much as I'd love to, I'm afraid I've got a public engagement and you know how it is, one doesn't want to disappoint your fans, but any other time would be lovelee.'

The Sir said firmly, 'Then there's nothing for it, it'll have to be dinner,' and that was that. No question of was I seeing anybody else that night, as a matter of fact I did have a date with cuddly indoor bowls commentator Ken King but he could easily be put off, sorry Ken but as I say we all have to make sacrificials in this life, I'm sure I passed up a reely great night but what else could I do, specially as The Sir himself was likewise making a sacrificial cos as he said, 'It means playing truant from the latest in a long stream of Education Bills but I'm quite sure the nation's standards of literacy such as they are don't stand or fall on the presence of one who can't even spell so there we are.' Though I had not the foggiest what he was jabbering on about I was glad to hear that The Sir could not spell, it brought him down to my level style of thing, you will not believe it but no one had ever had that affect before, all the men in my life had either wanted to make me feel stupid or tried to sound superious to what I was which comes to the same thing.

So I said very simplisticly, 'I'd love to have dinner, when and where?'

'If you'll be kind enough to jot down your address,' said The Sir, producing a little leather notepad with gold edges, 'I'll have my driver pick you up at eight if that's convenient.'

So began my whirlpool life with The Sir.

12

Champagne and Canopies All the Way

One of the worst things the *Sunday Shocker* put into my mouth was that in the bedroom stakes I rated The Sir only five on a scale of one to ten. Now hand on hat I never said those words, they were twisted by smear merchant Barry Butcher out of my answers to his questions. As I do not have excess to his tape recorder I cannot prove this but I want the world to know that I did not pass this remark in any shape or form. I am blessed with a very good memry and I have complete recoil of what I said to Barry Butcher in answer to what he said to me, and it was this, here goes:

BB: Right, so we've got it established that sometimes you ate out and sometimes you ate in, he'd send the chauffeur round to Fortnum & Mason's and you'd picnic off smoked salmon, paté de foie gras and other luxury foods washed down with vintage champagne, don't worry about the details my love I'll fill those in, but getting back to that day when he got you to serve him strawberries and cream wearing nothing but a frilly apron, high heel shoes, stockings and suspenders, that wasn't the first time you slept with him, was it?

MYSELF: Who says I slept with him?

BB: Leave it out darling, you didn't play effing Scrabble, did you?

MYSELF: Anyway it wasn't strawberries and cream, it was strawberry ice cream, he happens to be very fond of it, he always keeps a big tub of it in his fridge.

BB: Yeah, but for our readers strawberries and cream sounds better, I mean they eat strawberry ice cream themselves every day of the week but strawberries and cream has a classy ring to it, it says Royal Ascot, it says Wimbledon, it says the Henley Regatta.

MYSELF: He never took me to any of those places.

BB: Good thing he didn't, darling, considering what he made you do with the pudding course. What was it – you fed him the strawberries by putting them between your teeth and getting him to bite them, then he spreads the cream over his plonker and gets you to lick it off, am I getting this down right?

MYSELF: You're talking rubbish Barry, absolute crap. I've just told you, it was ice cream I served him so how could I of put it between my teeth, it would of dribbled down my chin, and as for putting it where you're trying to make out he put it, talk sense, the cold would of shrivelled it up, wouldn't it?

BB: Giving us one more good reason for making it strawberries and cream. So after that he makes mad passionate love to you on what kind of rug shall we make it and don't say tiger skin because the readers might be simple but they're not effing stupid, how about white fur say polar bear, no not polar bear we'd have effing Greenpeace after us.

MYSELF: If you reely want to know we always had our picnic meals in the bedroom and it wasn't a rug, it was a pink satin eiderdown if we're talking about the Brook Street place and a flowered duvet if we're talking about the flatlet in Westminster.

BB: Right, now we're getting somewhere darling. Now after you'd got in the swing of these champagne and caviare sex sessions, how did you rate him as a lover on a scale of one to ten?

MYSELF: I'm sorry Barry, I'm trying to collaborate but I've just never rated my men out of ten, I know a l ot of girls do but it just so happens I'm not one of them.

BB: Whatever score you do give them then – like red hot, average, piss poor, I'm trying to establish what he was like in the sack.

MYSELF: Well, I spose if I had to say anything I'd have to say average.

BB: Average. So we're talking about fifty per cent.

MYSELF: Fifty per cent of what?

BB: That's what average means darling, it means fifty per cent. So on a scale of one to ten, fifty per cent is five.

MYSELF: How do you make that out?

BB: I'm effing telling you. You just concentrate on remembering what you did in bed or better still on the kitchen table and leave the figures to me.

Swear to God, that is how I came to be quoted as saying, 'On a scale of one to ten sexwise I would definitely not rate The Sir higher than five, he was loving and gentle but you have to remember he was nearly old enough to be my grandfather so let's just say the earth didn't move and leave it at that.'

At least Barry Butcher didn't get it out of me when I first went to bed with The Sir, I let him think it was in a little room under Big Ben in the Houses of Commons, he went mad with joy, Barry I mean not The Sir, he said, 'I don't believe an effing word of it darling but it's a marvellous story' so he was quite chuffed with that particlar version. But the reel truth is that whilst I did once go to bed with The Sir at the Houses of Commons, though in his office not a little room under Big Ben, that was a little white lie designated to keep Barry Butcher happy, the first time we slept together was much earlier, in fact the first time he ever took me out to dinner.

True to his form Sir Monty had his Jag pick me up at Auntie Doris's when complete with peaked cap and leather gloves, Ted Nixon his faithful driver as I thought he was, pressed the doorbell at eight sharp – yes, the same Ted Nixon who sold the story of his employee's fling with top model Debra Chase amongst others to the *Sunday Stunner* which is how that virago of lies Debra Chase By Herself came to appear in the *Stunner*'s rival the *Sunday Shocker*, The Sir trusted that man and this was how he got paid back, talk about platitude.

Course, I had been ready half an hour when Ted rang the bell – it was ever so funnee when I got to know him better, turns out that not knowing the Sydenham area he had allowed himself a lot of leeway and had been cruising round the council estate for half an hour just to kill time, he daren't just park outside and wait cos as he said, round Auntie Doris's way they would twist off your aerial as soon as look at you but the point is I wish I had known he was out there cos I was so nervous at going out with The Sir that I could of murdered a Planter's Punch-up at Ciro's of Sydenham on the way to Mayfair, that's the same as a Planter's Punch but with twice as much dark rum.

I must say I did not see through Ted at first, he was much younger than I imagified the chauffeur of a Sir ought to be, about twenty-five I guess and I like that in a man, also quite good looking if only he would of let his black hair grow a bit but then he would not of been able to get his cap on. He did strike me as a bit familial to say we'd just met but I thought he was just being friendly. Anyway he chatted away saying, 'So where's he taking you Debra, the Ritz is it I wouldn't be surprised, he's very fond of the Ritz, all the first-class hotels in fact, Ritz, Savoy, Claridge's, anywhere that's a bugger to park excuse my French, do you smoke Debra, well you won't mind if I light up will you, so where did you bump into him then, party was it, he loves his parties Sir Monty, three and four in a night sometimes, I tell you, if I have just half his energy when I'm pushing sixty I won't complain, he's a lad, he is, he's wicked, wicked.'

Needles to say Ted only rabbited on in this way when I was by myself alone with him in the car, when he was driving The Sir he kept his trap firmly shut. Without being snobby I have got to say that after a while I did start getting the hump at Ted talking to me as if we were best mates when he was only the chauffeur, I bet he never talked to Lady Pratt like that and I am quite sure he would never of dared call her Pussy to her face like he did me, calling me Debra I mean.

At least Ted had his uses, he marked my card on The Sir, telling me quite a lot that otherways I would of had to of found out for myself, frinstance about his lavish Mayfair pad in fashionable Brook Street, this according to Ted was the company flat belonging to Pratt's Pork Pies Ltd, whilst The Sir had another flat belonging to himself personly in Westminister where he stayed when the Houses of Commons were rabbiting well into the night, The Sir later told me it was for the sake of convenientness but Ted said it was all down to tax, I must say I did not begin to figure out why anyone would want not one but two flats in Town within a ten-minute car ride of one another but it was to turn out a lucky break for Debra Chase I can tell you but no, I must not jump the gunner.

Whilst I had been inside a few luxuricant pads since living in London (as well as quite a few ratty ones, you would be amazed at some of the famous personalities who live like pigs but maybe I'll keep these revolutions for another book), I had never seen anything to match The Sir's munificent flat over a picture galleria in the heart of exclusive Mayfair. For openers it had its own private lift which let you out into the hallway where The Sir was waiting for me – not in silk pyjamas as the *Sunday Shocker* would have it, that was not till my third or fourth visit, but in a very tasty dark blue suit. Saying, 'There you are, how lovely to see you, now you look like a girl who wouldn't turn up her pretty nose at a very dry martini,' he led me into the lounge where he poured us drinks from a cocktail shaker, he certainly knew how to mix a dry martini, my first one ever it was, a bit like a Sock It To Me but without the glassy cherry. Then he took me on a conductored tour of the flat. Honestlee, it was like a hotel suit – parky flooring with Turkish rugs he said they were, antiquated furniture and old pictures with lights over them so you could see them better. Lovely big bedroom with luxuriant tiled bathroom leading off it, not exactly gold taps but not far off, fitted kitchenette, I thought 'I wouldn't mind moving in here!', little did I know that is exactly what I would be doing before long!

We polished off the dry martinis then The Sir said, 'Now I expect Ted has warned you to expect the Ritz, however I like nothing better than to prove my driver wrong from time to time, now how fond are you of seafood?' Never having been taken to the Ritz I was quite disappointed but course I didn't show it, just said I adored seafood specially lobster. The Sir then broke the news that he had booked a table at Spencer's, it is only the most expensive restaurant in London, Elton John goes there, you have got to be a somebody just for them to let you through the door.

The attentful Ted was waiting by the Jag down in the street and as we stepped out he threw away his ciggy and opened the car door, I felt like a princess which was just how I was treated when we got to Spencer's, as for The Sir you would of thought he was a lord or duke the way they danced attendants on him, but then that is the treatment he gets wherever he goes, even when they don't know him they can tell instinctfully that he is a VIP.

Whilst I did not see any famous faces you could almost smell the money in that room, there could not of been a man there under the rank of millionaire and there was enough fur hanging off the backs of the women's chairs to start a zoo with. The Sir seemed to know just about everybody in the room, as we were conductored to our table he was waving and nodding and backslapping like royalty on a walkabout, I felt proud to be accomplicing him. It was all very discreetful though, diffrent again from being out with a pop personalty in some flash nightspot where everybody stares at you, here they seemed to make a point of treating you as if you were normal. But I could not help noticing the crafty looks I was getting from some of the women, they would look at me then ever so sharply at their husbands as if to say, 'I hope this is not what you get up to when my back is turned', the older ones that is, there was a fair sprinkling of younger ladies who I would say they were definitely good time girls, as for the looks I got from them they were ones of pure enviousness.

We had another dry martini which they served up with what they called crudities being radishes and that, and then we ordered. I know it was a touristy thing to do but the menu was so fabulous I asked to keep it, The Sir was not in the least embarrassed, in fact he said, 'What a charming gesture, I'm sure Gavin, he's the chef, will be honoured to learn you've insisted on taking home a permanent memento of his culinary skills, wouldn't you agree Maurice?', this being to the Mater Dee who was hoovering about bowing and scraping and saying Yes sir, No sir, Three bags full sir. So still having that menu in my position I can reveal exclusively what I had for that first memorial dinner with Sir Monty Pratt, the *Sunday*

Shocker just did not want to know, all they put was 'Over a lobster supper washed down with vintage champagne, the naughty knight asked me to spend a naughty night with him', but that is not how it was at all, Debra Chase does not give her flavours lightly and I was not yet ready for that kind of committal, as to what reely did happen we shall see, meanwhile this is the true story of what I had to eat:

Oysters Spencer (6)
(same as oysters but cooked in some way)

Lobster Newburg
(lobster in a creamy sauce)

Salad Niçoise
(turns out it was a main course, couldn't eat it all)
Fingerbowls   Hot towelettes

Tulipe de Sorbet Spencer
(yummy sorbies and fruit in a little basket you could eat)

Café
Choccy mints   Brandysnaps

But getting back to that *Sunday Shocker* scandal story of how I spent the night with The Sir, it is a lie from start to middle as Barry Butcher admitted when I was protestful that he had got it wrong, he said and I quote, 'Come on darling, if we tell it your way we're going to get to the end of Part effing One without you getting laid, that's going to sell effing papers isn't it, who the eff wants to plough through all that effing crap, come on do us all a favour or let's all go home, I mean eff me Debra either let's get it down in words of one effing syllable or eff it.' Well now at last I am telling it my way no matter how many blankety words it takes and if some of them have more than one syllabus, though – but as to how Debra Chase top model reely did finish up that night, eat your heart out Barry Butcher, you were so eager to dig the dirt you did not dig deep enough, now I am ready to reveal all about that memorous night.

What happened was this. The Sir and me were chatting merrily away through our Good Food Guide recommendal four star dinner, as I think I already said he is very easy to talk to and we jumped with no awkward pauses from one tropic to another, like frinstance travel with me telling him about Paris and Spain and how I nearly went to Badedas though I was careful not to say who with, and him mentioning modestfully that he knew Paris quite well but had never been to either of the other places mentioned but had I ever been to New York where he had some business intrests and which he said I might enjoy, talk about understatement of the year, I told him it was one of the big unreelised ambitions of my life to visit New York upon which he said, I never dreamed he reely meant it but it transposed he did, 'Then we shall have to see what can be arranged.'

Then just as I was telling him – hint hint to all you handsome millionaires out there – that my other big unreelised ambition was to get to LA as part of my long-term plans to break into the movie business, up comes the Mater Dee to tell The Sir he is wanted urgently on the blower. By the Chief Whip no less, I thought 'Hello – kinky!' but it turns out as I was to learn during my crash course on policies that the Whips are just MPs who tell all the other MPs how to vote, I always thought they automatonly voted for their own side but there you go, you learn something new every day.

Instead of The Sir having to get up and go to the phone, the phone came to him being plugged into a socket in the table lamp, the only place I had seen this done before was in Bogie's Casablanca now Thatcher's in Seathorpe, where you saw people like power shower reps and wall-cladding contractors getting themselves rung up to make an expression. Picking up the white telephone with a comical sigh as if to say an MP's work is never done The Sir said into it, 'Yes Charles, not in the least unless you'd count interrupting supper with one of my more delightful former constituents an inconvenience, what can I do for you, oh dear oh dear oh dear, so it's all hands on deck is it, hardly a bolt from the blue, not at all, what will be will be, what time are we looking at for a division, I see, very well, no, as soon as I've dealt with a particularly succulent lobster I shall esconce myself in Monument Mews and wait for the bell, not at all, but I drive a hard bargain and shall expect a good conduct mark on my report card, not at all, goodbye Charles, not at all.'

What all that was about, The Sir confidenced to me as soon as the waiter had unplugged the phone, was that for reasons way over my fluffy young head the Parliament could not be sure of getting enough votes to pass this new education law he was about to tell me about till I made it pretty clear I did not agree with education, so he had to go down and put his cross on the billet form or whatever they have to do. The Sir said, 'Frightful nuisance, who'd be an MP eh, however I'll tell you what Debra, Uncle Monty has a game plan.' Then he told me about his little flat in Monument Mews, Westminister, that Ted the driver had already tipped me off about. The idea was we would go round there and he would leave me watching the telly while he went and made his vote, then he could come back and join me for a nightcap. As the night was still young or anyway not very old this suited me fine, I thought it was very nice of The Sir to trust me not to set fire to his flat or run off with the silver spoons whilst he was gone. I must say though I did not like the way Ted winked at me when he dropped us off, cheeky so-and-so that he was.

Monument Mews I was sprised to find was a shabby little dead-end which frankly I'm not being snobbish looked as if it was inhabited by cab drivers living over their garages, but The Sir said no, nearly all the mewses were occupied by MPs on account of it being within sound of the Derision Bell, this being a bell they ring when you have to go and vote. The flatlet itself when we got up the narrow stairs was lovelee though, but simpler and of course smaller than Brook Street, just a tiny lounge, bachelor-size bedroom though with king-sized bed that took up most of it, tiny little bathroom and kitchenette. But it was ever so comfy and The Sir said he preferred it to Brook Street where he said he never felt reely at home, you could of fooled me, he always made himself at home when he was there with me, so did I come to that.

So there we were all nice and cosy. The Sir switched on the telly, opened a bottle of bubbly out of the fridge and came and joined me on the sofa where we sat watching this old *Fawlty Towers* repeat and laughing fit to be tied, he loves Basil Fawlty so I always pretended I did too though quite frankly some of it was above my head, I like a joke but whoopee cushions and slapstickle are more in my line. Anyway, somehow his arm creeps around me and my head finds its way on to his shoulder and I am just beginning to think all this talk about having to go and vote is all a big come-on when all of a sudden this bell rings out in the little hallway. I thought, 'Hello, fire alarm, has he dropped his cigar down the side of the sofa and triggered it off or what' but no, seems this was the Derision Bell. For some reason I had been thinking it was a church bell style of thing like Big Ben that would ring out all over Westminister but there you go again, that was something else I had learned, it is plugged in like electricity.

Saying, 'Ah well, do not send to know for whom the bell tolls Pratt, it tolls for thee old lad,' and 'Now I shall be back at the earliest possible moment, do help yourself to anything you need, shampoo in the fridge, brandy in that decanter over there or if you'd like to make yourself some coffee or a snack you'll find the wherewithal in the kitchen, and I shall see you very soon indeed,' The Sir pecked me on both cheeks, this being our very first kiss not the long lingering necking session in the back of the Jag whilst Ted drove slowly round and round Westminister waiting for the car phone to summon The Sir to go and vote, this was made up by Ted for the *Sunday Stunner* and embroiderised by Barry Butcher for the benefice of his *Sunday Shocker* readers.

Now, with the aid of my Sex Romps Diary, I can reveal the exclusive truth about that night. Left to my own devizes I poured some more champagne, opened a tin of cheese footballs and switched over to an old horror movie on telly, *The Waking Dead* it was called. I watched this for a bit then began to feel pleasantly drowsy so I thought I would have a quiet lie down. After ringing Auntie Doris to tell her a little white lie, namely that The Sir had invited me to an all-night sitting at the Houses of Commons followed by a champagne and kipper breakfast at the Savoy, he had told me they sometimes did this, I went into the bedroom with the idea of grabbing a few Zs before he got back. I guess I must of taken my dress off before I zonked out cos it was in a crumpled ball on the floor when I woke up, The Sir would of hung it up if he had taken it off for me being neat in his habits. Anyway, cut a long story short, when I did wake up, must of been two in the morning, there he was on the bed beside me, stark staring naked and making violent love to me. When I say violent, this is figurative of speech, he was ever so gentle reely, in fact so gentle that he nodded off himself at one stage. But one way or another, with the odd Z in between, we made love all night long, must of been four times if you count the twice when he fell asleep in the middle and the once when I did. So began my six enchantful months with The Sir or what the *Sunday Shocker* called MY NIGHTS OF BOOZE & BONKING WITH RANDY MP.

Course, I could not keep it a secret from Dad and Babs that I was having a big fling with The Sir, Auntie Doris was not backward in letting them know I was hardly ever home nights these days, so rather than have them thinking I was sleeping around with any Tom Dick or Harry I told Babs it was The Sir knowing she would tell Dad who would say sunnink like, 'She goes looking for trouble that girl, she goes looking for trouble, we can thank our lucky stars we got out of Seathorpe when we did because God only knows what they'll be saying at Rosedene and Balmoral when they hear she's cavorting round London with their own MP,' but not to me thank goodness.

What Babs said was as usual sensible and constructional: 'Look love, just so long as you know it can't last,
these things never do, have your bit of fun by all means
but don't let yourself get hurt which knowing you I don't
think you will, you've been around quite a while now so
you must know what you're getting into, got into I should
say as you already seem to be in it right up to your neck.'
I could not of put it better myself.

The Sir was I will not say head over heels in love but
he was potty over me, my every wish was his demand.
Right from the start we were out every night that's when
we didn't stay in, excepting weekends when he had to go
down to Seathorpe to meet his consistents then on to his
place in the country to share his lifestyle with his ladyship
wife Pussy. I was not in the least jealous of this as the
Sunday Shocker made out, matter of fact I was glad of
a chance to put my feet up and have a night out at Bonks
with Suzie, being as how her millionaire scaffolder Fast
Eddie was likewise expected to go down to the country
at weekends to stay with Mummy and Daddy on their
ambling estate.

Catching up with her gossip, Suzie reely seemed to of
come up smelling of roses, as well as her lovenest in
Notting Hill she was now allowed to sign all her bills at
Bonks with Fast Eddie picking them up, so the Bonko
Zonkos were on her, him rather, that's the same as the
house cocktail which is a Bonko but in a tall frosted glass.
I asked Suzie if there was any chance of a permeable
relationship with Fast Eddie and she rolled her eyes a bit
but I gathered he had problems at home, whilst not upper
class like The Sir they were quite middle drawer and would
of looked down their noses at the very idea of their
precious son shacking up with a wannabee as they would

of regarded Suzie seeing as how she was still no nearer to being a top model, unlike yours truly who was at it from morning till night, modelling I mean!

But getting back to my steamy affair with Sir Monty Pratt MP and whatever his medals were, I know he had a lot of them cos one night when I met him back at the Brook Street flat after a regimenial dinner he had to go to he was wearing all these ribbons, not for long though as when he had to go out for the evening he always left strict orders for me to wait in the bedroom for him so after coming in to say hello and pour himself a glass of champagne out of the ice bucket that was always on the go he would invariously go straight into the bathroom and change into the famous silk pyjamas that Barry Butcher seemed so fascinating by, maybe he would of liked a pair himself, The Sir had four sets that I knew of, dark green, vermillion, dark blue and lemon, they were rather yukky colours frankly, course if I said as much this just gave him the excuse to take them off quicker! Sunnink else you did not read in the Barry Butcher version of Debra Chase By Herself.

I guess we had lunch two or three times a week and supper most weeknights, at first always in reely posho restaurants but then for a change when I thought he was looking tired we started to have the aforetomentioned indoor picnics, fetched in by Ted complete with snide looks specially if he chanced to glimpse me in the wispy black negligent The Sir had bought for me, not to mention a lot of other unmentionables, I had quite a wardrobe before long, some of it quite kinky, this was at the Brook Street flat, he would not let me leave so much as a lipstick at Monument Mews, he said Pussy sometimes used the place if she had to come up to Town for any reason, she would not use Brook Street as she said it looked like a high-class tart's boudoir, I wonder how she knew, takes one to know one I spose, anyway I think I have got good taste and I thought it was reely elegant, still do.

As Ted had already told me, The Sir loved partying, it was champagne and canopies somewhere or other every night. Most of these he took me to but a few he didn't, these usually being held at the Houses of Commons and to do with policies I guess, because he would say, 'You won't mind sitting this one out my dear, I have to work with the blighters therefore I'm obliged to socialise with them to some extent but there's no reason why you should suffer, I really don't think you'd take to them, they'd cramp your style.' On these evenings I would be picked up by Ted at wherever my last modelling assignation of the day might of been and driven to Brook Street where I would have a bath, change into something pretty, pour myself a glass of champagne and wait for The Sir to return.

As I say, I did not like Ted's manner at all, always coming out with things like, 'So it's staying in time again tonight is it Debra, you don't want to let him overdo it, you know he's got a heart condition don't you, one night of madness too many and it could be the end of the good life for you and me both, know what I mean girl?' I just didn't know how to handle these remarks, I spose I should of told him to mind his own business and not be so impersolent but I just couldn't bring myself to get on my high dungeon, way you're brought up I reckon, I knew whatever I said he'd be thinking, 'Don't you come the high and mighty with me girl, you're as common as I am and you know it' so I just used to sit it out in the back seat staring fixily in front of me and saying nothing, even then he could not take the hint, he'd just give his dirty laugh that he had then go 'Do I shock you Debra, eh, eh, eh, go on, you know what they say girl, if you can't take a joke you shouldn't have joined.'

Anyway, came the day, night rather, when Ted went too far. It was one of those evenings when The Sir had to go to some thrash he couldn't take me to, No 10 Downing Street respection for some visiting bigwigs from Russia or Bulgaria or wherever. We had had lunch together, a lovely lunch it was at the Savoy River Room, and over the coffee and port for him, brandy for me, he murmured in my shell-like what he would like me to wear that evening, something he always did if I was going to be waiting for him at the flat instead of going out with him.

Thinking I would give Ted's running commentary a miss for a change I made my own way to Brook Street by cab after doing a bit of shopping and having a quick drink with Suzie at the American Bar & Grill in Dover Street, somewhere else where Fast Eddie let her sign the bill I noticed, also the outfit she was wearing defnitely did not come from Chelsea Girl. Good for Suzie I thought, but I bet she did not have lunch at somewhere like the Savoy today or she would not be eating all those crisps which she could not afford to do anyway if she had ever made it as a Page Three Popsy. Knowing The Sir was due back around eight I got to the flat about half sixish, had my bubble bath and changed into the French maid's uniform he loved me to wear for our indoor picnics – saucy lace cap, even saucier frilly apron being completely seethrough, black basque, black net stockings and high heels. Then I arranged the smoked salmon canopies, shrimp boats and caviare on Ritz biscuits that Ted had fetched in from Fortnum & Mason's, and sat down in front of the telly to wait.

Just after eight the entryphone buzzes as I expected. No, he would not of forgotten his key, it was just that on our stay-at-home evenings when he had me wearing my French maid's uniform he liked me to go through this little ridicual of picking up the entryphone and singing out, 'I am sorree, ze mistress is not at 'ome but if you would like to come up you will find Fifi ze maid all alone and waiting for you,' which I had to do in a French dialect whilst pressing the buzzer to let him in. As I have already told the world in the *Sunday Shocker*, I did not mind these private games, they made him happy and they did nobody any harm so what was I doing wrong?

What I did mind though was that after going through the usual rigmoral when I was stood there in the hallway in my French maid's gear holding a tray of canopies and getting ready to curtsy as the lift came up, who should step out of it but Ted the driver, grinning all over his mug and his eyes sticking out like chapel hat pegs as Auntie Doris always says, I wouldn't of minded but he didn't even take his cap off.

Licking his lips and helping himself to a shrimp boat Ted said, 'Well well well so this is what the old bugger gets up to when my back is turned is it, stone the crows and I suppose other nights it's whips and thigh boots is it or is it black plastic macs?'

I wasn't so much frightened as furious, but stupid with it. I just stood there with my tray letting Ted feast his mince pies on what if he had had a camera would of cost him £1,200 minimum, I was petrifried I guess, the thought did cross my mind to drop my tray and rush into the bedroom, but then the other thought crossed my mind that if I did he would see my bare bum so I didn't move, there I was holding out my tray as if offering him another canopy so course, this gives Ted the wrong idea.

Leering at my boobs he said, 'Looks like your lucky night Ted, get in there my son, help yourself, to the food I mean Debra, coar these are good, you must invite me up here more often.' With this he was stuffing himself with canopies so fast I was afraid there would be none left for The Sir when he got back.

Still standing there like an unzipped nana I said, 'Where's Sir Monty, he was expecting to be back by now, why aren't you waiting for him coming out of No 10?'

Ted gave his dirty laugh. 'Coming out? Falling out more like. I've taken him back to Monument Mews, he's pissed as a fart, I tell you Debra I've seen that man arseholed in my time but never in this state, Christ knows what he was pouring down his throat in there but he was definitely feeling no pain, he couldn't even get out of the bloody Jag by himself, then I had to drag him up all those bloody stairs, anyway I got his shoes and tie off and laid him out like lamb and salad, he'll be spark out till morning. So.' And shoving another anchovy on toast in his mouth Ted starts rubbing his greasy hands.

I said, 'How do you mean, So?' though course I already knew the answer, I may not be quick but I'm not thick.

'So when the cat's away the mice get down to a bit of rumpoh. Now Debra, you know you fancy me, we're two of a kind so come on girl get them off, whoops, my mistake, you've got them off already haven't you, good, that'll save a bit of time.'

I did not mess about. I said, 'All right Ted, I'm only going to say this once. You lay a finger on me and two things'll happen. One, you'll get this tray of canopies right in the mush and two, I'll march straight to that phone in there, ring Savile Row police station and tell them you've raped me whether you have done or not, and I mean that Ted so if you don't believe it just try me.'

'Oh, I believe you Debra but there's just one little thing you haven't worked out girl, that's if you're going to ring the Old Bill whether you get screwed or whether you don't get screwed I might just as well get on with it because it's your word against mine either way, and incidentally I wouldn't give much for your word, not in that gear.' But Ted knew I wasn't bluffing, whilst I knew that he was.

I said very calmfully, though I don't usually swear, I don't believe in it, 'Eff off Ted, and we'll pretend this hasn't happened, now do yourself a favour, just get in that lift and go.' Which after a bit of chuntering about how I'd led him on and how I was going to get myself in big trouble one of these days, he finally did. It was only then that it hit me, I started shaking so much that as I carried the tray of canopies back into the kitchen I dropped it, luckily Ted had polished off so many there wasn't much of a mess to clean up.

Did I keep my promise to forget about what happened, or rather what would of happened if Debra Chase had not held her head? No I did not, I am not vindictious but I think men like Ted need locking up. I was straight on the phone to Monument Mews, I let it ring and ring being quite determinal to speak to The Sir if I had to hang on till five in the morning. At last he answered in a blurred voice. I said, 'Monty, it's Debra, I know you're sleeping it off but I've got to see you, it's important, I'm coming round at once.'

Course, when a girl says that to a man it usually means one thing and one thing only, sillee Debra, didn't think.

But the affect of it was that the shock must of sobered him up cos as my cab bumped down the cobbles of Monument Mews there he was in his shirt sleeves and red braces standing in the doorway, clutching a big tumbler of Scotch and looking worried.

He was still smashed out of his brains of course, there is no use saying he wasn't but he was not stupid with it, he never is, fact he once told me he had to make a speech on the Commons Market at this big dinner when he could hardly stand, he was so drunk that after he had sat down he could not remember a word he had just said yet there in the next morning's *Daily Telegraph* was this long report of his speech and as he said in his own words, 'and first-class it was too, one of the best I've ever made!' So when we got up into the lounge and he had poured me a brandy for my nerves, he had no trouble taking in the whole story as I sobbed it out. He didn't ask any questions, no did I invite Ted up or encourage him in any way style of thing, he just said very quietly when I had finished, 'He'll go first thing in the morning of course, I'm dreadfully sorry you've had this ordeal my child, I'm utterly to blame, had I not made such a pig of myself on two hundred proof vodka I should have twigged that Ted was bringing me back to Monument Mews contrary to his instructions.'

'So he had it all worked out, I hadn't cottoned on to that,' I said. Come in, Debra!

'Oh yes, it's happened before,' The Sir said. I didn't ask who with, just felt very special that when it came to his driver making passes at me that was it, he is out on his ear.

'Happily, apart from a very unpleasant experience you've come to no lasting harm or I should never have forgiven myself,' The Sir said. 'Now take off your coat while I pour us a little drink and let's try to forget all about it, shall we?'

It was only as I slipped my coat off I remembered I was wearing only my French maid's outfit underneath, minus the little cap of course, I had just thrown on my coat and rushed out of the flat and into a taxi.

You should of seen The Sir's face when he saw me revelled in my saucy uniform, he was so funnee, his mouth just dropped open, if he had been wearing an eyeglass it would of fallen into his whisky.

'You are magic, Debra,' said The Sir when he had got his breath back. 'There's no one to touch you, no one.' Then he gave a little cough which told me what was coming next as I had heard that little cough before. 'Unfortunately, after what I've taken on board today, I'm afraid it's one of those occasions when the spirit is willing but the flesh is weak.'

'Don't worree sillee, we'll just snuggle up and talk,' I said, and that's what we did, just sat there sipping our drinks and chatting about nothing in particlar, I felt reely peaceful and happy after my upset.

After a bit The Sir closed his eyes and went all quiet and I thought he had nodded off. We had been talking about how he was going to take me to the Ritz the next evening, I had been rather nagging him to I'm afraid, so I just sat there contentfully, thinking about what I was going to wear. Then suddenly, without opening his eyes again, The Sir said in this sad, distance-sounding voice, 'You know Debra, the more time we spend with one another the more I find myself wishing I were someone other than who I am. What do I mean by that, I mean that had I been I won't say an ordinary run of the mill sort of chap since no one is more ordinary or less bright than old Monty Pratt but let me say had I been plain John Smith without any of one's special responsibilities, perhaps you and I might have looked forward to a more permanent future.'

I don't know about The Sir being less bright than anyone else, he is one of the brightest men walking this earth, but he certainly did not have his wits around him this particlar evening, must of been the booze, because as I pointed out, 'But if you were plain John Smith you wouldn't be taking me to the Ritz tomorrow evening, would you?'

The Sir roared with laughter and cried, 'You're perfectly right as usual you little rascal, I should never have brought the subject up, let's have another drink and talk about something else, after all no regrets are worth a tear.'

Aren't they, Monty love? In that case why was one rolling slowly down my cheek?

13

Everything's Coming Up Rhubarb

I can pinpoint exactly when it all started to go wrong, it was when Dad and Babs had been back down to Seathorpe for the South-east Coast Bossa Nova quarter-finals and next time I saw Babs she said, 'Oh by the way, I'm afraid I've got some sad news for you, you remember that gay bloke you used to work for at Mr Scissors, well they were both gay weren't they but it's that Gerald I'm talking about, only I'm afraid he's dead, killed himself.' Seems that he and Mr Scissors had split up again, this time over a new slim-waisted blond apprentice Mr Scissors had taken on, Mr Gerald had blown his top again and it all got too much for him, he drunk a bottle of brandy neat then slit his throat with one of Mr Scissors' own razors, blood everywhere, it was horrible.

Now whilst I would not call myself supercilious I do believe in Fate, and it so happens that only the day before Donna Bella Rosa had read in her tallow cards that I was in for a bumpy ride on life's roller coaster and that my past would come back to hunt me. Now you do not reach the ripe old age of nineteen without having a bit of a past so I had no idea who or what this could mean, I had no way of narrowing it down. What I should of learned from the terrific death of Mr Gerald was that it was the Seathorpe connection, Babs's news was an amen.

Before the bad news though there was the good news. Well, bad and good I should say reely cos it involved a bit of a bust-up with Auntie Doris but as I had seen this coming for a long time I was not sorry to get it over with. One thing you learn when you are as successful as Debra Chase is that there is a lot of jealousy in this world and there was no shortage of it in Sydenham, particly in Auntie Doris's council block. Talk about the sniffy neighbours at Rosedene and Balmoral, these were ten times worse, you would of thought I was something that had crawled up out of the drains when I passed them on the steps. Instead of saying, 'Fancy us living in the same flats as the famous Debra Chase, she may be one of Britain's top models but it has not gone to her head, she is still not too stuck up to say good-morning, doesn't she look fantastic, wish I could wear a boob-tube dress and get away with it,' they seemed to be saying, 'Look at the little madam, have you seen the length of that skirt I wonder she bothers to wear one at all, do you know what time she came waltzing in last night this morning more like, talk about home with the milk yet you'd think butter wouldn't melt in her mouth.'

Personly I couldn't give a toss what they said, let them get on with it, if they wanted to be nice I would be nice back, if not they could do the other thing. Auntie Doris took the same line at first, she has always kept herself to herself and never had a lot to do with the neighbours anyway. But everything changed after The Sir gave Ted the big E and hired a new chauffeur, on my recommendal he took on Kanji who used to be my reglar driver with Sydspeed Minicabs, now if Kanji has a fault it is that he will slam the car door no matter how many times you tell him. So course, he's driving me home at four, five in the morning – even breakfast time if I've slept the night at Brook Street, and each and every time it's the same rigmoral – gets out, goes round to the passenger door and helps me out just as he has been told to by The Sir who always insisted on me being treated like a lady, then slams it shut fit to wake the dead or anyway the neighbours. Course, there is a lot of curtain twitching and what do the neighbours see, they see this coloured guy who they know used to be a minicab driver now swanning around in this gleaming black Jag, so they add two and four together as they think and start putting it about that Debra Chase has got a dark-skinned jiggler to who she has made a prezzie of about £30,000-worth of motor.

Now to me it does not matter if a bloke is as black as a hatter so long as his heart is in the right place and he has plenty of plastic in his pocket, joke, but I am afraid Auntie Doris is a bit prejusticed in that regard and sad to say she got very upset when the neighbours not only complained about being woken up at all hours but also started making sly insinuendoes about who I was coming home with. On top of this she had also got a letter from the council asking was it true she was taking in lodgers, I guess that was the neighbours' doing too, I tried to convict her that being her niece I was family so did not count as a lodger specially as I was not paying rent but this cut no ice at all with Auntie Doris, once she has got an idea in her noodle there is no shifting it, she grumbled, 'You don't know the council like what I do Debra, they can do what they like, they can throw you out into the street if they've a mind to and anyway there's no denying you are a lodger because that's what you do, you lodge here, it's a place to hang your clothes up that's when you do hang them up, besides which I'm not saying I agree with what the neighbours are saying behind your back, you've got your life to live and you're only young once as Babs always reminds me when I mention it to her in any way, but honestly I've got to say it Debra because it's beginning to prey on my mind, I really think it'd be better all round if you went your own way and found a place of your own where you can be among your own friends, it makes sense for you and it makes sense for me, I don't like upsets not with my chest, I just want some peace of my mind and besides I could do with that spare room back.'

'So what you're saying is it's time I moved on,' I said. No one can say Debra can't take a hint. 'I think you're right, Auntie Doris, I've assumed on your good nature too long and I'll start looking for a flat first thing tomorrow morning.' I would of gone on to of thanked her for putting up with me but she had started sniffling by now so I let her grab hold of her bag of mint imperials and disappear into her bedroom for a good farewell cry I guess.

First thing tomorrow I'd gone and said. Yes, well that was a bit difficult, wasn't it, cos flats cost money and at that moment in time the Debra Chase No 1 Account had exactly £917 83p in it, this being because though the money was still rolling in hand over heel I had put another few grand into the Debra, Babs and Eric Chase Academy of Dance to meet unexpected contagions such as Dad's and Babs's salaries which were not yet being met by what was coming in, plus I had made an investiture in another of Babs's business brainwaves, yes you've guessed it, the Debra Chase Diet Nibble Muffin. It was only selling in Mrs Aspinall's Bun in the Oven Bakeries in Seathorpe at prez, just to see how it went style of thing, so here again there was not a lot coming in, in fact there was zilch coming in, whereas what with paying the marketing consulate plus local advertising plus the special packaging plus the two-colour Debra Chase Diet Sheet you got with each muffin et cetera et cetera; there was quite a few bob going out.

Anyway, The Sir had once said to me, 'Now should you ever find yourself in any kind of trouble at all, Debra, I don't want you to imagine that because you're one independent lady and we happen to lead separate lives that you have to keep it to yourself, I want you to come and see me and then we'd sort it out and see what's to be done, is that clear, remember Uncle Monty's a Member of Parliament until rumbled by the electorate, I've some small experience in solving other people's problems and one does have certain contacts in this big bad world.' This was after that nasty turn with Ted when The Sir had got his wires twisted and thought for a while that I was in more trouble than what I was. So I did no more, I put my Auntie Doris problem on his plate. Luckily it was one of our indoor picnic nights so he was in a good mood, not that I ever saw him in a bad mood at least not with me, but I mean relaxed style of thing.

I must say The Sir was marvellous, there is nobody like him. He just listened to what I had to tell him then pouring us both a glass of champagne from the bedside ice bucket he said playingly, 'So that's the position is it, but I understood you had a problem, what problem, goodness me to hear you talk one would think you'd been reduced to living in a cardboard box on the Embankment!'

'But I have, practicly!' I wailed.

'Nonsense child! You've a roof over your head here at Brook Street for as long as I'm chairman of Pratt's Pork Pies Ltd, and you can jolly well move in your things tomorrow morning.'

He was so good to me, The Sir, I cry sometimes when I think how I paid him back for it, all I can say is that I never meant to let him down and it was for the best of motivations, but more of that in my last Chap, first let us get Debra Chase installed in her luxuriant Mayfair pad in Brook Street. Course, I had been half living there for ages but only when The Sir was in residents, frinstance I had never spent a weekend there. This was something else again, just the thought of being only a five minute cab ride away from Bonks on a Saturday night was pure bliss, I couldn't wait to tell Suzie.

'Only one thing, hardly worth mentioning,' The Sir said with that little cough he always gave when he had something embarrassful to say. 'Of course your life remains completely your own but by way of a proviso I'd as soon you didn't entertain anyone here in my absence, I'm quite sure the thought would never cross your mind but it's as well to have these things established, now up you get off that pretty little botty and crack open another bottle of shampoo.'

Now whatever Ted might of written in the *Sunday Stunner*, I never took anyone round to that flat, he had been sacked long before I moved in so how would he know unless he was up on the roof across the street with a pair of binoglers, wouldn't put it past him. All right, so I might of let the odd bloke take me out to supper if The Sir was away but no way would I of brought anybody back, in fact the only people ever to see me at home in my luxuriant Mayfair pad until I split with The Sir were Suzie and Barry Butcher of the *Sunday Shocker*, and I wish it had only been Suzie. Course, Dad and Babs came round once but they're familee, I invited them over for Sunday tea with smoked salmon canopies from Fortnum

& Mason's, Auntie Doris was asked too but she couldn't come, wouldn't come more like, Babs said she would of felt out of place. Must say Dad was most impressive though, he said, 'My my my, she has done well for herself, she has done well for herself, and you say he doesn't expect you to pay rent Debra, well that's one expense less, just as well with the bills we've got coming in.'

But I made mention of Barry Butcher. The Debra Chase story is coming up to the point where I first met him. This was one Saturday night at Bonks, where else, they say if you sit long enough in Bonks everyone you know swims before your eyes. I was sposed to be meeting Suzie so's I could take her back to show off my Mayfair pad but I guess she got a better offer from Fast Eddie. So there I was in the Magic Circle having a quiet Pussyfoot with ex-hellraiser Shakespeare actor Tony Trent who I once quite fancied but nothing ever came of it so I think he must of been gay, when in trolls Colin with this big burly bloke who if he had been wearing a tux instead of a blue lightweight suit with his belly flopping over his trousers I would of taken for one of the club bouncers. Colin of course looked a complete nerd as usual, it was the Chicago gangster look this time, pinstripe suit, black shirt, slouch hat, he looked like an infloatable George Raft. Having found a table Colin beckons me over, being as how whilst he was now a member of Bonks he was not allowed in the Magic Circle on account of being such a pratt, they would only let him in at all cos of being one of my staff.

Speaking conspirationally which took some doing as it is very difficult to talk out of the side of your mouth and chew a toothpick at the same time, Colin said, 'Debra, I want you to come over and meet Barry Butcher of the *Sunday Shocker*, he's a good guy, he's going to give you a big plug for the Diet Muffin, just wants a few quotes, you know the kind of thing, even Debra Chase worries about her weight now I want to share my secret, that kind of crap, it could be just the boost you need for going national with the product and I'm not even asking for a percentage now aren't I kind.'

'Lovelee,' I said, flashing a big smile at Barry Butcher who was sitting a few feet away. Never let it be said that Debra Chase turns up her nose at a bit of free publicitee.

'Just one thing,' said Colin. 'Whatever you do don't mention this Dial-a-Thrill Hot Line crap you've been doing on the quiet because it'll do you no good at all if that gets out, I only hope and trust it doesn't come to Rosa's ears, she'll go bald, I'm surprised at you Debra, I know what these people pay and it's peanuts, if you needed a few crinklies on the side you should've come to me and I could've got you the Bottom Line slot on *Stag Mag*, rear view only, pays in readies, no picture credit, Rosa needn't have known anything about it.'

I honestlee didn't know what he was going on about. Course, by now I had completely forgotten recording that Naughty Nurse demo with Julian James in his Earls Court pad whilst awaiting my Page Three debit, he had said I was not suitable so course I thought he had destructed the tape and that was that. How nave can you get.

Seeing me look blank Colin said, 'They've just started puffing you in this week's *Sunday Sleaze*, you probably didn't see it.' No I did not, the *Sunday Sleaze* is a rag I wouldn't touch with a barber's pole, it makes the *Sunday Shocker* look like the *Watchtower*. Colin goes on, 'It's just one little panel tucked away in the sex aids pages and they only run these tapes for four weeks so we might just get away with it unless you've done any more have you?'

I shook my head dazingly. 'And they didn't give you sight of the copy, Debra Chase tells her saucy sex secrets in I Was A Naughty Night Nurse, over eighteens only?'

I said spiritfully, 'This attempt to cash in on the name of Debra Chase has been done without my knowledge and without my permission and I shall be consulting my legal adviser first thing tomorrow morning.' This was one of the lines we had had to memorify at Donna Bella Rosa's School of Fashion in our lesson on how to deal with the meejah. 'Besides, Colin, I needed the monee.'

'That's your story and you're sticking to it,' said Colin. But by now Barry Butcher had got impatient and was lumbering across to us holding a big glass of whisky which he can drink till it comes out of his ears, saying, 'Are you doing this effing interview Colin or am I, hello Debra, stone me you don't get many of them to a pound,' this being a referral to my boobs.

'You have to take Barry as you find him,' said Colin smirkfully as he introduced us.

'I didn't find him, you did,' I flashed back.

Barry thought this was funny, one thing about him he never takes offensive. 'Right, eff off Colin, I've got an edition to catch, talk to you later,' he said, and with that he marches me across to his table where I ordered a wet martini, that's the same as a dry martini but with sweet vermouth on cracked ice. I thought we would at least have a bit of smalltalk till my drink arrived, someone once told me that good reporters like to lull you into a false sense of secureness style of thing but not Barry Butcher, he lights a fag, gets out his notebook and says, 'Right, we don't have much time Debra, this is for tomorrow's paper, so tell me all about this Diet Muffin, does it really work because I could do with losing a few pounds myself, now according to the leaflet anyone following the Debra Chase Muffin diet can lose up to fourteen pounds in a fortnight, now I find that very hard to believe so convince me.'

It's funnee how Barry Butcher gets results cos I knew exactly what he was doing, it was as if he'd dug a big hole in the ground and said, 'Right Debra, I want you to jump into this.' But like a fool I did just that.

Suddenly it was Get Debra Chase time. Course, I had a fairly good idea that Barry Butcher was going to do a knocking job but I had no idea what a slagging the Diet Muffin was in for. But that was not the only shock in store for me that Sunday morning.

I woke up early, well early for me on a weekend, tennish, put on the coffeemaker, then climbed into my jeans and went round to Berkeley Square for the Sunday papers. I get all of them except the *Sunday Sleaze* and the heavies – *Sunday Shocker, Sunday Screamer, Sunday Stunner, Sunday Mirrow, Sunday People* and *News of the World*. Course, as I picked the papers off the stand I had eyes only for the *Sunday Shocker*. There I was plastered all over page one under the big black headline, EXCLUSIVE! TRUTH ABOUT DEBRA'S MUFFIN! Then at the bottom of the page it said in more big black letters, HOW I PUT ON 10 LBS WITH DEBRA'S DIET, SEE MIDDLE PAGES. Luckily with my hair up and no make-up except for last night's mascara the newsvendor did not reconise his famous customer, I was not in the mood for the legpulling I would of got.

Tucking the other papers under my arm I skimmed the story on the way back to my Mayfair pad. The front page story wasn't reely all that bad except that everything I'd said to Barry Butcher was twisted round, like frinstance where I had said, 'As it so happens I can take you to a lady who did lose fourteen pounds in a fortnight but I've never said anybody can do it, in fact if you read my Diet Sheet you'll see it says it can be harmful to take too much off by eating the Diet Muffin and nothing else, you've got to have a proper balanced diet,' this came out as, 'Debra could name only one woman to back claims that followers of the Muffin Diet can shed fourteen pounds in a fortnight but she warned, "The way she did it was dangerous. I wouldn't recommend it." So why does her Diet Sheet make no mention of the dangers? Pouted the curvy top model, "It should have done but I didn't write it."'

But it was the middle page spread that was the reel gobsmacker. DEBRA, LOOK WHAT YOU'VE DONE TO ME was the headline, under it being these two full length pictures of the same woman, one of her looking fairly thin and one of her looking fairly fat. They were like those *before* and *after* pix you see in the slimming mags, except that here the *before* was the thin one and the *after* the fat one if you see what I mean. As I walked along looking at them I was thinking, 'Hello, I know that face.' Then I read the captions: 'Before the Muffin Diet, Jessie was a trim 8st 9lbs . . . After: plump Jessie tips the scales at a whopping 9st 5lb.' Yes, it was the one and the same cow who used to give me the runaround at Mr Scissors, well you waited a long time to get your revenge on your little assistant for becoming the success you could never be, didn't you Jessie? I only hope it was worth it cos I heard later that Mr Scissors fired her for losing one of his best customers namely Mrs Aspinall of Aspinall's Bun in the Oven Bakeries, Jessie took him to the Industrious Tribunal but she lost I'm happy to say, just serves her right.

The phone was ringing as I stepped out of my private lift into my luxuriantly-appointment flat. It was Colin wanting to say how sorree he was, I couldn't stop him babbling on, he was going, 'I feel really bad about it Debra, honestly I thought he was a mate, I've given him quite a few tips in the past and he's never let me down, I sincerely thought he was going to give you a plug, how he got hold of that Seathorpe woman I've no idea, I just happened to bump into him in the pub and he asked what you wer up to these days so I said the Debra Chase Diet, not a bad story, you can have it exclusive, all right Debra admitted I should have cleared it with you, what can I say except I'm sorry but as for that other story, I suppose you've seen the *Sunday Screamer*, I hope you don't think I'd anything to do with that, just one of life's coincidences I suppose.'

Course, in all the excitement of reading the *Sunday Shocker* exposal I hadn't so much as glanced at the other papers. I said, 'What other story, Colin?'

He said, 'You'd better take a look at it, Debra.'

I riffled through my bundle of tabloids and found the *Sunday Screamer*. DEBRA'S SLEAZELING SEX CHAT. The full steamy story of how sultry-voiced top model Debra Chase cashed in on her fame by teaming up with porn prince Julian James to make a sleazy 38p per minute Dial-a-Thrill Hot Line tape recounting the saucy sex romps of a nympho night nurse. Punchdrunk though I was I read it through to the very last paragram which was, 'Dirty-talk Debra was in hiding last night but a close friend said, "She did it when she needed the money before she found fame. But this attempt to cash in on the name of Debra Chase has been done without her knowledge and without her permission and she will be consulting her legal adviser first thing tomorrow morning.""

Only one person could of given them that quote and that was the person to who I had given it in Bonks the night before. I may not be very bright but I did not have to have a very high ID to figure out why Colin had been so keen for me not to mention the Naughty Nurse tape to Barry Butcher, it was plain as a pikelet – having sold the Diet Muffin exclusive to the *Sunday Shocker* he thought he would make another thirty pieces of loaves and fishes by selling the Dial-a-Thrill Hot Line exclusive to the *Sunday Screamer*. As for him not knowing anything about the Jessie angle in Barry Butcher's story, pull the other one, I later got it from Barry himself that it was Colin who suggested he should go down to Seathorpe and get a snap of the woman behind the Debra Chase Diet Nibble Muffin, namely Mrs Aspinall, I had stupidly told Colin how she was built like a barrel. So Barry goes down to sniff out the story and with the devil's own luck happens to pop into the Bun in the Oven Bakeries just as Jessie is making a big scene with Mrs Aspinall over having gained weight and wanting her money back. Thank you Colin, thank you very much indeed.

I was more sad than angry. Although he was a total nerd I had always looked on him as a mate. Shopping me like that was so ungrateful. All right, so he had done a lot for me but I had done a lot for him. Why Colin, why? Why kill the goose that lays the golden apple? Greed, I spose, plus all that stupid fancy gear he was buying could not of come cheap, plus I did hear he had begun to snort a certain white powder up his nostrils so he must of needed the money.

Sorree Colin, end of a beautiful friendship.

He was still holding on. I picked up the phone and said just three words, 'Colin, you're fired.'

That was a long Sunday. As luck would have it Donna Bella Rosa would have to of picked that particlar week in my life to go into hospital for some tests, don't ask me what, she didn't say and I didn't ask, I can't stand illness, so I couldn't look to her for comfort. Babs rang, having heard about the Diet Muffin exposal in a histrionical phone call from Mrs Aspinall, but all she was concerned about apart from our investiture going down the drain which was not her money anyway was what affect the bad publicitee would have on the Debra, Babs and Eric Chase Academy of Dance. Wait till you see the *Sunday Screamer*, Babs! Still no Suzie, turns out Big Eddie had taken her off for a dirty weekend in Paris to celebrate some important news, but more of that in my next Chap.

Until The Sir got back there was no one else to turn to. I was not going to slink my pride and call Brian, anyway who says he would be speaking to me after our bust-up, and though I had an address book bulging with names there was no one else I wanted to talk to. I never felt so all alone, reelising that apart from Suzie, The Sir and Rosa and all right Dad and Babs and my Mum if I knew where to find her, I had no reel friends, just acquaintals. Funnee how you can go to bed with someone and think you are best mates but when the crunch comes you reelise they were just ships that passed away the night as Babs would say. I guess I never had time to strike up any reel lasting relationships, that is the price of fame, it is lonely at the top.

Luckily for me, instead of coming back Monday

morning as usual The Sir was returning to Town that same evening as he had a meeting first thing, so I had his homecoming to look forward to. I tidied up the flat, I could of kept on The Sir's cleaning woman if I had wanted to but I did not want her prying into my things, then after watching a bit of telly and reading the rest of the papers over a box of chocs I prepared a simplistic supper of quails' eggs which he adores and smoked salmon, put a bottle of champagne in the ice bucket then made myself pretty for The Sir's arrival back.

Talk about a shoulder to lean on, he was fantastic. The before and after pix of Jessie in the Diet Muffin spread had him roaring with laughter so much that the tears ran down his face. For a few secs I thought The Sir was being unfeeling but then I saw that I had got everything out of perceptive and that there was a funnee side, as he said all it meant was that no way was the Debra Chase Diet Nibble Muffin ever going to be a rival to Limmits, it was not the end of the world, all right so I would lose a few grand but The Sir seemed to think I would of lost out anyway cos speaking as a businessman he said, 'Quite frankly my dear, had you asked my advice I should've said buy South Sea Bubble shares instead, however what's done is done, why not put it down to experience.' That reely made me feel better.

The *Sunday Screamer* sleazeline story he took a bit more seriously, after going on about the gutter press in his best tub-bumping manner he said I had a clear case for liable but here again he was ever so wise, he said if I went to court they would only start blackening my name whilst if I kept up a dignitised silence like the Royal family the story would die a natural death. Not a word of critical-ness about my stupidly having made the Naughty Nurse tape in the first place, you will notice. This not only made me feel better, it made me feel good.

But it was what The Sir had to say next that had me reely over the moon. Opening another bottle of champagne he said, 'The great thing is not to take this kind of nonsense too seriously, my goodness me when I think of the stick I've taken from the press over the years I could have spent half my days in litigation, yes and half my income in lawyers' fees, but life's too short Debra, stick those filthy little rags in the wastepaper basket and put them out of your pretty little head, that's my advice to you, besides you have better things to occupy your mind this week, I find I have to go to New York on Thursday and I really do feel I ought to have a secretary in tow but my otherwise excellent Miss Binns is afraid of flying so what do you say to that, wouldn't you like a few days in New York, hm, hm, hm, hm?'

The reason he had to keep hm'ing away at me like that was I couldn't answer, I just gawped at him, I was that numbstruck, it had come like a blot out of the blue, I could not take it in. Absolutely typified of The Sir to pronounce the news in that casual way of course, he took a delight in springing sprises on me like that. I could of hugged him – not could of, did. Then I leaped up and danced round the room singing 'New York, New York!' till I stubbed my toe on a potted plant, when The Sir strongly picked me up and carried me off to bed to kiss it better.

As The Sir said I had a lot to occupy my mind, so much that I had hardly time to think. I had an American visor to make supplication for, clothes to buy, shoes to get, lists of packing to make out, stuff like that. Then I had to cancel my modelling assignations for the time we were going to be away, luckily it was a thin week for once. As I say, Rosa was in hospital but by now she had an assistant, namely her sister Beryl who used to run a typing agency, she was her spitten image. So I popped into the office to tell Beryl airfully that as I was flying to New York I would have to cancel the two or three personable appearances Rosa had got lined up for me – they were only small fries, opening a Y-Pay-More discount landscape and patio centre in Maidstone and the re-launch of a park 'n' pick paint and d-i-y store off the M25 somewhere, plus dropping in on some joint called Minders out Watford Junction somewhere to give them a photo opportunism for the local press. Beryl gave me ever such a funnee look and said no problem, as it just so happened the first two had cancelled and as for Minders they had rung up to ask if I would mind some of the national smudgers sharing the photo opportunism if they upped the fee as they had invited porn prince Julian James to drop in, which Beryl even though she did not know much about the business had turned down, reelising it would not do much for my imagery.

Personable appearance cancellings are quite common in this business, either places that are going to have grand openings have to put them off because the plasterers are still in or somebody has run away with the takings or whatever, so I did not think any more about this, just thought myself lucky to get off the hook so easy. But then I had to ring ace photograprher Mike Mooney about a photo session I was sposed to be doing for the *Daily Stunner*, I knew it was for their Summer Scorchers series, this being a sly dig at the *Daily Scorcher*, but this was not due out for yonks so I thought no worries so long as he can use up his studio booking which for Mike he just has to raise his little finger and top models will be queueing all the way along Banana Wharf. But Mike too sounded all funnee, he said, 'Ah, right, yes, no you haven't let me down Debra, in fact you might have done me a favour because the editor's been having second thoughts about the Summer Scorchers, says we do the same thing year after sodding year and why can't we come up with something that doesn't involve sodding parasols, sodding sunglasses and sipping long cool sodding drinks through sodding bendy straws, you know how he talks, so tell you what darling, let's not fix another studio date right now, let me take a raincheck on the whole concept when I know a bit more about what's in the bugger's mind, all right, have a good trip, try to get into Costello's Bar in East whatever-it-is Street, ciaow darling.'

I felt uneaseful as Mike rang off, I knew there was something wrong, something he was holding back from me, and at any other time I would of said, 'Don't give me that bull Mike, pull the other one, what's going on, is it something I've said or what, come on I've a right to know.' But the truth is I was on such a high I could not contemplate on anything else but my dream trip to the Big Apple.

Dream trip, I said. I reely did think I was in a dream a couple of days later when without knowing how I had got there, being in such a whirl and having had so much champagne to drink in British Airways business class not to mention the VIP lounge beforehand, I caught my first glimpse of the Manhattan skyline from The Sir's hired limo which I am not kidding was the length of a London bus.

'There it is my dear, that's the Chrysler Building, there's the Empire State Building, those are the World Trade

Towers and if you can see that green roof there, that's the Knickerbocker where we'll be staying.'

'Knickerbocker, sounds like Knickerbox!' I giggled, being so happy. Then I took hold of The Sir's hand and began to sing again, ever so softlee, 'New York, New York . . .'

Little did I know that New York was to be the port before the storm.

14

What's It All About, Debra?

My fun-packed days in New York are just a blur now but I can remember the highlights as if they were only last week instead of last month. Sipping cocktails in the Rainbow Room on the 65th floor I think it is or maybe 56th, anyway ever so high, of the Rockyfellow Centre. Going up the Statue of Libertine, I never knew she was hollow. Getting called Lady Pratt at the Knickerbocker Hotel cos of course that's who they thought I was, I asked The Sir what they would say if he came to New York with the reel Lady Pratt and he said they wouldn't say anything as he always stays at the Pierre. Seeing a Broadway show, forgotten its name but it was a musical and I know The Sir had to pull strings to get tickets, then having a late-night snack at the Stage Deli where all their sandwiches are named after stars and celebs, I had a Frank Sinatra, that's the same as a Dean Martin but on a different kind of bread, maybe one day I'll be able to go to the Stage Deli and order a Debra Chase, you know you have reely arrived when they name a sandwich after you.

What else? Lunch at the Russian Tea Room where I had cold bosh soup for the first time ever. Watching the Rockets at Radio City Music Hall, honestlee it is massive, I'm sprised they don't divide it up to make it into a cinecentre. Shopping in Bloomingdale's where The Sir would sometimes drop me if he had a business meeting, stuffing a big bundle of dollars into my hand and saying, 'Now off you go and buy yourself something silly, then take a cab back to the hotel and I'll see you in the suite as soon as ever I can.' Course, I knew what he meant by something silly and made sure he got a nice sprise when he returned, which he usually did in quite a bad temper for The Sir, saying, 'Blessed red tape, they're ten times worse than we are.' He didn't tell me much about who he was having his meetings with but from what I gathered the trip was not a success businesswise, he was hoping to launch Pratt's Pork Pies and Sizzlers in a big famous grocer's that they have like Fortnum & Mason's but apparently there were all sorts of snags in the food laws. Still, The Sir did not let it get him down and as soon as he had got back from his meetings and had a bit of a chunter he was ready to relax in our sumptial suit on the 29th floor of the Knickerbocker and then hit the town.

But all good things come to an end and all too soon we were sitting down to our last meal in fab New York which was brunch at the famed Waldorf Astoria. The Sir was a bit depressive at first being as how he said his board of directives would not be best pleased when he got home emptyhanded. Whether his gloom transmuted itself to me or whether I was feeling sad because our dream trip was nearly over or whether I had a forbidding of what was in store once we got home I couldn't say, maybe it was a bit of all three, but I was a bit down myself. Soon enough though we began to chirp up as the champagne took its affect, so The Sir ordered a second bottle then we had quite a few zonkos at the airport and in short got on the jumbo so squiffy that I zizzed off straight after dinner, missed the movie, shame cos it was a Jack Nicholson, and did not wake up till they were bringing round breakfast.

The Sir and me had agreed to part company at the luggage carousel, he was a bit nervous in case the airport papa ritzy were hanging about which matter of fact they were, they were snapping away like mad when I came out of Customs so it is just as well Debra Chase did not waltz out on the arm of Sir Monty Pratt, not that it made much diff at the death. Considerable as usual, The Sir had arranged for a limo to pick me up, so I was looking round for a driver holding up a bit of cardboard with my name on it when who should I spot with a fag dangling out of her mouth as usual but Donna Bella Rosa, looking grimmer than I have ever seen her. I thought, 'Hello, trouble!' and was I right or was I right!

'Come on, I've sent your driver away, we've got a lot to talk about,' said Rosa, grabbing one of my two matching suitcases and hustling me out of the arrivals lounge. I said, 'Should you be doing that when you've just come out of hospital?' but she just grunted and coughed ash down her front.

She didn't say a word till we were out of the short-term car park and heading for the M4, she reminded me of that time Dad had to pick me up at Southampton police station. I thought it was my nipping off to New York for a week without telling her that had got her throwing a moody but she didn't even mention it. All she said after a bit was, 'Well I hope you had a good trip Debra, sorry to be the one to bring you back to earth but Sunday's papers are on the back seat, you'd better have a look at them.'

I leaned over and scooped up the heap of papers, the *Sunday Shocker* was on top and I could see my picture in a big box at the top of the page and course, it is a follow-up to their Diet Muffin exposal, it was all over page seven with the headline MUM USED DEBRA'S MUFFIN AS DOORSTOP. Apparently readers had been writing in with their Diet Muffin experiences and seemingly they had all gained weight on it, well maybe they did and maybe they didn't but as for using it as a doorstop that was just plain ridiclous, you would of needed at least five Diet Muffins to hold a door open, I bet that letter was written by Barry Butcher in the office.

'And when you've digested that you'd better turn to the *Sunday Stunner*,' said Donna Bella Rosa as I skimmed through the story. I didn't reely care about the *Sunday Shocker* stuff any more, the damage was done now, so I slung it on the back seat and turned to the *Sunday Stunner*. Well, I guess you know what is coming. Small picture of smirking Ted in his chauffeur's cap. Big picture of The Sir wearing just bathing trunks and smoking a cigar, they must of got it from Ted, he had a key to the Brook Street flat for when he had to deliver the canopies and that from Fortnum & Mason's and I bet he went through it with a fine toothbrush before he left, come to think of it the snap was probly one of the ones that Babs developed for The Sir at the Seathorpe 24-hour Foto Developing Service, small world. The headline was EXCLUSIVE: MP'S NIGHTS OF PASSION BY THE CHAUFFEUR WHO SAW IT ALL. BEGINS TODAY ON PAGES 5, 6, & 7.

I won't tell you what I heard myself saying to Ted as I turned to page five but it was something I could of been arrested for if I had screamed it after him in the street which was what I felt like doing. Page five had the headline WHY PORK PIE BARONET WANTED JELLY FOR THE BELLY DANCER complete with pic of said belly dancer, she looked a right slag. The story, sposed to of been written by Ted, began, 'As chauffeur and gofer to millionaire pork pie king Sir Montague Pratt, Bart, Tory MP for Seathorpe, I was used to getting strange orders at any hour of the day and night. Once while entertaining a TV make-up girl to lobster and champagne at swish Spencer's he had me called into the restaurant and sent me to Soho to buy a certain kind of sex aid she had told him about. Another time when he was having a wild fling with an American House of Commons researcher he had me combing the West End for a two-gallon drum of whipped cream. But the weirdest request of all was when the bonking baronet took up with Jasmine, the belly dancer from Birmingham . . .'

I didn't want to read any more cos it was making me car-sick, specially with Rosa's driving, you would of thought we were on a flipping dodgem track. There was nothing I needed to know about The Sir's little piccadil-loes, I was quite aware I was not the first young lady in his life any more than he was the first man in mine, as to what he got up to with them that was no more of my business than it was of snake in the grass Ted's.

'Turn over the page,' said Donna Bella Rosa, noticing that I was not lapping the story up like two million other *Sunday Stunner* readers.

'I don't want to read it,' I said.

'I'm not asking you to read it, I'm asking you to turn over the page,' said Rosa insistfully. So I did, and there like a smack in the eye was a picture of yours truly and in big black letters the chillful words, NEXT WEEK: DEBRA'S FRENCH MAID FROLICS.

My heart turned to ice. Then I thought What a cheek, kicking the series off with a Birmingham belly dancer and not getting round to top model Debra Chase till the second week. 'They can't do this,' I said.

'They're doing it,' said Rosa.

'But the *Sunday Stunner* must know I've got a contract with the *Daily Stunner*,' I said, I mean they were under the same owners, I could only think their right head didn't know what their left head was doing. 'I'll call Mike Mooney and ask him to sort it out.'

'He's already called me, and you no longer have a contract with the *Daily Stunner*, they've cancelled,' said Rosa. 'Now I don't want you to tell me anything the whole world won't know on Sunday but your MP friend took Polaroid pictures of you in this French maid outfit, didn't he?'

'Quite a few,' I had to admit. And course, ratbag Ted had it away with them.

'So Mike Mooney told me,' Rosa said. 'They must be pretty explicit for the *Daily Stunner* to pull out.'

'I spose they were quite raunchy,' I confessionalised, and why not? What two people do in the privatisation of their own bedroom, or their own lounge, kitchenette and bathroom come to that, is nobody's business but their own, those snaps were for our eyes only, or rather for The Sir's since they turned him on more than me. 'Anyway,' I said carefreely, 'who needs the *Daily Stunner*? There's always the *Daily Screamer*.' I did a lot of their Bingo promotionalising, this being worth quite a few bob, so I saw no reason why we should not go the whole honk and become their Page Three Pet as well.

'There *was* the *Daily Screamer*,' said Donna Bella Rosa grimfully, tooting her horn at the police car in front of her. 'They're dropping you too, let's face it Debra, you're not exactly flavour of the month at the moment, it's that sleazeline story that's done the most damage so far, the Diet Muffin saga didn't help but God alone knows what the clients are going to think when the *Sunday Stunner* hits the fan, I'll be frank with you, there's a borderline in this business between going topless and going over the top, and I'm afraid it looks as if you've gone over the top.'

No mention of Colin's betrayfulness I noticed, no, it was all down to Debra, wasn't it? Still, no use crying over spilled ink.

'So what have we got lined up at the moment?' I asked Rosa. I was just itching to get back to work and put all this garbage behind me.

'As of this morning, an offer of a full frontal in the *Sunday Sleaze*, and another offer you'd do well to refuse, a place called Rambo's in Leicester want you to parade up and down their catwalk in your French maid's uniform.'

I was reely aching to meet up with The Sir again so he could pat my hand and reinsure me it was just a storm in a teapot as I knew he would. 'It'll blow over,' I said.

'Let's hope it will,' said Rosa as we zig-zagged off the motorway.

The Sir was on the phone as I reached Brook Street, he was saying, 'Very well Henry, I'll be guided by you, I'm sure you're absolutely right as always, as for the other business that's between me and my board but obviously I'll keep you posted, yes, nasty affair all round but as we've had occasion to say before let sleeping curs lie or should one say let lying curs sleep, ha, what, goodbye Henry and my thanks to you as always, goodbye.'

Seems he was talking to his lawyer who had told him that though he could take out a conjunction against Ted for stealing our Polaroid snaps, fact he could get him arrested for it, it would finish up in a big court case with his name being dragged through even more mud than it was already, mine too come to that, he said they reely put you through the mangle in these cases so his lawyer's advice was same as I had already said to Donna Bella Rosa, keep schtum and it would blow over.

I asked The Sir what Lady Pratt would make of it all but he didn't seem bothered about that angle, just chuckled roguefully and said, 'Pussy? She claims not to have read the bilge which doesn't mean to say she's not been made fully conversant with it, I expect it's the sole topic of conversation around the village, however there's little enough she can't already have heard about in one way or another, so long as I don't frighten the horses or get caught in a paternity suit she's quite tolerant of my little peccadilloes bless her heart, probably the more so because I turned a blind eye when she was having a torrid affair with the gardener's boy some years ago, shades of *Lady Chatterley's Lover*, what?' As for his consistents down in Seathorpe, seems his local Conversative party had already had a meeting and they had passed a vote of confidentiality in him, they were going to stand by him. Talk about leading a charmed life, The Sir could get away with blue murder. Only one thing bothered him and that was that the directives of Pratt's Pork Pies Ltd were not best pleased, they had called a special board meeting, still, touching wood he reckoned he could talk his way out of any trouble.

Then he said something reely sweet to me, he said, 'I'm sorry if your name is about to be dragged into that blasted man's cesspit of lies and half truths my dear, if only because it would seem to put you on a par with those other passing fancies whereas I think you know you've always meant far more to me than that. As to what I'm supposed to have got up to with those fillies I hope you'll take it with more than a grain of salt.'

I said all innocent like, 'So it's not true then, pity, I was just wondering where I could get my hands on a two-gallon drum of whipped cream,' which had him falling about. On which happy note we put the lid on our problems and took ourselves and our jet lag off to bed with a bottle of duty free champagne.

There were two messages for me on the answering machine, one from Barry Butcher asking me to give him a bell, he could take a running jump for a start, and the other from Babs saying Dad would like a word, this did not come as a trific sprise, would like a thousand words more like. The Sir had his special board meeting the next morning so rather than have Dad ranting away at me down the phone for an hour I thought I would pop over and see him and Babs with a few souvenirs from New York I had got for them, just little things like his'n'hers matching pink and blue sateen Big Apple baseball jackets, but you cannot reely shout at someone when they have just filled your arms with prezzies so I thought it worthwhile going over personly.

Although I no longer had wheels owing to my little Mini having become a write-off, The Sir said I could ride with him to the City and take the Jag on and he would get a cab back, absolutely typified of him to think of me when he had problems of his own.

Not that Debra Chase did not have problems, as I reelised soon as Kanji pulled up outside the Debra, Babs and Eric Chase Academy of Dance in Tulse Hill, cos that's just what it wasn't any more, it was now the Babs and Eric Chase Academy of Dance, yes they had taken my name off the sign.

I went down to find Babs and Dad giving dancing lessons to this old couple, honestlee they must of been about sixty, they were so gaga they would of been better off having themselves pushed round the floor in wheelchairs never mind trying to do the Liberty Two Step. Spotting Debra Chase sitting herself quietly down in the corner they both gave me ever such a filthy look, and as they finished staggering round the floor and took themselves off, this being the end of their session, the bloke said pointfully to Dad, 'I was going to ask you where I could find a decent pair of dancing pumps Mr Chase, these suede shoes seem to act like suction pads, but you've obviously got family business to discuss so we'll leave it till next week.' Cheeky sod and that's swearing.

The second he had got rid of the two old wrinklies Dad started. 'So, the wanderer returns, the wanderer returns, you might well wear dark glasses my girl, it seems we can't pick up a paper these days without you're splashed all over it.'

I let him have his rant for a bit then gave him and Babs their prezzies and that quietened him down, though I could tell he still had a lot to get off his chest. But first it's Babs's turn. 'You know I believe in live and let live flower, but you see there comes a point when what one person does can affect other people, what's that saying, no man is an island, and I'm afraid with all this bad publicity you've been getting that point's been reached.'

'Is that why you've taken my name off the sign outside?' Ask a silly question.

'We'd no option love, that kind of thing might be good for your image, I don't know, but one thing's for sure it's certainly not good for ours, the clientele we're trying to reach out for they just don't want to know about that side of life.'

'It's ballroom dancing they're looking for, not Bacchanalian orgies,' grumbled Dad, getting into his stride again. 'There's no use beating about the bush Debra, you may be my daughter but so far as this particular enterprise is concerned your name has become a liability, a liability.'

Course I was hurt, I'm not going to say I wasn't but I wasn't going to show it, not Debra Chase business lady, I was going to keep this on a strictly commercialised footling, so I said, 'Does that mean I don't have a share in the profits any more then?'

'Profits, what profits?' snorted Dad. 'There's barely enough in the kitty to pay this quarter's rent, that couple you saw going out are the only booking we've got till next Monday.'

By the sound of it the Babs and Eric Chase Academy of Dance as it was now called was doing badly enough without any help from me. I'd already gathered as much from Babs, as whenever I asked how they were getting on she would say, 'Oh, give it time' or 'Oh, it should pick up soon, we're just waiting for the dark nights.' So I thought it was a bit unfair to put all the blame on what the press was saying about their partner. Still, I wanted to be constructional so I said, 'Well, if I can help in any way,' even though I had very little laid by having plunged nearly all my spare cash into the Diet Muffin business.

Babs said, 'Well that's very kind of you petal, if you could see what you can do we'd appreciate it, just to tide us over, what we'd like to do is get a really nice colour brochure done, something high quality, you know all glossy, and then really blitz the neighbourhood with it but of course it all takes money and as your Dad says there's the running costs to keep up with, we don't want to keep crawling to you cap in hand for another sub but I'm afraid at present just till we've found our feet there's very little coming in and a lot going out.'

So the top and bottom of it was that I left Tulse Hill promising to find more capital as Dad always calls money, even though the Babs and Eric Chase Academy of Dance had nothing to do with me any more and even though for the moment I had even less work coming in than they had. Story of my life, that.

The Sir had already returned from his board meeting when I got back to Brook Street. He was sipping a zonko Scotch and looking tired and a bit glum. I asked him how it had gone and he gave a big sigh and said, 'Why oh why can't blasted people leave other people alone, my dear were we doing any harm?' I said I agreed with him all the way but that just because we were being beseeched by the press for their latest bit of scandalmongering I didn't see what business it was of Pratt's Pork Pies Ltd, it was me The Sir was asking to dress up as a French maid, not his board of directives.

The Sir shook his head saying, 'That's not quite the position, no one cares a button about my private life so long as I deliver the goods in my annual report, what concerns our great dynasty of Pratt's and all their hangers-on is your name above all others being linked with mine, you see my dear their great fear is that the Great British Public will think there's a connection with that blasted Diet Muffin venture of yours and Pratt's Pork Pies Ltd, do you see what I'm driving at?'

'But that's ridiclous!' I said protestfully. 'Just cos they're both food, I mean to say how can anyone connect the two, I mean for one thing who's going to eat pork pies when they're on a diet, pork pies make you fat!'

'So do your diet muffins by all accounts,' said The Sir patting my hand smilingly. 'But we shall see what we shall see. I'm already in my board's bad books over failing to bring home the bacon from New York, if our sales go down after the press have done their worst then they'll want my head, it's as simple as that, now let's give a cooling bottle of shampoo its freedom and leave the matter be.'

The Sir had to go down to the Houses of Commons straight after lunch, he said everyone was going to pull his leg about what Ted had put in the *Sunday Stunner* so he might as well get it over with, he was so brave, no wonder he had all those medals, so I rung up Suzie and invited her for tea at the Ritz, all right at that moment of time I could not reely afford tea at the Ritz but so what, I did not want Suzie to know that and anyway you only live once as they say.

I was just bursting to tell Suzie all about my fab New York trip and so even up the score for her having been to Badedas with Fast Eddie, and course we had to catch up with one another's news, I wanted to know what the buzz was down at Bonks about all the latest Debra Chase exposals. Some hopes. Trust little Suzie, she is full of her own news, isn't she? Seems Fast Eddie is going to set her up in her own swish nails boutique off fashionable Knights-bridge, that is what they were celebrating when he took her off on that Paris jaunt, she has always been interested in nail care so she was over the moon. Reading between the lines whilst Suzie burbled on I guessed this meant goodbye to any hopes she was clinging on to that Fast Eddie would ever marry her, you do not make a girl a prezzie of a nice little business if you are about to make her your wife and keep her in luxuries but so what? Suzie had now got securefulness whilst still keeping her freedom, talk about having your cake and chewing it twice.

I was glad for Suzie, she deserved a break but I could not help thinking Here am I, top model Debra Chase, and after nearly a year's hard work what have I got to show for it? A share in a diet muffin business that's just about to be bankruptured and an ex-partnership in a dance school that looks like going the same way. All right, so I am living a life of luxuriance in exclusive Mayfair but that is no more than my due, if I had of thought that after all that graft I would still be kipping down in the spare room of Auntie Doris's council flat in Sydenham I would of put my head in a bucket. But that plus a wardrobe full of clothes was all I had to my name, whereas look at Suzie, nice flat, accounts all over town and now this poncey nails boutique, lucky for some is all I could say.

But course, I didn't say it to Suzie, just said how knocked out I was and promised to be her first customer, then started to steer the conversation off the subject of Suzie and on to the subject of me. This was not all that difficult once she had told me all there was to tell about her nails boutique cos natch, Suzie had lapped up every word of what the tabloids had been saying about me and she couldn't wait for Ted's disclosals about my French maid romps, she wanted me to give her the full story ahead of the *Sunday Stunner*, so's she could be first with the news down at Bonks I spose.

But bless her, Suzie could see I was unhappy about the whole thing so she said comfortably, 'Don't worree Debs, it's all good' – meaning it was all good publicitee which course after my heart to heart with Donna Bella Rosa I knew it wasn't, but no way was I going to tell Suzie I was worried about the work stopping coming in so I told her what else I was worried about, or anyway what The Sir was worried about, namely people thinking the great Debra Chase Diet Nibble Muffin flop was tied up in some way with Pratt's Pork Pies.

So at this Suzie has one of her brainwaves, she said, 'That's easily taken care of, all you have to do is just.'

'Just what, Suzie?'

'Tell your side of the.'

Tell my side of the story. Got it in one, Suzie.

Well, I know now it was the most stupidest idea she had ever had in her life but at the time all I could say was 'Good thinking, Batbrain' cos it seemed to solve a lot of problems. There were no worries about who would listen to my side of the story – that I guessed was why Barry Butcher of the *Sunday Shocker* had been trying to reach me, so's he could get some spicy quotes and put a spoiler on Ted's stuff in the *Sunday Stunner*. I also knew they would pay good money. But that was not my motif for returning Barry's call right there from the Ritz. All right, the £25,000 he straightway offered for my story would come in useful to pay the bills for the Babs and Eric Chase Academy of Dance for a while as well as covering our losses on the Debra Chase Diet Nibble Muffin, but my reel reason was to help clear The Sir's name. Through the pages of the *Sunday Shocker* I could tell the world that the Diet Muffin was cooked up by that silly fat cow Mrs Aspinall and Babs between them, that every penny of the money that went into that business came out of my purse and not out of The Sir's pocket, and that he didn't even know about it till I showed him the stories in the *Sunday Shocker*, so where was Pratt's Pork Pies Ltd sposed to come into it? Course, there would have to be a bit about our love life cos that's what the readers expect but the point I wanted to get home was that though The Sir is the most generous man in the world he is not one of your Fast Eddies who sets a girl up in business just to stop her banging on about getting a ring on her finger.

That's what I thought I was going to say, anyway. Course, Barry Butcher knew different.

He was round Brook Street within the hour, bringing with him a cheque for £10,000 and saying I would get the rest when I had dished up enough for three juicy pieces. Plus his tape recorder. The Sir was going to be at the Houses of Commons till late so we had plenty of time, though I was a bit nervous that he might come back unexpectantly and stop my wonderful idea, Suzie's rather, being a sprise when I showed him next week's *Sunday Shocker*.

I said to Barry, 'Right Barry, first and foremost I'm not going to say anything about the rotten trick you and Colin between you pulled on me over the Diet Muffin, that's washing under the bridge, but there's some things I want to put straight.'

'Eff the diet muffin darling, done all that,' said Barry, switching on his tape recorder. 'The big question is what have you got to tell me about this titled Pratt you've been laying?'

All my training at the Donna Bella Rosa School of Fashion came back to me.

'We're just good friends,' I breathed.

*

What's it all about, Debra? That is the question I have been asking myself whilst telling my story like it reely is after how it was slanted by Barry Butcher. All along I have been hoping I would be able to report a happy ending but it is not to be, at least not for the time being.

First off my *Sunday Shocker* series blew up in my face from Day One. The Sir called me up from the country, something he had never done before, to say the fat was reely in the fan, he had already had three of his co-directives on the blower asking what the blue blazes he meant by lending the company flat to a blasted bimbo – cos of course, Barry Butcher had made a big mench out of my luxuriant lifestyle in the Mayfair pad or lovenest as he chose to call it. Also, it seemed Lady Pratt was not best pleased to say the least, as The Sir put it, 'Pussy has always been willing to turn a blind eye God knows, but really my dear, to overlook this stuff she'd require a white stick and a blasted guide dog.' Good old Sir, never loses his sense of humorousness.

I said, 'I'm ever so sorree if I've upset anybody Monty, particly Lady Pratt, I hope you don't feel I've let you down, I only wanted to tell the world that you had nothing to do with the Diet Muffin, but course what with all the stuff about the reel truth about the French maid outfit they were so insistful on it must of got left out, ever so sorree, maybe I can get it put right next week.'

'Don't do anything next week!' barked The Sir down the phone, highly sharpish for him I thought. 'If you value our friendship Debra, don't utter another word to those blasted guttersnipes!'

With a gulp I told him as tactiley as I could that it was

a bit late for that as Barry Butcher had already got everything he needed on tape. 'Still,' I said looking on the bright side, 'a lot of it is about other men in my life like soccer players and DJs and that, I think the only mention of us next week is where you show me a good time in New York.'

At this The Sir just gave a groan and said, 'Oh my God, now look here, I intend to lie doggo for a few days, I'll be in touch, don't worry my dear I know you meant it all for the best but it's rather a pity it's had to work out like this, however there we are, I have to ring off now my dear, bye bye, we'll speak soon.' He had hung up before I had a chance to ask him what he thought of Ted's stuff about us in the *Sunday Stunner*, talk about sizzling, as for the pix I am sprised they dared print them in a family newspaper.

Then comes a call from Babs to thank me for the money I had promised out of the *Sunday Shocker* series, she said Dad had said he wished it had come from a more respectful source but as I tartily reminded her, beggars cannot be choosers.

But this was not all Babs had to say, she went on, 'You're more than generous pet, only your Dad and me have been taking a long hard look at the books and reviewing the situation in the words of the song and what we don't want you to be doing is throwing good money after bad, now don't get me wrong we both still think the dance studio idea's viable to use a favourite word of your Dad's, never more so, only it's a case of have we bitten off more than we can chew? So we've talked it over and talked it over and what we've come up with is this, what the heck are we doing in Tulse Hill where we're not known, why don't we go back to Seathorpe where we *are* known and re-launch the Babs and Eric Chase Academy of Dance there? The more you think about it the more it makes sense love, thanks to you we've still got Oceanview so that's somewhere to live taken care of, and with what we can get on the flat plus what you've very kindly said you'll put in to tide us over we should be able to find a nice studio and this time get the thing on a proper footing and let's hope it takes off and we make a go of it, as your Dad says we can only learn from our past mistakes so what do you think blossom?'

What I thought was that nobody cared what I thought so long as I came up with the money, no that's not a nice thing to say, guess I was feeling low at that particlar moment in time. But I did think that if Dad and Babs had started their Academy of Dance in Seathorpe in the first place I might of had a few more bob left in the bank than I do now, and who knows maybe I would not of been in such a hurry to tell my story in the *Sunday Shocker*, I could have been more insistful that Barry Butcher put over the Diet Muffin angle I wanted before giving him the rest of the stuff, specially as when I met his editor in Bonks a few nights later he said that so long as he had DEBRA CHASE BY HERSELF splashed across his front page so's he could get it advertised on telly, he did not give a toss what was in the story, he said, 'We're not selling what's in the tin, we're selling the tin.' Wish I'd known that. Course, all I said to Babs was I wished her and Dad luck again and they would have a cheque as soon as my *Sunday Shocker* money cleared through the Debra Chase No 1 Account.

I was hoping to hear from Donna Bella Rosa, I had not had a peep out of her since she had driven me in from Heathrow after my fling in New York. But as

Monday morning came with still no word I thought no harm in giving her a bell, see how she reckons my chances of getting back into the big time after all this sleaze. I got ever such a shock. Her sister Beryl answered the phone, saying I was lucky to find her as she had only come in to pick up the mail, Rosa had been taken into hospital again, this time for a big operation and it was Beryl's belief that she would be off sick for a very long time, between you and I that sounded to me like for ever. Anyway, seems Rosa had wound up the business and one of the big agencies in New Bond Street had taken over most of her clients. Funnee I thought, nobody's called me. Then the penny dropped. Most of her clients, not all of them. Meaning that as regards Debra Chase they did not want to know. Thank you very much for telling me Donna Bella Rosa and get well soon. No, I reely mean that, she was reely good for my career but I reckon we had to go our seprate ways sooner or later.

So there I am with no work and without an agent and thinking, 'Here we go Debra, something tells me it is going to be another of those days.' I did not know the half of it.

Over the months The Sir had given me quite a bit of jewelry, not diamonds and pearls as both the *Sunday Shocker* and the *Sunday Stunner* would have it but nice pieces all the same like a turquoise brooch and an enamel and gold necklace with matching ear-rings, so to cheer myself up I thought I would go and get them valued. For the record they were not worth half as much as I thought so I still have them, I would not part with them for the world unless I reely had to as they are of great sanctimonial value. After that I did some shopping down

Berwick Street market, I was amazed how much cheaper it is than Fortnum & Mason's, then I had a spot of lunch at a Soho brassiere, no one reconised me as I was incongruous in blue jeans, dark glasses and scraped-back hair.

When I got back to Brook Street I knew at once that The Sir had been in, I could smell his cigar smoke. Funnee I thought, he said he was going to be lying doggy and would not be back for a while. I went into the bedroom and spotted straight away that his two spare pairs of shiny black shoes were gone, he loved polishing those shoes, it was his hobby I guess. Then I opened the wardrobe and saw that he had taken all his clothes.

There was a letter on my pillow, written in proper blue fountain pen ink on Houses of Commons notepaper. I still have that letter and this is what it said:

My dear,

Having popped in to pick up a few things I was frankly somewhat relieved to find you 'not at home', since what I have to tell you is rather difficult, and perhaps this way is best.

I'm taking Pussy off at once to New Zealand where she has a sister. We shall be gone perhaps three months, by which time I expect the gutter press will be turning its poison pen to other targets. Pussy's family have some business interests down there and it may be I shall make certain decisions about the future while I am there.

However, all that is very much in the air until I have looked at such opportunities as may present them-selves. What is certain is that we – that is you and I – I am afraid must now come to the parting of the ways.

I am sure you understand. It has been great fun while it lasted and as I said to you on a previous occasion when I was waxing sentimental and you very properly brought me to task, no regrets are worth a tear.

Please do not feel that you have to pack your bags and move out of Brook Street at once. You have all the time in the world to find alternative accommodation – I do feel I owe you that much. Thank you for making an old dodderer feel young again.

Much love, my dear, Yours aye, Monty

PS I am sure some rag would offer you a high price for this missive but I know I can trust you not to divulge it, that is to say to keep it to yourself. I think you'll agree enough harm's been done.

Although it was a sad letter to read, fact it is stained with my tears if anybody wants to know, that PS made me feel highly proud. The Sir was right, he could trust me never to show that letter to a living soul, hand on heart until this moment only one other person in the world has ever set eyes on it and I did not show it to him, he picked it up off my dressing table. This was a young publisher I had got to know called Mark, I met him down at Bonks where I had drifted feeling a bit lonesome a few days after The Sir had legged it to New Zealand. I guess I let him give me one Jumbo Mumbo too many, that's the same as a Mumbo Jumbo only in a bigger glass, and cut a long story short we finished up back at my place, I am not proud of this, I am just making the statement what happened. Mark is a nice boy but nosy with it and as I say he picked up my private letter and read it whilst I was in the bathroom. When I came out he said smirkfully, 'You know, there's a book in you Debra.' And next day he bought me this Marilyn Monroe lips tape recorder.

So there we are. Debra Chase, This Is Your Life. I do not know if anyone will print it as Mark has been fired in some office shake-up and has gone into advertising, so we shall have to see. Also I do not know if a book can have a PS like The Sir's letter, but this one has. The very morning after I had finished getting all this down on goodness knows how many hours of tape, I must of been burbling away for a fortnight, I open my *Daily Stunner* to read BONKING BARONET GETS THE BOOT. The story began, 'Bonking Baronet Sir Monty Pratt, the playboy Tory MP whose bizarre sex frolics with kiss-and-tell top model Debra Chase made headlines, has been ousted as chairman of the famous pork pie firm founded by his father.' I did not see how they could do that seeing as the firm was in his name but seems they had a special board meeting and voted him off, fancee waiting till his back was turned all those hundreds of miles away.

But that much was all I had the chance to read cos just then the entryphone buzzes and I hear this posho voice saying he is from Pratt's Pork Pies Ltd and can he have a word. Course I cannot say no seeing as I know they own the flat, so I press the buzzer and up comes not one bloke but two, both dressed like undertakers and carrying black briefcases. One of them said, 'Good morning Miss Chase, good of you to be sensible about this, I'm Mr Potter the company secretary and this is Mr Trotter the company solicitor, now I think you know why we're here, we're required to repossess the flat which as I'm sure you're aware is company property, perhaps you'll be good enough to take acceptance of this document,' with which the company solicitor shoves this big sheet of thick paper into my hand, stamped with red seals and full of howtofores and wherewithals.

Funnee, all I could think of was that this was the first time I had ever met a man secrety, I guess Lady Pratt wouldn't let The Sir have a girl company secrety knowing what he would get up to behind the filing cabinet.

I said very dignifried, 'You can't expect me to follow all this legal rigmoral but I don't want to cause any trouble, I've had a good run for my money, you can have your flat, just give me time to get packed and I will be on my merry way.' They both gave these big heavy sighs and mopped their foreheads, I have never seen two people so relieved, what they were expecting I do not know, maybe they thought I was going to break out into histrionics.

They both looked as though they could use a drink and I know I did so I said, 'There's one bottle of champagne left in the fridge, now is there anything in this sheet of paper to say we can't give it its freedom whilst I'm packing?' Made me choke a bit saying that, cos 'give it its freedom' was one of the phases The Sir used to use when opening a bottle. Anyway, Mr Potter the company secrety chortled, 'I think that's an excellent idea Miss Chase' and Mr Trotter the company solicitor chortled, 'I don't believe there's any mention of Moët & Chandon in the inventory' as he opened the bottle, and that's how I said goodbye to my luxuriant pad in the heart of Mayfair, with a glass of champagne in my hand.

Finding somewhere to live was no problem, even though Auntie Doris did not want me back and I could not afford anywhere else at prez, cos I knew there would always be a room for me back at Oceanview where Dad and Babs were already living again. So that is where Debra Chase finds herself at this moment in time, talk about going round in full circles. All right, so to some it may seem like back to square one but I do not look at it like that, you have got to remember that I am not yet twenty and that is still quite young in the life of a top model. Everyone has their ups and downs and I reckon I have had my share of both but this is not the end of the Debra Chase story by any means, it is only

THE BEGINNING

Join a literary community of
like-minded readers who seek out
the best in contemporary writing.

From the thousands of submissions Sceptre
receives each year, our editors select the books
we consider to be outstanding.

We look for distinctive voices, thought-provoking
themes, original ideas, absorbing narratives and
writing of prize-winning quality.

If you want to be the first to hear about our
new discoveries, and would like the chance to
receive advance reading copies of our books
before they are published, visit

www.sceptrebooks.co.uk

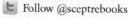 Follow @sceptrebooks

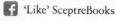 'Like' SceptreBooks

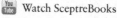 Watch SceptreBooks